ZODIAC DRAGON BROTHERHOOD

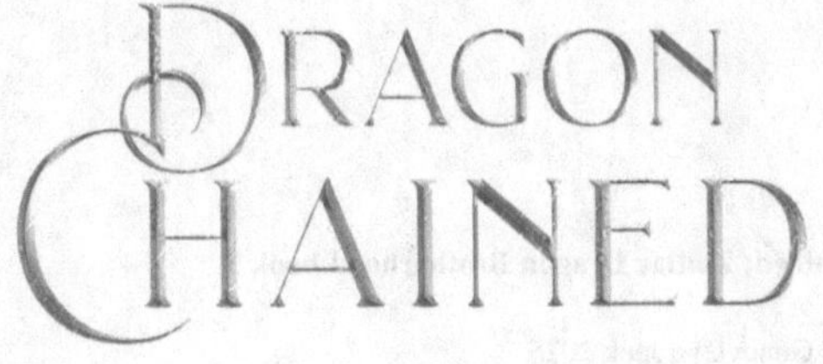

DRAGON CHAINED

USA TODAY BESTSELLING AUTHOR

GENEVIEVE JACK

Dragon Chained: Zodiac Dragon Brotherhood book 3

Copyright © Genevieve Jack 2025

Published by Carpe Luna, Ltd. Bloomington, IL 61704

First Edition: November 2025

ISBN: 978-1-962757-40-9

eISBN: 978-1-962757-17-1

v 1.6

The cake was late. Maggie smiled at her guests as she doled out more tea sandwiches and sparkling pink punch. An expectant dragon was always something to celebrate. Successful dragon pregnancies, after all, were far rarer than the human kind. Her best friend, Katie, had tried for years for this baby—a girl, the doctors had predicted—an incredible blessing indeed. Everything had to be perfect for her special day.

Maggie had ordered the cake, a full sheet with raspberry filling and buttercream frosting, decorated with pale pink roses and baby bottles, from her favorite bakery, Honey Cakes on Elm Street. But when she swung by to pick it up that morning, she'd been deeply disappointed to find the cake was missing. The baker, Mr. Honey, was certain he'd fulfilled the order, but it simply wasn't in the cooler. The man seemed beside himself at the mistake, but Maggie struggled to show him any sympathy or understanding. The party was that afternoon. She needed the cake.

Normally, she was a level-headed dragon. Maggie worked among humans as an accountant, a position that easily blended into the background, and didn't enjoy calling attention to herself. But she'd spoken up about the cake. How could she throw a baby shower without one? She'd even gently pressed into Mr. Honey's mind, using her psychic dragon abilities, and was disappointed to find he was telling the truth. Either one of his employees had misplaced the cake or given it to another customer by mistake.

"I'll make it right," the baker had promised. "I'll decorate one from the case and deliver it to your house for your party, free of charge."

Maggie had agreed, but here she was, surrounded by fifteen dragon women dressed in pastel florals and drinking foamy pink punch from crystal cups as the mother-to-be opened her second-to-last gift, and still, there was no cake. What if it didn't come? Everyone would understand, she knew, but Maggie couldn't let it go. She was a perfectionist who prided herself on her organization and planning skills. She'd ordered that cake in plenty of time, Creator damn it all. She swore to never order another thing from Honey Cakes bakery.

The chime of the doorbell lifted her spirits. At last! She excused herself from the room and opened the door to find a human man holding a big white cake box. "Finally," she said, taking it from the stranger. Weird. As her hand brushed his, a feeling of immense dread washed through her, the hair on her arms standing on end. He drew his hands away quickly, pivoted on his heel, and strode toward his car at a fast clip.

She was relieved. Something was wrong with him. She'd sensed...darkness. With a shake of her head, she dismissed her instincts. She had a party to attend to. Maggie peeked into the Honey Cakes box to check that the cake was what she'd ordered.

And that was when the bomb went off.

Chapter One

SEB

Everything about the recording studio feels small today, but the truth is, it's the same size as always. It's me who's bigger. Who feels bigger anyway. I've entered my alignment, the month of my dragon's birth and my star sign. I'm a Taurus dragon, which means on April 22, midnight tonight, my inner dragon will rise to the surface. For the next thirty days, I will be the most powerful of my kind. My senses will be sharper. I'll be faster. Stronger. And I will rise to lead the Zodiac Dragon Brotherhood, the brotherhood of twelve warriors responsible for protecting my kind.

But a side effect of that privilege is my appetites rise in kind—and not just for food and drink. Our dragons can only procreate during our alignment, which means even now, on the cusp of my star sign, my biology is sending me a steady stream of lusty daydreams, and my inner dragon is squirming to be free of my skin. I'm fidgety, hot, and horny as hell. It's all I can do to remain in the moment, listening to a band called Spun Arrow, who are trying their wicked best to impress me right now. I can barely concentrate through the thunder of my thoughts.

"I think the bass line is off." Crew, my assistant producer, sends me a disappointed scowl. We both had high hopes for this group. "He's lagging."

I hear it too. As distracted as I am, the part of my brain that has always spotted true musical talent is cringing at what's happening in the live room of the recording studio. I force myself to focus because Full Throttle Records is counting on me, and I owe it to this band to give them a shot. But once I've given them a few more bars, I nod at Crew. He's right.

Crew holds up a hand, signaling to the band through the soundproof glass to stop playing. They do, but I can see the bassist is already copping an attitude. His hip pops out, and he tips his head as if he's annoyed by the interruption.

Over the intercom, Crew corrects him, tells him to internalize the beat and keep up with the drummer. It's a common problem with young musicians. On his own, the bassist's skills are likely passable, maybe even commendable. No doubt some music teacher some-where told him he had what it takes. But when you play in a group like this, the goal is to not stand out. You need to blend. You need to hit the beat like it's coming from your own heart. Lagging like he is, it's coming across as amateurish.

I know we've done the right thing calling him out when the guy's ears turn red. You've got to have a thick skin in this business. You've got to be a fucking ice cube when it comes to criticism. This guy, I know his type. Big ego. Hair trigger. He's the type that probably deals with his frustrations with booze, women, or drugs. In other words, capital T trouble. Not ready for the big time.

He's probably a Leo.

No thank you.

Spun Arrow starts to play again, and it's better. Bassist is gritting his teeth, really trying to show Crew what he's made of. Trying. Trying too hard. At this level, this stuff has to happen naturally. On tour, he'll have to play perfectly whether he's hungover, hungry, distracted, in bad weather, or half asleep after traveling on the bus for days. His muscle memory has to be perfect. We can't rely on focused effort.

Another producer might take the risk, but not me. As a Taurus, I thrive on predictability and stability. There's a reason the symbol of our sign is the bull. We're reliable. Steady. We hate the unknown. This guy is an unknown.

I gesture to Crew and shake my head once. He nods. "Yeah. Not good enough."

"Needs some time in the barrel," I mumble. Five more years working the clubs and forcing himself to mesh with his fellow musicians might turn this guy into pure gold. He's just not there yet.

Crew nods. "Got it, boss."

My phone interrupts any further conversation. It's Connor's ringtone, and my stomach forms into a tight ball before I answer it. I bring the device to my ear as Crew waves me off. He'll take care of letting Spun Arrow down easily.

I slip into the hall. "Seb," I say in lieu of hello.

"Brother. Have you seen the news?" Connor's voice cracks. Connor is an Aries dragon and the leader of the Zodiac Dragon Brotherhood for five more hours, until my alignment. Then it's my turn. Normally, I wouldn't mind stepping up, but considering everything that's happened in the last month, it's a hell of a time to be at the wheel.

"No, I've been in the studio all day. What happened?"

"The Order is at it again. There's been an incident. A horrible incident."

I hustle toward the room I've been using as a remote office here and close the door behind me. "How is that possible? I thought you killed Roman."

"I did. Someone else must've taken the wheel."

"Already?"

"Already. The Order bombed a baby shower, Seb. They targeted a dragon in her own home. On her own property."

"What?" Heat rises in my blood. Thank the creator I'm alone because I have the strongest urge to knock someone's head off. I did not need this today. "The mother and baby—"

"They're alive. Some of the older dragons covered her with their bodies."

"Thank the creator."

"But six others died. The host and the women closest to the door. An order member posed as a delivery driver and hid a cursed bomb inside the cake."

"Fuck, Connor. Six! Shit. Was there anything we could have done? Any forewarning?"

"None. As far as we know, it was a random act of violence."

I scoff. "It was an act of war. When Donovan died, the accord died with him. I just thought we'd have some time while the Order regrouped and named a new leader. I thought we'd have a few months to strategize on how best to protect our people."

"I know. I didn't see this coming either. I've convened the four as my last order of business." The four are the subset of dragons that take on the brunt of decision-making. Since we each lead for a month, the next three signs after us have to be closely involved in anything we do for continuity. Connor is an Aries, which means I, as a Taurus, Remus as Gemini, and Ellison as Cancer make up the four right now. The remainder of the twelve are brought in if necessary, after the four have convened.

"Right. We're going to need Remus and Ellison."

"And Lucas. As of tonight, I'm transitioning the crown to you. The four now includes Lucas as Leo."

"Fuck. That's right."

"Look, unlike a month ago when Solomon stepped down and I rose to this position as Aries, I'm not going anywhere. I'll help you as much as I can, just as long as it doesn't put Fiona in danger."

As much as I appreciate Connor's help and am glad

he's able to transition things to me properly, I know better than to take his generosity for granted. His mate Fiona has been through enough over the last month. She's been lucky to avoid another major fibro flare after all the stress she's been under. When Connor says he'll help as long as it doesn't put Fiona in danger, that includes excessive stress or worry. Those things can land her in bed for weeks recovering. I won't be the cause of that. Besides, it's customary for the last leader to get a break from the heavy lifting. It's why we operate the way we do. It's an ancient system and one I've been intimately associated with for a decade, since the last Taurus brother stepped down.

"So, Cardinal Island tonight for the handoff?"

"Can't. We have to do this on world. I can't bring the ring through the portal. We're coming to you." He means the cursed ring we obtained earlier this year, the same kind as is worn by every member of the Saint's Order, the secret society that exists for the sole purpose of enslaving or killing dragons. The magic of their rings is toxic to us.

"You're bringing the ring here, to LA?"

"I am. I'm not going to miss being in charge of this thing, Seb. It gives me nightmares. Makes my skin crawl having it in the same room as me."

"Fan-fucking-tastic. Really looking forward to taking possession of the evil jewelry."

"Just wait. I have something else for you. Something I didn't see coming."

"So where are we meeting?" I ask.

"Beverly Wilshire. Penthouse. One hour."

"See you then."

Chapter Two

SEB

"About time you joined us," Connor chides through a teasing grin as he lets me into his hotel room. Correction, suite of rooms. This place could be someone's very high-end apartment. The enormous Viking of a male pulls me into a hug and thumps me on the back. Fiona, his human mate, stands just behind him, and I greet her with a warm smile. Although I'm tempted to pull her into a hug, it's a bad idea to touch a dragon's mate, especially when the relationship is as new as theirs.

She meets my eyes and offers a little wave. "Hi, Seb!"

I'm relieved to find the others are already here. Remus doesn't get up from where he's tipping his chair onto its back legs at the table, but he waves two tattooed fingers in the air like a sloppy salute. I reflect his greeting back at him and add a warm, "Remus."

Although he's naturally charming and articulate, he's also as clever as they come, and in his case, that manifests in economizing his words. When Remus speaks, you listen, because he probably has something important to say. It's a personality type that serves him well at the tattoo parlor he owns, where being a good listener and confidant is popular with influential clients.

"Brother." Ellison stands from his seat, extending one manicured hand toward me. I shake it formally, noticing the Cancer-sign has his laptop in tow. If there is one person on this earth who works harder than I do, it's Ellison. He's a partner at a law firm, which comes in handy now and then in our fight against the Order. But he's also the overly cautious and sometimes pessimistic type. He's never the first to jump at a solution, but once he commits, he's as reliable as it gets.

"Glad you could make it." I grasp Ellison by the shoulder.

Just then, the sound of a door opening turns me toward what I assume is the bathroom. Lucas Oliver, the Leo member of the brotherhood, strides out, still smoothing his hair. I haven't seen the actor turned director since he left for Singapore to film his latest movie, but I catch my jaw tightening.

"If you're done primping, Lucas, maybe we can begin."

He gives me an arrogant smile and delivers a warm-hearted hug that I return, because we are brothers, after all, even if he annoys the hell out of me.

"If you had hair this good, you'd keep it looking its best too," he says through a perfect smile.

I groan. The truth is, the dragon does have perfect golden-brown hair that, along with his gleaming, straight smile, makes him a charm factory guaranteed to woo any woman he chooses. I'm no slouch in the looks department, but I've always been more interested in getting the job done than being flashy or outgoing. Basically, the opposite of Lucas the Leo.

His ability to put others at ease would make even the most confident dragon envious. People tend to find me intimidating, especially when I know I'm right. Which is most of the time.

Lucas takes a seat next to Ellison, and I sit down at the head of the table. "So, where should we start?" I ask. "What do you know about the bombing?"

Ellison leans forward. "The host of the baby shower was a woman named Maggie Freely, the wife of a Peter Freely, who runs a little independent bookstore in Maryland. Maggie worked as an accountant. Both were extremely careful with their dragon identities. Peter told us that Maggie had shopped at Honey Cakes, a local bakery, for at least seven years and never had a problem. She ordered the cake for the shower in person, the same way she always did. But when she went to pick it up that morning, it was missing from the cooler. The owner of Honey Cakes says he still doesn't know what happened to it. He's grilled all of his employees and searched the store. While it's possible the cake was given to another customer, it's highly unlikely because there wasn't a cake left in the cooler at the end of the day."

"Right. If the orders had been switched, the customer who took the wrong cake would have left behind the right one."

"Exactly. So this guy, Frank Honey, he made Maggie a replacement cake, but he doesn't normally do deliveries, so he hired a DashCab delivery person to take her the cake. A man with DashCab identification came and got the cake, and by the time it was delivered to Maggie, there was a bomb in it. But get this, Mr. Honey says a second DashCab delivery driver came to Honey Cakes after the first one and was confused that the cake was already gone. Mr. Honey chalked it up to a mix-up at DashCab, but now, after authorities told him what happened, he is distraught that he might have given the order to someone targeting Maggie."

"So, it's fair to say that an Order member somehow discovered that Maggie or Peter was a dragon, stole the original cake, and used the circumstances to deliver the bomb. Anyone get a description of this delivery driver?" Anger throbs in my veins. I desperately want to disembowel whoever is responsible for this.

"Frank described him as a Santa Claus look-alike. White hair and beard with a big belly. Was wearing a black leather vest over a white T-shirt and jeans."

"Do we have anyone on the list who fits that description?" I ask Ellison. We have a long list of people, mostly billionaires and politicians, who we know are in the Order. For years, under the accord, Saint's Order members were supposed to register their properties so that dragons could avoid them. But now that the accord's been broken, who knows how complete it is. It's possible one of them would pose as a delivery driver to pull this off, but the conservative billionaires who end up in the Order usually have a penchant for designer suits, gold watches, and oversized yachts. They don't tend to look like Santa.

Ellison shakes his head. "No one. It was either a new recruit, or someone hired this out."

Remus shakes his head. "New recruit. I analyzed the security footage from the camera at the front door. He was wearing an Order ring."

"Fuck!" I slam my palms down on the counter. This situation is so far out of my comfort zone, if it were a line of music, it wouldn't even be in the same song.

"Can anyone take the lead on going to Maryland and trying to track down Santa Claus?" I ask.

Lucas raises his hand. "I'm shopping for filming locations for my latest project. It's a great excuse to nose around the area. I'll run this asshole down."

"Thanks. If they're hunting us again, and they could randomly target someone like Maggie, anyone could be next. It's like the deaths of Roman and Stephen haven't created so much as a speed bump in the Order's plans." I rub a hand over my face while the implications soak in.

Ellison rubs a finger across his chin. "If anything, Donovan's death, by dissolving the accord, untied their hands."

I look to Connor for some words of wisdom. He's been uncharacteristically quiet this entire time. Beside him, Fiona looks just as grave. Mates don't usually participate in these things, but at this point, I'm open to ideas from anyone who wants to give them. "So, what do you think we should do? Do we take this to the Oracle?"

Connor shakes his head. "Already have, brother. She said our future lies in the gifts of the past."

"What the fuck does that mean?" I ask.

He rubs his jaw. "I can't say for sure. But we think it has to do with the Saint's Order ring Reagan's father left us when he committed suicide. I brought it tonight to pass on to you for safekeeping."

"Gee, thanks." I scowl.

"We've learned something about the ring, something we need to show you before we hand it off. Something we didn't see coming. Fiona, would you do the honors?"

She stands and moves toward a credenza across the room, where a jewelry box waits beside a set of barbecue tongs. "Technically, I can touch this because I'm human, but Connor would prefer I use these." She clicks the tongs together a few times. Carefully, she pops open the wooden box and plucks a heavy silver ring from inside with the tongs. It looks like a men's high school class ring, except there's a St. George Cross engraved on the face of the heavy platinum. Although the font is too small for me to read from this distance, all of us know that the cross is surrounded by an inscription: *Astra inclinant, sed non obligant*, meaning the stars incline us, they do not bind us. The Latin quote is a way to poke fun at dragons who hold tightly to the guidance of the stars and were made by the creator out of the celestial cloth. This ring is an abomination to my kind.

Fiona leans over the table and holds the ring over a decorative silver tray at the center. "Don't let it touch you. It burned Reagan when she accidentally came across it in her father's secret safe."

When she drops it, the ring hits the silver tray and revolves on its edge with a hollow metallic sound before settling on its side. Every dragon in the room, including me, draws in a sharp breath and scoots his chair back. Being this close is like standing beside an electric fence. You don't have to touch it to hear and feel the static buzz that threatens to zap you. If that ring could grow legs, it would hunt me. I know it in my bones.

"I don't think you have to worry about anyone touching that thing, Fiona," I say softly. "There isn't a dragon here whose skin isn't prickling right now." As if to prove my point, Remus tips his chair back again and stays that way, trying to put even more room between himself and the ring. Ellison is uncharacteristically fidgety. Lucas's movie-star smile is no longer in the room with us, replaced by a tight-lipped sneer and narrowed blue eyes that fixate on the ring.

Connor, who is now standing protectively next to Fiona, clears his throat. "This is the first time we've had access to this magic. Even before the accord, when we were at war, dragons never kept the rings for study or experimentation."

"Why not?" Lucas asks. I was wondering the same thing.

"As far as I know, from my ancestors, Order members were always very careful to protect their rings and destroy or reuse them when a member died, but also, there was the fear that the rings could be tracked and lead the Order straight to us. That hypothesis has officially been tested with this specimen and proven false. They came looking but didn't find it."

"So this is our first real shot at understanding this thing," I say in wonder.

Connor nods. "Never in the history of our kind have we succeeded in obtaining an Order ring. With it comes the unprecedented opportunity to learn how it works and how we can defend ourselves against it."

I scoff. "Only problem is that none of us can even touch it. How exactly do you expect us to Mr. Science this thing?"

"Mr. Magic." Conner corrects me. "All reports suggest these things are cursed with a dark enchantment. And there's something else. Something we haven't shown you yet."

Fiona digs in her leather bag and retrieves a vial that, even in the brightly lit room, seems to glow in her hand. When she takes off the lid, I smell sunlight and honey. The other dragons must smell it too because Ellison leans closer to her and whispers, "What is that?"

Fashioned onto the underside of the lid is an eyedropper. Fiona draws up some of the liquid and holds the dropper over the tray. She releases a single drop that lands on the ring. The thing jumps onto its side, spinning like a top. The metal must get hot because the liquid sizzles then steams off in a puff of white smoke. Dry again, it falls onto its side, revolving in tighter and tighter circles until it comes to a full stop.

"What the fuck was that?" Seb asks.

"We don't know," Fiona says, returning to Connor's side. "When my sister died, she left me a sliver of property that includes a chapel and a well. This water came from that property. We knew the Saint's Order had been trying to gain ownership of the land but didn't know why until now. The water has properties we don't understand. Properties that seem to be in opposition to whatever makes that ring poisonous to all of you."

Connor brushes one eyebrow with the back of his nails. "No dragon can understand the magic of the ring or the water. We need a witch."

Remus and I exchange glances. We both know the witch he means, but she's not the answer. "If I could find the witch you're referring to—and that's a big if—I doubt she could or would help us."

"We talked about this, Seb. You are in the best position to convince her."

"You mean manipulate her." The witch in question is Zoe Willow, lead singer of Raven's Wish. Connor wants me to hold out a record contract like a carrot on a stick. It's unconscionable.

"Hey, witches are rare and highly secretive. We're lucky even to know of one, let alone have an in with her."

I shift in my chair. "I don't have an in with her, okay? Actually, my label rejected her and her band a little over a year ago."

Connor growls. "You didn't mention that before."

"I didn't know. It was my partner's call. Apparently, Zoe Willow showed up at an audition a strung-out mess. She's a drug addict. Ruined her music career. Since then, she's fallen off the map."

Remus scratches his stubbled jaw. "She wasn't high when I did her tattoo. I won't work on anyone under the influence."

"How long ago was that?" Ellison asks like a detective trying to run down a timeline. Damn it, once that dog gets hold of a bone, he won't let it go easily.

"A few months. Maybe five or six. Venomous Ink is a busy shop. I only remember her because I usually project a little on to my clients to dampen the pain of the needle. She was mentally strong enough to push me out of her head."

I raise a hand. "Well, there you go. Remus can contact her and see if she'll help us. He, at least, has seen her in the flesh. I only know of her. We've never even been in the same room."

"Remus doesn't have what she wants. You, presumably, do," Connor says.

Ignoring Connor, I stare across the table at the tattooed brother. "Remus? Any way you could give it a go first? I don't even know where to start looking for her."

Remus shakes his head. "My contract protects my

customer's privacy. Unless they owe me money, I don't keep their personal information. You have as much of a chance at finding her as I do."

"*Fuck.*" I glance around the room, my gaze catching on Lucas. "Zoe Willow can't be the only witch we know. What about you? You must have worked with a few witchy actresses in your day?"

Pretty boy snorts. "Sorry, no. Not even one that I suspect might be." He shifts in his chair, his hands spreading. "Sorry. Besides, I'm going after Santa Claus, remember?"

Connor shakes his head. "We need this figured out yesterday, Seb. We're in the eye of the storm here. The Order is going to be careful while the authorities are investigating this bombing. But they will eventually strike again. Understanding the magic of this ring and the water in that vial is paramount."

"Think what it could do for us, Seb," Ellison chimes in. "If we understood the magic, maybe we could make an antidote for the poison or a shield against their weapons."

Lucas piles on. "And if this doesn't work or it happens again, what's next? Declaring a code red and sending civilians into hiding? Battling Order members in the streets like we did a hundred years ago? It's going to be different now that there are cameras everywhere."

Connor frowns. "We may need to do both those things, with or without the witch."

I plant my face in my palm. "I have a bad feeling about this."

Connor grips the shoulder of my suit jacket. "As of tonight at midnight, this is your circus and your monkeys. You can decide how you want to proceed, but no one is in a better place to force Zoe Willow to do what we need her to do than you."

Chapter Three

ZOE

I'm not saying this job is completely without merit, just that the work is emotionally soul-killing and that security should take your belt and shoelaces each morning as a precaution. Everyone in my row of cubicles is one tough call away from snapping. Even the ancient building I work in is depressing. It's never the right temperature, smells mildly of blue cheese, and rumor has it there's still asbestos in the walls. We work in a gray world of half-sized cubicles constructed in two rows, on a floor that used to serve as an orphanage a hundred years ago. Every time someone coughs, I hear echoes of long-forgotten children suffering from consumption.

I am leashed to my workstation by a headset with a long curly cord, circa 2010. My conversations are being recorded for quality assurance. Going off script is strictly prohibited. During the pandemic, the company allowed people to work from home, but the second employees could get the jab, they scrapped that program. Too hard to monitor bathroom breaks, I guess. According to management, there is absolutely no reason a person should need more than fifteen minutes untethered from their computer.

The ping comes in my ear, and I speak even before I register the meaning of the words I'm saying. It's like I'm in a trance or something, half asleep and reciting from rote memory. "Regal Health. How may I help you?"

"You denied my wife's claim. She's very ill and needs chemo to save her life. The hospital says Regal is refusing to pay." The voice on the other end of the line is male and trembles with barely contained rage. I'm betting he's called before, and I'm betting that I won't be able to give him a different answer.

"Can I have the name and address on the account, please?" He gives it to me, and I bring up his claim. Jesus Christ, he has called before. Like fifty times. Wife has a rare form of cancer excluded from the policy. He's insured by Regal and is up-to-date on his premiums, but his policy doesn't cover her specific illness. My eyes go blurry as I recite the canned response the system gives me, redirecting him to his insurance agent to review his policy.

"You people are heartless!" he seethes. "How do you look at yourself in the mirror in the morning?"

Everything feels heavy. This isn't my fault, but I feel complicit in what's happening to this man. Maybe a few years ago, I could work a little magic on the system and help him without Regal ever knowing. I come from a long line of powerful witches after all. But I pushed too hard and abused my craft. I've been cut off. I've got nothing anymore. I can't even conjure myself a cheese sandwich.

"I'm sorry," I mumble into my microphone. "I'm just a call representative. There's nothing I can do."

He sniffs. "Right."

The call disconnects.

"That's going to get you fired," pink-haired Emily says from behind me. We all call her pink-haired Emily to differentiate her from brunette Emily who works down the hall.

I squeeze my eyes closed. "I know," I whine. "I just couldn't kick him when he's down with a trite 'Thank you for calling Regal Health.'"

She rolls her chair closer to me. "They all sign the contracts, Zoe. It's not our fault that no one reads them. Exclusions are exclusions. It helps if you don't think about the human element."

I lift an eyebrow. "You pretend the person calling you isn't human? What, like they're all robots or something?"

She sniffs. "No. Just...there are charitable agencies that will help them, eventually. Regal Health is a business. Just because we don't pay for something doesn't mean they won't eventually get treatment. I picture them figuring something else out once they know their policy won't cover them. Like, we're doing them a favor providing them with closure on that."

I stare at her for a few long moments, but she's actually serious. She's convinced herself that everything always works out for people, that somehow, someone other than the people our customers paid to insure them will swoop in and solve this man's problem.

Unfortunately, I know better. I don't believe in heroes or guardian angels. The only thing at rock bottom is the rock and you. I would know. I've been there. And the only person who can push you off that rock and start the long and arduous climb back to ground zero is also you.

That man on the other end of the line is probably going to lose his wife. She's going to die because he didn't read, or maybe didn't understand, a fifty-four-page contract written in a way that is beyond most people's comprehension. She's going to die because he probably didn't have any other option anyway when he signed that contract. People's employers often choose these accounts. She's going to die because they're poor and can't pay cash.

"You're probably right," I say stiffly and turn back to my computer. Three more hours until my shift is over. I glance at the clock. With every tick of the second hand, it feels as though my energy is slowly being leached from my body. I'm being drained of my blood, one drop at a time. I close my eyes. I can do this. I have to do this. I need the paycheck. I need the health insurance.

"Hey, Zoe, is this you?" Pink-haired Emily rolls her chair into the aisle again, her wheels squeaking and knocking against the linoleum floor.

With a sigh, I pivot slowly, almost wishing another call would come through. Almost. I cringe when I see what's on her screen. It's a picture of me in a slinky, disco-ball dress, sitting on a stool with an acoustic guitar in my lap. The Barrel Room is advertising my show tonight. Of course I'm using a stage name: Aimee Oliver. I look different now that I'm healthy. Along with my decision to switch to folk-inspired pop music, more conservative clothing, and smaller venues, it's given me a second chance at a baby music career. It's nothing like the one I had with Raven's Wish, and the opportunities and money are nowhere near what they were and probably never will be. But at least I have the smallest sliver of light in my life to look forward to. I'm rarely recognized as Zoe Willow these days, which is for the best.

"Uh, yeah. It's just a hobby."

"Oh my gosh! I was just out looking at places to take Gary for his birthday, and there you were. I didn't know you were a singer."

I snort. "Well, you know..." I don't mention that there was a time that I thought I could be the next Taylor Swift. That dream has died a slow, painful death. Only a few venues in the area will schedule me since my personal implosion and fall from grace, and, again, the pay barely covers transportation to the venue. Singing, truly, is something I do only for personal fulfillment these days.

"Exciting, though!" Emily says. "Maybe I'll head down there tonight with Gary. Have a few drinks. Cheer you on."

"Oh, don't put yourself out." I would never invite anyone from work to one of my shows. It's awkward, especially considering the one area of magic that hasn't left me is my voice. Things always seem to get out of hand when people who have heard me sing see me in real life. And I need this job. If things go wrong here, it could mean trouble for me.

"I'd like to watch you perform, and I know Gary would too," she says sweetly.

I frown. "Here's the thing, Emily," I start, digging for a good lie. "I'm not very good as it is, and if you were there, I'd be really nervous. I know you want to be supportive, but honestly, you'd make it ten times harder for me."

"Oh." She tucks her chin and extends her lower lip as if she can't believe I've just suggested that her presence might not be welcome. "Well, okay. I guess being an amateur is hard. I get it. I was once in a play in high school, and every time I was supposed to go onstage, I suffered major anxiety."

"Right. So... Tell you how it goes on Monday?"

She looks completely deflated. "Sure. Of course." She holds up a finger as a call comes through, and she turns back to her computer to answer.

Bullet dodged.

I may have burned all my bridges in the music industry, but I intend to sing until the day I die. My big dreams may be dead, but my talent isn't. And I will protect this tiny niche of happiness with everything I've got.

I glance at the clock. Two hours, fifty minutes until I can log out.

Chapter Four

SEB

As far as I can tell, Raven's Wish dropped off the map after Full Throttle rejected them. Off the fucking planet, it seems. Crew has been trying to run them down all day, and I've done my share of Googling too. No one has updated their website in eighteen months. No one has posted about them on social media in over a year. I've searched for each of the members separately. The drummer, Alex, made a go of it for about six months with a band called Marxigram, but even he is a ghost these days.

"Are you sure you even want to find this girl?" Crew asks. "I'm not questioning your judgment—"

"I literally pay you to question my judgment. I just... have a friend who remembers her and was interested in hiring her for a private event."

"Tell your friend to reconsider. Gregg and I thought

she was the most tragic case we'd ever seen in this business, and we've seen a lot of addicts."

"That bad, huh?"

"So bad we had to call an ambulance. I wouldn't be surprised if she were still in rehab or the psych ward."

I cringe. Magic shares a razor's edge with mental illness. Hell, I've been in my alignment less than twenty-four hours and I already question my sanity. My skin feels too tight, and my body feels pressurized like a champagne bottle ready to pop. I'm not crazy, though, and I'm willing to bet she isn't either.

Undeniably, something had its teeth in her back then. It might have been drugs. It might have been booze. Witches are human, after all, a human capable of magic, and unlike dragons, they can become addicted to drugs and alcohol. They can overdose. Their magic only complicates things.

I knew this was a bad idea.

"Thanks, Crew. I'll consider her a lost cause."

"Probably for the best."

He leaves my office, and I stare at the picture of Raven's Wish on their website. Even the photo makes her look strung out, like she's there but not there. She's too thin, the type of thin you see when someone is skipping meals to do drugs. I can make out the outline of her ribs where the neck of her dress falls off her shoulder. Bleached white hair falls in a harsh, asymmetrical line across her prominent cheekbone. It's too hard and cold of a look for a girl who probably still has a prom dress in her closet. But it's her eyes that unsettle me the most.

Unfocused and glazed, she stands on that stage, but she's not really there.

"Where are you, Zoe Willow?" I mumble, and then an idea comes to me. I screenshot her photo and do a reverse image search. Dozens of photos pop up. I zoom in on each of them until one is too close a resemblance for me to dismiss. "Well, I'll be damned. Looks like you didn't fall off the map after all, *Aimee Oliver*."

I jot down the details of her next show. If all goes well tonight, Zoe Willow is about to have the opportunity of a lifetime.

THE BARREL ROOM IS A DIVE IN HOLLYWOOD THAT DOES NOT live up to its name. It looks neither like a storage room for whiskey barrels nor like a place for fermenting wine. If, instead, you picture a family of rats building a bar inside a barrel, you might get closer. The place has the vibe of a basement decorated by frat boys on spring break. The decor has a decidedly yard-sale feel, and what counts as a stage is just an elevated circular platform at the center of a room of velvet sofas and thrift-store chairs. This is the type of place where you thank fuck for the poor lighting because you don't want to know about the overall cleanliness.

I find a shadowy spot in the back to stand. No sense in taking one of the few chairs. As a dragon, my feet won't get tired like a human's, and there are a surprising number of humans here, given the ambiance—or lack of it. The place is packed. Zoe Willow may have been a washed-up drug addict, but her pseudonym, Aimee Oliver, has amassed a following. People are buzzing with excitement to take in a show by the *undiscovered* talent. If they only knew.

A server comes around, and I order a bourbon, neat. The woman's eyes rake over me as she takes my order, and my inner dragon sniffs at her appreciatively. She's a divine specimen of a human, and given that my mating drive is through the roof, I'm tempted to return her small talk with an invitation. But I'm not the type to be easily distracted. I'm a Taurus after all. We're known for being stable, work-oriented, and attentive. Tonight, I have a job to do. The Zodiac Brotherhood is counting on me. I need Ms. Willow's witchy help, which means I need to know exactly what I'm dealing with when it comes to this witch.

On second thought, I grab the server's arm as she's walking away and order a second bourbon. They're both for me. I'm going to need them to take the edge off.

The sound of applause and appreciative whistles moves my attention from the server's ass back to the center of the room. Zoe Willow is taking the stage, and sweet goddess, she is not the same woman I saw in that picture on Raven Wish's old website. Gone is the waifish, heroin-chic physique, replaced by a curvy but fit body wearing a short, flowy white dress with puffy sleeves that twinkle under the stage lights. Her hair is a natural shade of dark blond and falls in soft waves around her shoulders. When she smiles, bright-red lipstick frames flawless white teeth.

She arrests me. Even from the back of the room, her ocean-blue eyes seem to draw me in. I can't look away. My dragon comes to attention and presses against my skin, warming my blood. She is enchanting. A siren. A wanderer of dreams. A passing angel.

The server arrives with my two bourbons, and I barely look at her as I hand her a wad of bills and toss both drinks back, grumbling as I wrangle my dragon into submission. Fucking alignment. Major pain in the ass.

Zoe brings her lips to the microphone. "Thanks for coming, everyone. I'm Aimee Oliver, and I'm so happy to be here tonight."

Her voice is a caress, and I watch as everyone in the room leans forward in their seats as if they want to get just a bit closer to her. Her gaze travels from one person to the next as her fingers pick out a tune on the acoustic guitar hanging from her shoulder strap. She boosts herself onto a stool behind the microphone and crosses her legs.

"This first one is about when something gets its claws into you. It could be love or drugs or alcohol or something we don't think about, like anger or fear. But those claws sink in, and sometimes we have to cut a chunk off ourselves to get free. And every time we fall back under the spell of that thing, it takes a bigger chunk, doesn't it? Takes a chunk and makes us smaller. That's what I call this one—Smaller."

Creator, her voice is hypnotic, and she hasn't even begun to sing yet.

"Promises.
You promised me,
you'd set me free.
Make things easy.
But all I've seen
is claws in deep,
slicing off a piece,
of my soul asleep.

Am I getting smaller?
Am I losing my way?
Is it any better when
you succeed in stopping the pain?
Or are you just a monster,
saving it up for a rainy day?
Who brings it all down heavy in
the most unbearable way?
Forcing me smaller...
Your promises...promises...
Crushing me smaller."

I shake my head to clear it. Fuck! No question she's a witch. I stand taller when I realize that I've leaned toward her like everyone else. All of us motionless on a giant, collective inhale. Even the servers have stopped working, paused in their journey toward the kitchen or bar to stare, gap-jawed and glassy-eyed. The bartender holds a bottle aloft in one hand as if he's forgotten what he was doing with it, as a single tear frees itself from the corner of his eye. He notices me watching him and swallows, then continues making his drink.

For the life of me, I can't tell if this is a spell or just her. She's talented. If this had been the audition a year ago, Crew and Gregg would have signed her immediately. I snort. I'm getting ahead of myself. I'm here to get her help as a witch. Then again, hearing this, makes it far easier to offer her something in exchange.

> *"Your claws*
> *They scrape and tear*
> *Sink deep*
> *Catch me unaware*
>
> *I cut you out*
> *All you're about*
> *Cut out parts*
> *I never knew I needed.*
>
> *Am I getting smaller?*
> *Am I losing my way?*
> *Is it any better when*
> *you succeed in stopping the pain?*
> *Or are you just a monster,*
> *saving it up for a rainy day?*
> *Who brings it all down heavy in*
> *the most unbearable way?*

Cutting me smaller...
I'm cutting...cutting...
cutting me smaller.
Until I fade away."

I ORDER ANOTHER DRINK AT THE BAR. THE BARTENDER POURS IT and pushes the glass across the counter toward me. "She's really good," he mumbles.

I'm about to agree when my inner dragon grabs my psychological wheel and gives a possessive growl.

"Huh?" The bartender holds a hand to his ear.

I clear my throat and say, "Thank you." With a lift of my glass, I slink back to my spot against the wall. What was that all about? Was my dragon really just jealous of Zoe's distant praise by the bartender? Fucking alignment. I shove him down deep, lean against the wall, and concentrate on Zoe.

For the next hour and a half, I listen to her sing song after song about freedom and sacrifice, about addiction and recovery, about sin and redemption. Her music is moving but also has a hypnotic beat. I catch myself tapping my toe more than once.

She's just reached the bridge of her latest number when a man near the front storms the stage, reaching for her. She shakes her head at him and steps away from his grabbing hand, never missing a note. But another fan, emboldened by the first, rushes the stage. Zoe backs up again, but the stage is a circle. A young man behind her steps onto the platform and places a hand on her waist.

She jerks away, but things are getting out of hand. Doesn't this place have bouncers? Security?

As if they've read my mind, the guy checking IDs at the door shoves his way through the crowd and starts pulling people off the stage. But there are just too many. Touching her. Grabbing her. She stops singing.

"Stop!" she yells when a hand grips her thigh. My drink hits the nearest table, and then I'm moving.

Dragons like me have a couple of innate powers. We can camouflage ourselves until we are practically invisible. We have incredible strength and speed. We can enter people's minds under certain conditions. As I stride toward Zoe, I push fear. I push distance. I part a path through the crowd as easily as a hot knife slices butter. And when I reach her, I lift her into my arms, guitar and all, out of range of the crowd's grasping hands.

Her head whips around, searching for the security guard.

"I won't hurt you." I project the thought into her head, and she feels it. She narrows her eyes and scowls. "Where's the dressing room?"

"Behind the ladies' room," she says.

I kick and shove and mentally coax the crowd to part, and I have her out of there before most of the audience knows she's gone. But when I reach the location she described, it's actually the door to a broom closet with a vanity set up next to the mop. I scowl as I set her down in the small space.

She's out of my arms, across the room, and holding the guitar up between us like a weapon before I can even close the door behind us.

Chapter Five

ZOE

"You're not allowed in here. Turn around and go back to your seat," I command, but unfortunately, there's no magic in my voice anymore. No spell or special influence, just a tremble of fear that makes me sound breathless and the twang of a string as I grip the neck of my guitar. Shit. I really can't afford a new guitar right now. I hope to God I don't have to break my baby over his head.

He holds up both hands and backs against the door. I hate that. If his back is against the door, he's not positioning himself to open it and leave. "I was only trying to help. The security in this place is severely lacking."

I don't lower the guitar. "Thank you," I say tersely. "If you could just show yourself out now, I'd like to be alone for a moment to compose myself." Compose myself. Right. Try breathe into a paper bag. I think I was one strong shove away from being trampled to death or torn to pieces out there. In one way, I owe this guy. He did get me out of a dangerous situation. But he's the size of a fucking bull. He takes up all the space in here. I don't feel any safer with him looming over me right now than I did on the stage.

He sticks his hands into the pockets of his designer jeans, pushing a jacket with an expensive-looking drape behind his hips. Who is this guy? Not your average Barrel Room attendee based on the watch he's sporting. Is that a Vacheron?

A charming smile splays his lips. "Actually, I was hoping we could talk. I'm Seb—"

Shit. Is he hitting on me? "No. Now isn't a good time. B-but you can send me a message through my website tomorrow."

"Uh, this can't wait." While I attempt to protest, he reaches into his pocket and pulls out his card, holding it out to me.

Confused, I lower my guitar and take the card between my fingers. I read it, then read it again. "Full Throttle Records? I don't understand." I've auditioned for Full Throttle before. They *don't* come to you. You go to them, *after* you've grown to a level of popularity they can't ignore and sent in a demo. Aimee Oliver hasn't existed long enough to attract the label's attention, and they didn't get a demo from me.

"Sebastian York." He extends his hand, and I shake it, ignoring the warmth that infuses through my arm from the touch. I'm suddenly aware of him for other reasons than his size. His presence is...intense. "I'd like to talk to you about an opportunity, one that could benefit both of us."

A flicker of hope moves through me. Could he have simply been visiting the Barrel Room and heard me sing? Could this all be some kind of karmic reward for finally hauling myself out of the gutter? I rest my guitar against the wall and sit on one of the two small chairs in the room. "Mr. York—"

"Please, call me Seb."

"Seb, you should know I wasn't expecting to play for a recording exec today. I have a set that could better showcase my range."

"I thought you were magnificent," Seb says, and I'm surprised how sincere he sounds. Maybe he genuinely finds me talented. "The connection you had with that audience was pure magic."

I frown, a tingle of misgiving radiating along my spine. No active magic was involved in my show today. I haven't practiced witchcraft in over a year, the entire time I've been sober. But passive magic remains in my voice. It's something I can't control, which is why I hate the way he says it, as if he knows I'm a witch and what he's after is the magic. If so, he's going to be gravely disappointed.

It also worries me for other reasons. If he suspects I'm a witch, then he knows witches exist, which means he has ties to the supernatural community, ties that might mean he knows about my past. "Tell me more," I say evenly, hoping I'm wrong.

He leans back against the door, taking a moment to find the right words. "I have an object in my possession with some unusual qualities. I'm looking for someone who can analyze it, tell me how it works. If someone could do that for me, I'd be incredibly grateful. I'd definitely open some doors of opportunity to reward that person for their help."

"You want me to analyze an object? I am no chemist, Seb. I think you have the wrong person." I hold his card out to him between two fingers.

He slides his bottom jaw from side to side. "I think you are exactly who I'm looking for, *Zoe Willow*."

I tilt my head and feel the blood drain from my face at the sound of my real name. "Who are you, really?" I lower my outstretched hand, frowning down at the card. Is this even real?

"I am the co-owner of Full Throttle, like the card says, but I'm also a dragon."

"A dragon." I squint up at him. I've heard of dragons. My mother told me about them when I was growing up, but I've never actually met one. Or maybe I have and just wasn't aware. He looks remarkably human. Now that I think about it, there was one person, the man who did my calf tattoo. His mind had pressed against mine, and I'd thought he might be a dragon. I'd never confirmed as much, though. If you don't ask personal questions, you rarely have to answer them.

Besides, my understanding is that they are extremely secretive about their identities and blend in seamlessly among humans.

You know what I am. The words run through my head, but they aren't my thoughts. I hear them in his voice, as if he's speaking directly into my mind. I raise my mental shields and shove. He starts and blinks a few times. "I don't have the wrong person. You're a witch, and I need your help."

I crumple the business card in my fist. "I can't help you. I don't use magic anymore."

He waves a hand. "You just did when you pushed me out of your mind. And don't tell me your voice doesn't ring with it. I practically felt it dance across my skin out there."

I shake my head. "That's intrinsic power. I am a witch. Magic lives in me. But I can't cast spells. I certainly can't analyze the magic in this object of yours."

His brow rumples. "Why not?"

My fist squeezes the card tighter, the edges of the cardboard digging into my skin. I don't owe this dragon an explanation. The reason I can't use magic anymore is as humiliating as it is personal. It would take me hours to explain, hours that I don't have. It's late. I have work in the morning. I raise my chin and look Seb in the eyes. "Suffice it to say that I overused my magic a year ago and fried my circuits. Actually, auditioning for your label with Raven's Wish was the low point in that journey. I haven't used my magic since."

"You look better now," he mumbles.

I sigh. I do feel better. Almost normal. And I won't jeopardize that. "My healer says I may be able to practice again someday, but honestly, I'm not interested." I don't like the way Seb's studying me, almost as if he's sympathetic. Almost as if he cares deeply. He doesn't care. Seb is not my friend. He's a stranger who wants something from me, just like everyone else. I hate the way I'm charmed by him. I hate the way I feel like I owe him something for carrying me in here. Most of all, I hate how my heart still clings to the tiniest bit of hope that my singing career isn't over, that he could be the key to my redemption in the industry.

But that's impossible. I can't do magic, which means I can't do what he wants, which means he won't give me what I want.

"There are ways," he says softly. "Working together, we may be able to revive your magic sooner. Dragons have healing energy—"

"I said no." I don't mean for it to sound like a hammer falling, but it does. I am not going to allow this stranger, this species of supernatural whom I don't even know or trust, to tempt me into using my magic again.

At least the no seems to work. Seb bows his head for a moment. When he looks at me again, he seems resolved. "Okay. But if you change your mind, here is what I'm willing to offer you: a two-album contract with a top-tier advance and a full PR and advertising budget."

I snort. "I don't even have enough songs written for one album, let alone two."

He smiles almost smugly. "You will, once I start working with you. You'll be given a cottage with a recording studio you can live in and work in around the clock, chef and housekeeping included." He smiles a little. "And honestly, after what I saw out there, you don't need any help with your stage presence. I'm picturing a tour of twenty or so cities once the album drops. Something to really maintain the momentum after release."

My eyes sting with gathering tears. Goddess, damn it all, what he offers would be a dream come true. But I shake my head. "Sorry. I just can't."

He studies me again, shakes his head, then stares at me harder. Takes a step closer. Fuck, his eyes are...glowing, and he's sweating, like he might be ill.

I raise a hand and almost touch him. When did he move in so close? "Hey, are you okay?"

He shakes his head and turns away from me. "Yes. Just need some air." Fumbling with his wallet, he throws a fifty on the small counter next to a can of hair spray.

"What's that for?"

"A drink. Dinner, if you need it. I'm sorry I upset you, Zoe. It truly was an amazing set." He turns and slips through the door, leaving me staring after him, surrounded by the sandalwood and spice scent of his cologne.

SEB

So much for the witch idea. Zoe Willow will not be helping us. Whatever occurred before, she's either lost her ability or lost her drive to do magic. Either way, she's not a good fit. It's hard for me to imagine what scenario would cause this to be true, but I know she wasn't lying. Her voice may reverberate with magic when she sings, but it couldn't hide her disappointment. And her expression as she turned down what was obviously her dream offer was nothing short of devastated. The scent of salt in her tears lingers in my nose. If Zoe had any choice, I am sure she would have said yes.

As it is, I'm afraid I destroyed her tonight. I picture her crying in that insult of a dressing room, and my dragon roils inside my skin, begging me to go back there and kiss her tears away, push that short white dress up around her waist and pound into her until she can't remember any sadness at all. I growl.

What an incredibly inappropriate thought.

I am not the type of executive that has affairs with the talent. I've always lived by the motto that you do not dip your pen in the company ink. That's a good way to get into some serious legal and ethical trouble. My inner dragon may be a horny, unrefined beast, but even in my alignment, I know better.

Any relationship with Zoe Willow would be an unpredictable and complicated mess, and that is something my dragon and I do not need in our life.

Unfortunately, my body disagrees. I glance down at my growing erection as my car and driver pull up, readjusting myself as William hops from the driver's side and opens the door for me. I slide into the back seat, and he returns to the wheel, adjusting the cap of his uniform.

"Remus called while you were indisposed," he says as he pulls into traffic. "Sounds important."

I pull my phone from my pocket and see several missed calls from Remus. I'd turned off the ringer during Zoe's show and been so enraptured by her performance and our discussion after that, I hadn't even noticed the vibration in my pocket. I hit the call button and bring it to my ear.

"Seb, thank the creator," Remus says in lieu of hello. "I need you to get down here right away. It seems we underestimated what's going on with the Order."

"Hmm? What are you talking about?"

"There's been another murder, and it has the Order's

calling card all over it. It's just you and me on this one. Ellison is back in New York with Connor and Fiona, and Lucas went to Maryland to try to track down the bomber. I need your help making sense of this. I'm sending you the address now."

"I'm on my way." I groan as I end the call and forward the address Remus sends me to William's phone. "Sorry. There's been a change of plan. We need to head to the Laguna Beach area immediately."

"No problem, sir. I'm on it." He taps a few buttons on the console, and the directions to Remus's destination come up.

We travel in silence for a few minutes, me shifting uneasily in the back seat as my partial erection presses painfully against my zipper. I consider putting up the divider and rubbing one out in the privacy of the back seat, but I know from experience it won't help. A dragon in his alignment needs sex, preferably with their mate. No other medicine will do.

William glances at my squirming in the rearview mirror and clears his throat. "Do you need me to make a stop on the way? Mia's residence is en route."

Mia is a fellow Taurus dragon and does indeed live in the area. We've used each other before in years past to stave off the strong mating instincts our dragons force on us during our alignment. William has been with me long enough to know, and it's not a bad idea, actually. Among dragons, it's perfectly acceptable to have such arrangements. It's just sex, after all, not mating. A salve that barely eases the pain of an open wound. A no-strings-attached arrangement. I'd have jumped on the suggestion in the past.

So why do I find that the moment I consider saying yes, my erection is gone and my dragon is suddenly uninterested, almost repulsed, by the idea? My brow furrows. Problem abated. "Thanks, but no. I'm fine. Remus needs me there as quickly as possible. Brotherhood business."

He sends me a little nod. "Understood. I'll have you there in no time."

I lean back in my seat, surprised as my inner dragon sends me mental images of carrying Zoe, the scent of her hair, the way her arms had wrapped around my neck. That's weird. Crap, I hope he's not developing a fixation on the singer. If so, he's going to be sorely disappointed.

I redirect my attention to my email as my blood heats again. It's done. The decision made. I will not bother Zoe Willow again.

Over an hour later, we pull up the drive of a beachfront property past a small contingent of police cars. I recognize Remus's army-green Jeep by the VENMINK plates. I hurry inside.

Remus meets me at the door. "It's a crime scene. I influenced the lead detective to let us in. Gave an insane excuse of being insurance investigators. Best not to draw attention to yourself," he mumbles. "If he starts asking questions, we're screwed."

"What happened here?" I whisper.

He gestures with his head toward the hall. As we walk, I watch him fade, camouflaging himself before we enter the bedroom. I follow his example, stepping quietly into a crime scene that stinks of blood and the smoky scent of dragon. A man's naked body lies at the center of the room, surrounded by crime tape and forensic labels.

His head is missing.

Remus elbows me in the side and points to the wall. Nailed to an enormous oil painting of a dragon is the head. Blood tracks from the severed neck to a pool on the floor that still looks wet. Painted to the side of this grisly scene are the Latin words, *"Astra inclinant, sed non obligant."* The same inscription that appears on each of the Saint's Order rings.

Remus nudges me and gestures toward the hall. We creep past the investigators, down the hall, and into an empty bedroom where we can close the door.

"Who was he, and why do you think he was targeted?"

Remus frowns. "Reed Follis, art professor. Popular among the local gay community."

"How do you know that?"

Remus holds up his phone and starts showing me social media and Grindr accounts. "His last post was about meeting someone for a drink." He holds out his phone. On the screen, a social media post by the deceased reads, "Sometimes love requires you to take a leap of faith."

"You think someone seduced him and came back here with him to kill him."

"It's a theory."

I lower myself into one of two leather chairs in the

room. I feel as though someone has delivered a serious blow to my gut. "Fuck. Do you know what this means?"

Remus crosses his tattooed arms over his black T-shirt. "It means the Saint's Order has targeted another dragon in the general population, unprovoked and on their own property. He must have concealed his ring too, or it was an initiate who didn't have one yet."

I nod. "Two attacks. Days apart. On either side of the country. We knew the Order stopped observing the accord the moment Donovan died, but this is bigger than that. This is war. They are actively hunting us, Remus. This will not be the last attack."

Rubbing his jaw, Remus asks, "What do you want to do?"

I hate that it's my call to make, but this can't wait for another gathering of the four. "Let's send out an alert to all registered dragons. Code red."

Remus's eyes flare. "You'd send the entire species into hiding?"

I square my shoulders. "What other choice do we have? After these two murders, it's clear that any interactions our people have with humans pose a risk."

"You're talking about shutting down businesses. Pulling children out of schools." Remus grabs his head. "What about the witch? Did you get her to agree to help us?"

I shake my head. "It was a false lead. She can't perform the magic we need."

Remus frowns. "Can't or won't? I could have sworn I felt her power in my head."

"She said no, Remus."

"What about a referral? Did you ask her for the name of another witch?" Remus's hands land on his hips.

I become intensely interested in an imperfection in the arm of the chair. "It didn't occur to me in the moment."

Remus scoffs. "Maybe you can track her down again. Get inside her head. If we find out where she lives, we can enter her dreams and strongly encourage her to help us."

It's a completely unethical and unjustified idea. Zoe isn't our enemy, and entering her head without consent would be wrong. Funny, Remus is usually the easiest brother to get along with, quietly intelligent and articulate. But a dragon born under the sign of Gemini is as unpredictable as an evil twin. When he's triggered, you never know what you're going to be up against.

I stand and stride toward him until we're face-to-face. "You wouldn't even use your customer files to contact her, Remus, because you felt it would cross some ethical boundary. Don't expect me to invade her psyche without her consent and force her compliance. I won't do it. I'm a dragon, not a monster."

He lifts his chin in a gesture of agreement and acceptance. Silence stretches between us. "But what about the other part? Will you ask her to help us find an alternate witch?"

My dragon suddenly roils, excited for an excuse to see her again. "Yeah, I'll ask her. That's a good idea. The logical next step."

He shakes his head. "I'm scared, Seb, for our families. For our futures. Do you think this is what the Oracle saw coming? Why she had Solomon step down?"

I shrug.

"What do we do now? How do we protect our people? It's been decades since we've had to fight. How do we tell them they're not safe anymore? How do we protect them all? They're counting on us." Remus rubs his temples.

Since the day I ascended, I've been proud to be a Zodiac brother, but right now, I lament my alignment. I'm the one in charge, and I have to make the call. "We have to be honest. Even if I can find a witch, it will take them time to work their magic. I know you don't like the idea of issuing a code red, but I haven't changed my mind about that. It's the only way to keep everyone safe. When we leave here tonight, we need to activate the warning protocol. Get the word out that every dragon needs to go into hiding until further notice. Tell them we don't have a way to protect them just yet."

"That's not a permanent solution." Remus shakes his head. I understand his frustration. This isn't going to be easy on any of us.

"No, but it's the only one I've got."

Chapter Seven

ZOE

My breath is coming in huffs as I drop into the chair in my cubicle at five minutes to seven Sunday morning. Made it! I'm so tired from staying up late playing my set Saturday night, and then agonizing about Sebastian and his unexpected offer, that the only thing holding me upright is caffeine and willpower. I must have smoothed out his card five hundred times before crumpling it again and throwing it away. Somehow, though, I always ended up picking it out of the trash. I don't know why. I can't help him. Doing so could kill me.

But I'm here, with my headset on, logged in exactly on time.

I cheerfully answer call after call, until my boss, Rachel, comes in, looking flustered. She's an older, heavyset woman who always wears a brown cardigan, even when it's ninety degrees out and eighty in this old building with its faulty air conditioner. She reminds me of a fifth-grade schoolteacher who's been in the game for decades and is just riding out the years to retirement. I get the sense she doesn't want to be here any more than I do. Her expression is always sour, and I have never once seen her short, meticulously curled hair move.

"Emergency meeting. Please log out of the system when you finish with your call," she whispers behind each of us. I hit the button and check my watch. Midmorning. Must be a promotion announcement or other news from corporate.

As soon as everyone is off their calls, we all gather at the front of the room where Rachel raises her two brown arms and wiggles her sausage-like fingers to get our attention. "Is everyone logged out? I have a very important announcement."

The last stragglers join us, and the questioning whispers die down into anticipatory silence.

"Before I start, I just want to preface this by saying that I'm very proud of this team, and this announcement has nothing to do with the quality of the work performed here. Regal Health has just announced a strategic initiative to lower costs by leveraging offshore call centers. Under a new relationship with Chennai Teleservices, Regal Health will outsource all call center positions to India. Our West Hollywood unit is closed, effective immediately."

A murmur rises among my coworkers. "But I need

this job! How can they do this with no notice?" pink-haired Emily cries.

I can't bring myself to say a word. My cheeks feel cold, as if all the blood has drained from my face. I don't just *need* this job. It's a lifeline. Regal is the only company, after more than four hundred applications, that would give me a chance, given my poor work history. And I applied for everything.

Rachel raises her hands again. "Regal is offering a voluntary severance package. If you agree to part ways with the company in the next forty-eight hours, you will receive four weeks' pay. If you choose to stay on, you may apply as an internal candidate for a select few positions in our Omaha office. However, if you choose that option and are not offered one of those few positions, you will lose the offer of severance, and your employment will be terminated."

Omaha. Jesus. I rub my face. I'm sure there's a music scene in Omaha, but the idea of uprooting my entire life and leaving everything I've built here behind, to do a job I don't want to do, in a state where I don't want to live, is just too much for me. My eyes burn, and then my cheeks grow wet as I can't hold back the tears any longer.

"What are you going to do?" pink-haired Emily asks, as everyone heads back to their desks to pack up the few things we were allowed to have here.

"I've only worked here six months. My chances of getting one of the few coveted positions in Omaha are almost nil. I'll have to take the severance," I say.

She nods. "Me too. I mean, I've worked here longer

than you, but Gary is the primary earner in our household. It wouldn't be worth it for us to leave the state for a job that pays minimum wage."

I slip my purse over my shoulder and grab the crystal obelisks of rose quartz and black obsidian I keep on my desk for protection and healing. That's it. That's all I have. Other workers have photos of their families, children's drawings, plants, and drawers full of snacks. Not me. I'm not in a relationship, and I don't have kids. The only people who might have made my wall are my parents, and honestly, after everything I put them through last year—how much I cost them—it's been a long time since we enjoyed a photo opportunity. I slip the crystals into my bag, hug Emily and a few of my other colleagues on my way out, and reassure Rachel that I'll complete the electronic form opting in or out of the severance package within two days.

Goddess, this sucks.

I ride the bus to my apartment building and enter the stairwell to climb the stuffy staircase to my third-floor apartment. When I moved in several months ago, the landlady, Mrs. Everett, said the elevator would be fixed "in a few days." It isn't. And the stairwell isn't air-conditioned. To make matters worse, Mrs. Everett's second-floor apartment is just inside the door to the stairwell. She can hear me coming and going, and she loves to stick her head out to inquire about my business or tell me the latest on the other tenants. She's an awful gossip. I try my best to step as quietly as possible as I pass the second floor, but even on my tiptoes, the floor creaks.

Sure enough, the door to the second floor opens, and Mrs. Everett steps into the stairway. "Ms. Willow, I'm so happy I caught you."

"Hi," I mumble, my throat still thick from crying on the bus.

She holds out a piece of paper. "What's this?" I ask as I take it from her.

Hands folding in front of her hips, she tucks her chin and frowns. "As you know, the estimated cost to repair the elevator is significant."

In fact, I did not know this. All I know is that the repair is well overdue.

"To afford it, I have to raise the rent. Your lease is up June first. If you want to stay in your unit, we'll need you to come in and sign a new lease agreeing to the new monthly rate by May first. Oh, I hope you do. We'd be so sorry to see you go, Zoe."

I look down at the paper in my hands, remembering that my lease is almost up, and I've procrastinated signing the new one. *Shit.* "This is $400 a month more than I'm paying now!" I say, my voice rising with my mounting panic. Even if I hadn't just lost my job, I couldn't afford this.

She frowns. "It's commensurate with other rent in the area with similar square footage."

I hold up the paper, fighting back tears, but I don't know what to say. I can hardly breathe through my constricting throat. I open my mouth, thinking that I should advocate for myself somehow, but no words come out. I finally give up, just shake my head, and continue up the steps.

She calls after me to "have a nice day," and I refrain from giving her the finger, which I feel makes me a candidate for sainthood.

Pushing into my minuscule efficiency apartment, I flop onto my sofa. There is really only one option. I'll have to move back home. I have no other choice. It could take me months to find another job in this market, and finding one that pays enough to cover this rent increase is going to be a major challenge.

I reach for the phone while the idea is fresh in my mind and before my brain has a chance to talk me out of it. Moving back in with my parents is going to be humiliating, especially since they covered the month I spent admitted to inpatient rehab. Technically, I owe them tens of thousands of dollars. They forgave the debt, but whenever I see them now, I sense a weariness in them. I required too much. I tested their faith in me. I was a blight on their reputation within the coven. It's going to take time to rebuild their trust in me.

So, even though I'm better now, asking them for help feels wrong. It feels like failure. It's an enormous step back. I dial my parents' number, and my mother answers on the third ring.

"Zoe? What's wrong?" Her voice holds a note of dread, as if she expects me to ask for bail money or for her to come to the hospital because I've overdosed again.

"Nothing. Mom, I'm fine. I'm safe. I mean, it's just..."

"Oh, thank the goddess." She breathes out a sigh of relief. "You know, I'm sorry to say, I still worry about you, Zoe. You've done so well this last year, and Dad and I are incredibly proud of you. But you must understand, I might never get over the fear of your relapsing after everything that happened. Are you still seeing Jeremy?"

"Yes. I haven't missed an appointment all year." Jeremy is one of the coven's healers, part doctor, part psychiatrist, part witchy herbal and energy expert. He's both physically healed me over the last year and mentally helped me to manage my addiction to gold dust, the powdered potion I once snorted to boost my power. All witches draw power from the goddess, but it takes years of practice in the craft to draw enough power to change our circumstances. Gold dust is a shortcut. It gives instant access to a level of channeling that would require decades of persistent practice in the craft to attain naturally.

Gold dust itself isn't problematic for witches. All young witches use it to help advance their magic, and I'll likely have to use it again someday to do the same. But the way I abused it to propel Raven's Wish to the brink of fame and fortune almost destroyed me. While it opened doors for us and increased our talent tenfold, it almost destroyed me.

Gold dust is addictive. I started out just using it before an important show, here or there. Then, I couldn't perform without it. The effects wouldn't last as long as expected, and I needed to use more to get me through the set. One day, it didn't work at all, because the amount I took stopped my heart. That's how I ended up losing our record deal and in a rehab hospital. Once they started my heart again, it took three days for me to come out of my gold-dust-induced coma. Since then, I've been unable to access my natural magic. Jeremy says it's still there, but the trauma of everything has left me blocked.

"I'm so glad to hear it," Mom says, pulling me back into the moment. "Jeremy will have you back on track in no time, honey. Just trust the process. Now, enough about all this, what did you want to talk to me about?" I picture my mother with the phone to her ear, holding my father's hand and smiling, relieved that I'm not in any sort of trouble. I squeeze my eyes shut. I can't do this. I can't disappoint them again. I *can't* tell her I lost my job, even if it isn't my fault. I can't ruin her day and have her up all night agonizing over whether I'll ever practice magic again. I can't hand over my adult problems to my parents when I have long since flown the nest and am old enough to be a parent myself. It isn't fair.

No, I have to handle this situation myself. I owe it to them.

The break in conversation stretches on for a few seconds longer than it should, and things turn awkward. "I...I was just wondering what you knew about dragons?" It's the first thing to pop into my head.

"Dragons?" Her inflection betrays her surprise. "Not much, honestly. Witches and dragons don't cross paths very often, and when we do, we stay out of each other's way."

"Right. Why is that exactly?" It's never been something on my radar. More of a truth I simply took for granted.

"Dragons have been fighting a war with a group of humans for generations. Witches have always tried to remain neutral. It's an ugly bit of business. A group of humans who've gotten their hands on some celestial magic have been hunting dragons for centuries."

"Hunting them? Like animals? That doesn't sound like a war. It sounds like an unprovoked attack." I try to imagine a man like Sebastian York being hunted and can't wrap my head around it. He definitely came across as the hunter last night. My heart skips a beat just thinking about the way he looked at me.

"You might think so, but to the Order, dragons have been undermining their success for centuries. A dragon's proximity inspires humans. If you're an entrepreneur, you might desperately want one to work for you, but it would be your undoing if they went to work for your competition. I think the Order feels like dragons are chaos agents whose very existence threatens their wealth and prosperity. Witches have always remained neutral in the matter. We stay out of their business and out of their way, and usually, they leave us alone."

I'm instantly sickened by that explanation. It sounds like dragons are being punished by this group for existing. Sure, their inherent abilities might cause disruption, but it sounds unintentional. Not something worth killing them over.

"I met one last night," I say. "I played a little gig at

the Barrel Room, just for fun, and one introduced himself to me. He looked human, but he had psychic abilities. Beamed a thought into my head."

"You're kidding!" She snorts. "They tend to be extremely secretive about their identities. That dragon must have felt he could trust you to admit what he was. What did he want?"

"He, uh, liked my music. Owns a label. I think he was interested in potentially signing me as a solo artist. Left me his card."

She sighs into the phone. "Well, if the opportunity is right for you, go for it. Dragons possess healing powers for witches, on top of enhancing creativity. Might be a boon for you. I met a dark witch once in my twenties who claimed to have a dragon scale he used in his rituals. Apparently they are very powerful. Just be careful. The psychic powers you mentioned are formidable. Dragons can influence your mind without you even knowing it. Even slip inside your brain while you're sleeping."

"Ugh, that sounds scary. Not interested in being mind-raped, thank you."

"No...no... I think most dragons are benevolent unless you're an Order member. But you just have to be careful. As I mentioned, they're at war. You don't want to get caught up in the gears of something you never intended to be a part of."

"Right. Thanks. Well, I'll keep that all in mind if I decide to pursue it."

"Any time, sweetheart."

I end the call and stare at the wall. *Shit.* Well, that didn't go as planned.

If moving home isn't an option, I need to get serious about finding something that is. I have no savings. No nest egg. Regal might have been soul-draining work, but I needed that job. Which means I have to find another like it that pays even more or I'll lose this apartment.

There's no way I can risk pursuing one of Regal's positions in Omaha. Even if I wanted to move, there's no way I'd get chosen for a position with my experience. And trying means I'd miss out on the severance that just might be the only thing to keep me afloat. I'll have to live on it while I find another job.

I *have* to find another job.

My eyes drift over to the urn that rests on my book-shelf. It holds an emergency supply of gold dust. If I snorted just a little, I could probably have a job before the day is over, but then, who knows how my body would react to it. I might not be able to work the job as I recovered from it.

I shake my head. "Not worth it," I mumble.

What I need is to make a list. Any place I can think of with employment potential. Maybe I could tend bar at one of the venues where I sing. I stand to grab a notepad and a pen, and that's when I see Seb's business card flat-tened on the counter.

Top advance, studio, place to stay, hands-on help... Seb had offered me the world.

All it would cost me is my sanity and possibly my life.

I sigh and start making my list of places to apply. But for some reason, my eyes keep darting to Seb's card squared on my counter. I've got to get out of here and clear my head.

I grab my jacket and keys, and I leave the card and hopefully my worries on the table.

Chapter Eight

SEB

My thoughts are heavy as I make my way to a little diner called Alice's in the boonies outside LA. It's a hole-in-the-wall, the type of place where the floor is always sticky, even when it's clean, and the paint job has seen better decades. Regardless, Alice's makes the best pancakes and is a safe place to be a dragon. For one, it's usually empty. Plus, it's not the type of place that richy rich Order members tend to hang out.

It is, however, exactly the kind of place I need right now. The coffee is strong, the servers are friendly, and the regulars are quiet. I need time and space to think. I need a plan. Today, I activated the code red. All dragons are going into hiding. That includes my brothers and me. This might be my last meal as a free dragon.

The bell above the door rings as I walk into the diner,

the smell of floor wax and warmed coffee hitting my nose like a kiss from an old friend. There's no one at the hostess stand, so I turn left to follow the row of booths deeper into the restaurant. And what do you know, the creator is playing games with me.

In an otherwise empty restaurant, Zoe Willow, dressed in a T-shirt and bomber jacket that make her look both casual and iconic, like the girl next door you always dreamed might love you, is sitting in one of the booths. She looks up at me through the steam from her cup of coffee, her brows rising as if she's as surprised to see me as I am to see her. I offer her my best attempt at a charming smile and walk over to her.

"Is this seat taken?" I ask, sliding in across from her.

Her lips sag in an exasperated frown. "Are you following me?"

I smooth my hand across the edge of the table. "No. Of course not."

"It's just that you carried me offstage last night and propositioned me with a very scammy-sounding offer—"

"That was not a scam."

She arches a brow skeptically. "You would offer me a two-album deal and a place to stay with a recording studio, in exchange for me doing a little magic for you."

"One hundred percent. The offer is still open, by the way."

She takes a sip of her coffee, which I notice is as pale as hot cocoa. "Why are you here, Seb? I can't imagine many music producers frequent this place."

"On the contrary. I come here for the pancakes."

"They're the best in California," we say in unison. The jinx lightens the mood, and we both laugh.

"I had no idea you'd be here," I say seriously.

"Really?"

At that moment, Sally comes through the swinging door from the kitchen and sees me. "Hey there, Seb. You want the usual?"

"Yeah, Sally."

"Full whip?"

"Always. How's Ken?"

"Doing better now that the chemo's done."

"Glad to hear it." She disappears back into the kitchen, and I give Zoe an intense look that can only mean I-told-you-so.

"All righty then, I guess you come here for the pancakes." She shrugs and turns her attention to her coffee.

"Are you waiting on an order?" I ask, noticing she doesn't have any food.

"No." Her voice drifts off, and she doesn't offer an explanation. I can't leave it alone.

"If you acknowledge that Alice's has the best pancakes in the universe, then why aren't you eating any?"

She sighs heavily. "I lost my job today."

"Did that asshole from the Barrel Room fire you over what happened last night?"

She snorts. "No. I haven't lost any gigs, thank the goddess, but unfortunately, those don't pay the bills anyway. They barely pay for my Uber to get there. No, I was let go from my real job as a call center rep. This cup of coffee is my treat to myself for remaining upright and not collapsing into a pile of tears, but it's all I can afford right now."

"You can't afford pancakes?"

She shakes her head.

"This is unacceptable," I pronounce. "I cannot eat pancakes alone. Sally!" I call toward the back.

She pokes her head out of the kitchen. "Yeah, Seb?"

"Double that order!" I look back at Zoe. "Do you want whipped cream?"

"Who doesn't want whipped cream?" she says as if it's a foregone conclusion.

"Extra whip, Sally!"

"You got it!" Sally yells. She comes out a few minutes later with two orders of blueberry pancakes with whipped cream and pours me a cup of coffee, then tops off Zoe's cup.

"Thanks for this," she says. "It would have been torture watching you eat those." She points her chin at my plate, her blue eyes flashing, then shovels in a massive bite of butter-and-syrup-soaked pancakes.

"So...I've got an idea," I say. "How about, since you don't have a job, you take me up on my offer and come live in the free apartment and accept the advance I'm going to pay you on that two-album deal?"

She brushes her bangs out of the way, and her eyes go misty like she might cry. "Look, Seb. I don't think I explained things well enough last night. I think I'd better give it to you straight."

"I wish you would."

"Young witches like me, we're not strong enough to perform the type of magic you're asking for. To deconstruct a magical object made by another witch is advanced magic."

"You *can't* do it?" My eyes narrow. It's hard to believe. I felt the power in her voice last night.

She presses her lips together and shakes her head. "There's a potion that young witches like me take sometimes. It's sanctioned by our coven. Think of it like training wheels for advanced magic. It's called gold dust, and it would allow me to do what you're asking."

"Then let's get you some gold dust and make this happen."

She licks her lips. "The problem is, I overused gold dust when I was singing for Raven's Wish. It's how the band got an audition with Full Throttle to begin with. When I collapsed during that audition, that wasn't from addiction to some street drug. It was the price I paid for using too much gold dust too often. That's what gold dust toxicity looks like in witches."

"Your heart stopped," I say, because I remember Crew telling me.

She nods. "I was revived, but it took three days for me to regain consciousness and weeks for me to be mentally myself again. I lost all my power. I can no longer do any magic, not even a simple spell, without it."

"So, you can never use it again?"

She takes another sip of coffee and glances out the window. "It's been a year, and technically, I could try again, but I'd have to be very careful. As someone who has struggled with it before, my side effects would be severe. I might code again. And if I did, it would be a far more serious situation." She uses her fork tines to make holes in the edge of her pancake.

I take in the set of her shoulders and desperately wish I could help her through what she's going through. I'd hand her a wad of money if I thought she'd take it. But maybe there is a way we can still help each other.

"What about a referral? If you hook me up with another witch who can do the job, I'll pay you a sizable bonus."

"How sizable?" she asks without missing a beat.

"Fifty thousand." I don't know what makes me say it. It's way more than a simple introduction is probably worth, but it will keep her afloat.

"I'll try."

"You'll try?"

"Hey, witches aren't all fans of dragons. I can't ask just anyone. I have to find someone who is dragon-friendly and also powerful enough to do the job. It's a delicate situation."

I nod. "Yeah, we kind of have to be careful right now about our identity."

"Exactly."

"But you'll try."

She shovels in another bite of pancakes loaded with whipped cream. "Yeah, I'll try, and not just because you've won me over with free pancakes."

I chuckle. "It was the whipped cream, wasn't it?"

"Definitely."

Chapter Nine

SEB

While my mind keeps drifting back to pancakes with Zoe, Remus is staring at me like he wants to hurt me.

"Have you gotten a referral from the witch yet?" The Gemini sits across the table from me in my heavily guarded cabin in the San Gabriel mountains, sipping a cappuccino out of a mug that reads "Treble Maker." I'm sure my Firetender Patrick chose that one on purpose. Totally coordinates with the death rays Remus is sending in my direction.

He's pissed because he's had to shutter his tattoo parlor temporarily under the guise of suffering a long-term illness to conform to the new dragon lockdown. It's the only way for us to stay safe. We're playing a game with the Order, and all the rules have changed. Our only defense right now is to see them before they see us. That means living in properties owned by investment firms with no identifying dragon information and staying out of the public eye.

I, too, have taken a leave of absence from most of my duties at Full Throttle in order to hole up in this cabin in the mountains. Every person on this property is either a dragon or a Firetender, a human sworn to serve us. Every security guard here also carries a gun and monitors the gated property electronically. This place is safe, but it's not a long-term solution.

"She hasn't contacted me yet, and I haven't had a chance to follow up. I've been a bit busy fielding questions and protests about the new safety protocols."

"Go today, Seb. I know it scares you. You hate walking into situations where you don't have control. But it has to be done."

I rub my eyes. He's right about me having reservations. "It's possible she couldn't find anyone. Considering what I offered her, I think she's tried her best, but she made it sound like not all witches feel favorably toward dragons. The only thing worse than not having a witch is having a witch who wants to kill us."

"Don't think like that. You've got to try. If we understood the magic of their rings, it could change everything for us."

I sigh heavily through my nose. It's only been a couple days, and I'm already getting complaints. People are going to come out of their skin if I don't do something soon. "Look, she's performing again on Saturday. I can check with her then."

"Saturday?" Remus curls his lip. "People have turned their lives upside down for you, Seb! You can't wait another five minutes, let alone five days."

I run a hand through my hair. It's getting long and I seriously need a cut, but I'll have to wait until I can get a private barber in, preferably a dragon. "What would you have me do, Remus?"

"Seek her out tonight. If you know where she's been performing, there must be someone there, a manager or something, who knows how to reach her." He points an accusing finger at me. "This is your job, Seb. Get it done."

I rub my chin with the side of my hand. Fuck, I need a shave and a shower and a weekend off. "Fine. I'll go today. But I've been thinking, Remus. Witch or no witch, we need to take action. Whatever we learn about the ring, it's not going to be a quick fix, which means we've got to be strategic about what we do next."

"Fuck. Why do I feel I'm not going to like this idea?"

"It's well past time we turned the tables on the Order. So far, we've been at war, but only they have been fighting. We've been running. We need to fully activate the brotherhood. Have everyone, all twelve of us, pair up and start rotations. Take them out before they take us out."

He raises an eyebrow. "You want us on the offensive?"

I nod. "Ellison has the list of order members from our rolls. I have a feeling that won't be accurate any longer, but Mason's mate Reagan is a journalist, and her friend Imana works for a vigilante organization. Last month at

Connor's, I heard she has her own list, and if I were a betting man, I'd put money on that one being more up-to-date. She's some kind of tech genius."

"You want me to talk to this woman?"

"Yeah, I need you to go to Thornsboro and convince Imani to share what she knows, any information she has on the Order. Get Reagan to help you. Then we can call the team together and start targeting members to neutralize."

"You mean, we kill them." He frowns.

"That's one possibility, but it isn't the cleanest, given how powerful these guys are. I think we aim to cut off their rings, even if we have to take their hands. They're helpless without them."

"We either collect bodies, or we collect rings," he mutters. Remus sets down the mug. "My father told me stories about the war, before Donovan brought about the accord. I never thought it would come to this."

"Me neither."

He nods and stands from the table. "I'll find Reagan and Imani and get that list."

"Thanks."

"And you're going to find a witch, right?" Remus's bright eyes bore into me.

"Yeah," I promise. "I'll find someone to help. I won't quit until we have someone."

"Good."

Patrick shows him out, and I grab my keys.

"Should I call William, sir?" Patrick asks.

I shake my head. "Not this time. I'll drive myself."

"Are you sure that's safe?" Patrick frowns.

"Safer for William," I quip. Patrick starts, his expression filling with fear. "Don't worry about me. I'll check in regularly and stay on high alert. Is it okay if I borrow your truck?"

"You're paying for it." He shrugs.

"That may be so, but I'd still like your permission. It's less conspicuous."

"Take it." Patrick grabs his keys out of the dish near the door and tosses them to me.

I jog out to the garage and skim past my Venom F5 to the much less flashy Ford Maverick and slide behind the wheel, praising the creator when I find the tank full. Then, I take off toward East Hollywood.

The truth is, I already know Zoe Willow's address. While she was playing her set, I cornered the manager and, with a little psychic pressure, got it out of him. I didn't want to admit it to Remus, but I found the witch enchanting and thought the address would come in useful at one point or another. Part of me may have even fantasized about standing outside her bedroom window, perhaps attempting to enter her dreams. But no, that would be wrong. Tempting but wrong. Still, she fascinates me, now more than ever. I'm not entirely put out at having to see her again.

But when I roll up to her address, I think I have to have the wrong building. The place doesn't look inhabitable. There's garbage on the front lawn and graffiti sprayed across the corner of the brick. I check the address twice. It's correct. Unit 304. I park the truck and walk in a door that doesn't close properly, into a lobby with a brown stain on the ceiling ringed with wet plaster, as if whatever problem is causing it has been festering for months. None of the security features on the building are maintained. The door doesn't lock. There's no one at the front desk. A sign on the elevator door says it's out of order.

I duck into the stairwell, climbing past peeling paint and loose handrails. As I pass the second floor, an older woman sticks her head into the stairwell and seems surprised to see me. She scans me from head to toe, her eyelids flaring when she sees my watch. When I give her a look that says mind-your-own-business, she disappears back behind the door. I continue to the third floor. The hallway is in similar disrepair. Wallpaper peels from the walls, and a few lightbulbs are out, making the entire place look shadowy and dated.

What. The. Fuck. This place should be condemned.

I knock on the door to unit 304, wishing that this is all a big mistake. Maybe the manager gave me the wrong address and Zoe does not live here. But I hear footsteps and then a familiar voice.

"Can I help you?" Zoe asks through the door.

I clear my throat. "It's Seb... I need to talk to you."

Several long moments go by. "I, uh...thank you for the pancakes and everything. I enjoyed spending time with you, but, uh, this isn't a good time. I'm sorry."

I stare at her door for a minute, until something scurries across my toes, and I break my staring contest with the peephole to follow a blur of brown into the corner.

"It'll only take a minute, I promise. Please don't leave me out here in the hall with what I hope isn't a rat. I'm not particularly scared of rats, but what I have to ask you is none of his business."

She snorts, and then I hear a beleaguered moan. "Um...just...hold on a minute." My dragon hearing picks up a flurry of activity inside. A shirt flutters through the air. A glass clinks into a sink. Some papers rustle. A cabinet door opens with a squeak and closes with a thunk. I snicker when I realize she's picking up the place...for me. Entirely unnecessary. If I thought it could convince her to help me, I'd dig her out of the bottom of a dumpster.

At last, the lock clicks and the door opens. This is not the Zoe Willow I saw the night before last. Her eyes are puffy and red, and she smells like she hasn't showered today. It's not a judgment, just a fact. She's dressed in white joggers and a burgundy sweatshirt that reads College. Not a specific college. Just the word College. Her dark blond hair is in a messy bun at the top of her head.

My dragon rouses, and heat flutters along my skin. *We could clean her,* he rumbles. *Lick her clean.*

"Well?" she asks.

Fuck, I'm staring. I shove my inner dragon down deep and step inside. She closes the door behind me. "Is everything all right?" I ask softly.

She looks down at herself and then at me. "Hunky-dory. Fan-fucking-tastic."

I slide my gaze to the left, where I find a collection of Chinese takeout containers shoved behind the microwave. "It seems like, maybe, you're being sarcastic right now and that something is, in fact, amiss."

She tips her head to the side and narrows her eyes on me. "Don't judge me. I'm sure that in whatever ivory tower you live in, everything is perpetually pristine, but here, in real life, sometimes people get busy and forget to take the garbage out."

My nostrils flare. "For three days in a row?"

"Are you serious right now? Why are you here, Seb? How did you even know where I live?"

I clear my throat and brush invisible lint from the sleeve of my shirt. "The manager at the Barrel Room shared it with me when I told him I had an opportunity for you."

She licks her lips. "Is this the same opportunity we already talked about—twice—or something else?"

I sigh. "You said you no longer practice magic, but I... We...dragons desperately need the help of a witch. Lives are at stake. Many, many lives. I respect your refusal to help, but I was wondering if you'd had time to think of another witch who might."

She sighs. "I haven't, Seb. I'm sorry. I've been...busy... and haven't had a chance to speak with anyone in my coven."

"All I need is a name. Any witch who might help us, please." I'm very close to begging.

"Why can't you find them yourself? You found me."

"Your voice betrays your magic." I see her brow twitch at the corner. She likes what I've said, so I continue, taking a step closer. "It's like hearing silk, you know. Like notes transform into something that caresses you from the inside. You may not practice the craft anymore, but your magic lingers in your voice like a siren's. I listen to hundreds of voices a year, Zoe, and you are truly a rare talent."

Her mouth works like she doesn't quite know what to say. I look away when a tear rolls down her cheek. I hadn't meant to make her cry.

"Was that what you've been doing in here for three days? Writing music?" I ask.

Her cheeks heat to a delicious shade of pink, and she swipes her fingers under her eyes. She doesn't answer my question, though. "Say I did refer you to another witch who could analyze the enchantment on this object you mentioned. What would you offer them in exchange? I have to tell you, there aren't many of us who could use a recording contract."

"I'll offer them whatever they want, within reason. And if they help us, there will be a bonus in it for you, of course, for making the connection."

"Only if they agree to help you."

I nod. "Yes. I'm a generous man, Ms. Willow, but I won't pay you for a referral to someone who has no intention of giving us what we need."

"Call me Zoe."

"Zoe."

She paces to the window. The glass is clean on this side, but the outer panel is dingy and cracked, framed by curtains that I presume were ivory when they were new but are now an uneven shade of tan.

"I think..." She closes her eyes and takes a deep breath. "I'd like to try to help you myself, if the offer is still open."

My heart leaps inside my chest, and my fingers tingle with the desire to touch her, to pull her into my arms and celebrate this turn of events. To have her in my cottage! My dragon roils under my skin with excitement. "The offer is still open."

"There's only one thing. As I mentioned to you at Alice's, I'll have to use gold dust. There's a risk that if I try this, I will need care to recover from the side effects. I need your promise, whether I succeed in cracking this enchantment or not, I need you to promise you will care for me until I'm back on my feet. I'm talking medical, rehab, a place to stay...whatever is necessary. I won't do it unless it's in the contract."

My dragon is as excited as a dog who's had a raw steak thrown into his bowl. I don't consider for a second that this is a terrible deal, that I'm promising everything for someone who has told me straight out she probably can't deliver. "Done," I say, without a second thought.

She holds out her hand. "Then you have yourself a witch."

Chapter Ten

ZOE

When my hand connects with Seb's, it's like I've extended my arm through a portal into some tropical paradise. It's instantly warm. Aruba, Jamaica, ooh my arm is taking me to a sunny beach somewhere. Is that a dragon thing? It must be.

So why does he look like he's been punched in the gut? He's bent over, holding his stomach, almost as if he's bowing to me. Is he holding his breath? Sweat breaks out on his forehead.

"Hey, are you okay?" I ask.

He releases me, and it's like the agony I saw only a moment ago was a trick of the light. He goes back to being as calm, cool, and collected as before. What was that all about? Maybe that's a dragon thing too. Maybe they all bow when they strike a deal. Who the fuck cares. It's done now.

But the feel of his touch lingers on my palm. Several truths tick themselves off in my head at that feeling.

1. This is going to hurt. Using my magic again will drain me and make me ill. Resorting to gold dust could kill me.
2. I have no choice. I can't support myself. I've applied everywhere and have no prospects. I will end up crawling back to my parents or be on the street if I don't do this.
3. I'll never get an opportunity like this again.
4. I have no idea if I can trust this dragon. He's not like me. He's not even the same species.
5. I am weirdly and undeniably attracted to Sebastian York, and I would regret to my dying day giving this opportunity to another witch.

Those last two mark me as a complete idiot. I'm putting my life in this guy's hands. This entire thing might be a suicide mission. But at least there's a mission to it. After my last application was auto-rejected, doing something riskier for work was looking more and more like my only option. Things like selling pictures of my feet on the internet or learning to dance with a pole came to mind. Jobs that would probably upend my life. At least this is for a good cause. I could end up saving someone.

I rock back on my heels as an awkward silence unravels between us. "So, um, do you want to give me the address or..."

He shakes his head. "I thought you could come with me now." He looks around the place, focusing on a moldy black stain growing in the corner of the kitchenette that has refused to budge, no matter how hard I've scrubbed. I've been willfully ignoring it for the better part of the year.

"Now?"

"Feel free to pack only the essentials. I'll send one of my assistants to get the rest of it once we have you settled. We can have your furniture moved into storage."

"Storage?" I'm confused. "Why can't it just stay here, in this apartment?"

"This offer comes with a place to live and a studio, remember? I promise you, the accommodations will be completely acceptable. I assumed you would want to let this place go."

I tuck my hair behind my ear. "I know you said that, but like, what if I can't do it? What if I try and fail? I haven't even been in the same room as this object yet. I can't promise you—"

"All I'm asking is that you try."

"But this apartment is the only affordable place for miles," I say. Even after the rent increase, I will never find a better apartment at this price.

He moves in closer, studying me, his eyes reflecting the light in a weird way that turns them gold like a cat's. His nearness is intense, and I almost give in to an instinct to rise up on my toes and sniff his neck.

"Perhaps we aren't understanding each other clearly. I will provide you with a place to live, Zoe, until such time as you choose to leave, if you choose to leave. You need not ever return to this building again." He darts another glance around the place. "It would be preferable to me if you didn't."

I swallow hard. He could be lying, but my gut tells me he's not. Besides, I can't afford the rent anymore anyway. "All right." I nod slowly. "I'll just be a few minutes."

He slants a charming smile and clasps his hands behind his back, waiting.

I shift my weight from foot to foot. This place is an efficiency unit, which means there are only two doors. One leads to a bathroom with a toilet, shower, and sink, with just enough space to turn around. The other is the way he came in—the front door. I almost ask him to go wait in the hall and then decide that would be rude. Instead, I open the drawer to my dresser that doubles as a TV stand and pull out a change of clothes. Then I head into the bathroom for a quick shower.

When I come out a good twenty minutes later, I feel like a new person in a skirt and a kelly-green top. Seb is on his phone, mumbling something about reports and working remotely. I pull my suitcase from under the credenza and start throwing in everything that will fit.

He excuses himself off the call and comes to my side. "It helps if you roll them," he says, taking one of my T-shirts and folding it in half before rolling it from the bottom up. He slides the now cylindrical shirt into the corner of my bag.

"Um, I can do this," I say, incredulous.

"I don't mind helping." He pulls another handful of

clothing from my drawer. As he turns to me, a thong swings from his pinkie. My cheeks heat.

"Really," I say, grabbing the clothes from his hands. "I'll get this. If you want to wait in the hall or downstairs, I swear I'll be right out."

His eyes snag on the thong I just tore from his hands, and the faintest red tinge colors his cheeks. I lift a brow. "I'll be in the hall."

Ten minutes later, with my guitar in one hand and my rolling bag in the other, I join him in the hall, noticing one of the wheels isn't working right. He hoists it like it weighs nothing, tucking it under his arm when he notices the handle threatening to break under the weight. Together, we descend the stairwell.

As we reach the second floor, Mrs. Everett appears, blocking our path. Her gaze slides over me and then Seb, lingering on the fine quality of his clothes, his watch, and then his shoes. She adjusts her glasses on her nose. "Ms. Willow, will you be signing the new lease? I really need to know as soon as possible. If I don't have a new lease, agreeing to the new terms, I'll have to evict you at the end of the month."

I glance at Seb. Here goes nothing. "No, Mrs. Everett. I won't be signing the new lease. I'll be out by the end of the month."

The old woman grows cross, her finger rising between us. "This is unacceptable. Your current lease requires thirty days' notice before leaving the apartment. You have not given notice. You will owe for one more month's rent. Plus the lease breakage fee."

Seb rolls his eyes. "Let's settle this right now, Mrs. Everett. How much does Ms. Willow owe you if she's out by May first?" A lock of his hair falls over his forehead, and I think I might swoon.

"$1,500"

Seb sets my bag down and pulls his wallet out of his pocket.

"I shouldn't owe that much money!" I protest. "My lease is up at the end of the month."

Mrs. Everett raises a wrinkled eyebrow. "No notice."

"Your notice was me not signing the new lease."

She shrugs again.

Seb counts fifteen crisp hundreds into her hand. I have never seen that much cash in one wallet. What sort of person even carries that kind of money around with them? My anxiety peaks. Seb is a partner at Full Throttle. I did my research and confirmed who he is. But does he do drugs on the side? Hire prostitutes? Why would someone, who should easily be able to rock a platinum Amex, carry so much cash?

"Zoe?" He's staring up at me from the first-floor landing, my suitcase tucked under his arm, the door to the stairwell propped open. Mrs. Everett disappears through the door to my left to her second-floor apartment.

"Coming," I say, pretending to adjust my shoe before jogging to his side. Damn it, Zoe. What have you gotten yourself into?

I get even more nervous when he sets my bag and my guitar in the back seat of a Ford Maverick, then holds the passenger door open for me. I stare inside. It's clean enough, new enough; it just seems odd.

"What's wrong?" he asks when he sees me hesitate.

"I guess I just don't expect someone who carries $1500 in cash in his wallet to drive a Ford Maverick. Or maybe I do, and that's the problem. Who exactly are you, Sebastian? Why do you carry so much cash? What do you plan to do to me now that I'm at your mercy?"

He laughs and moves closer until I can feel the heat of his body. "This isn't my car," he whispers in my ear. "It's my...housekeeper's. And I don't usually carry this much cash, but, as I mentioned, it's really dangerous to be a dragon these days. That's why we need your help. I can't leave a trail, even a credit card transaction. Not now."

"Because you're being hunted by the Order."

His eyes become slivers, like he's surprised I know about the Order and a little suspicious. He glances down at my hands coupled in front of my waist.

"I asked around after the first time I met you. My mother told me some things."

He helps me into the truck. "I will tell you everything you want to know, as soon as we're safely back at the house."

Chapter Eleven

SEB

Fuck.

Fuck. Fuck. Fuck, fuck, fuck.

Everything about Zoe is as intoxicating as the finest wine. As I slip behind the wheel, her scent fills the cab of the truck, a combination of clean linen, fresh-cut pear, and clementine. It might as well be pure pheromones. I'd been attracted to her before, but this is off the charts and highly unusual. I've got to pull myself together.

"Seb, are you okay? You're sweating."

I laugh and roll up my shirt sleeves, running a finger along the inside collar of my shirt and unbuttoning the next button. "It's a little hot," I mumble.

My dragon wants her. Wants her like he's never wanted anyone. A delicious daydream fills my head of what it would feel like to grab that tiny waist of hers, pull her over to my side of the cab so she was straddling me, and show her exactly what it's like to be with a dragon.

Mine.

No, no, no, no, I tell my inner dragon. Alignment or not, Zoe Willow is not mate material for so many reasons.

Mine, my inner dragon insists.

I swallow and turn the key in the ignition.

"Oh." We both reach for the air conditioning at the same time, and her hand brushes mine. She grabs my forearm, then moves her palm to my forehead. "You're burning up. And God, your eyes are…"

I blink and start going over first-quarter sales figures in my head. Gently, I remove her hand from my head. "I'm fine, really. Thanks, though." Shit. My voice is a rusted-out scrap heap, all rough grit. I start the car and pull into traffic.

Her hand is still hovering between us, her ruby lips parted. She blinks and reaches for her seat belt. "Is that a dragon thing?"

"Is what a dragon thing?"

"When you touch me, it's like…"

I raise an eyebrow. I know exactly what it's like… for me. Like someone just plugged me in. But I'm curious what it feels like to her. "Like what?"

"Hot." A cherry blush creeps up her neck to her ears, and her eyes widen. "I mean, like really warm and tingly and like—"

"Maybe it's just a man and woman thing," I say,

flashing a seductive smile. "I can't help it if you find me hot."

"I didn't mean—"

I break the tension building in the cab with a laugh. "I'm fucking with you, Zoe. Dragons run hotter than the general population. That's what you're feeling."

She doesn't say anything, but she leans back in her seat and seems to relax a bit. "So, where are you taking me? You mentioned a cabin with a studio."

I nod. "A private property in the San Gabriel mountains."

"How far?"

"A couple hours."

"Goddess."

"It's important, Zoe."

"You keep saying that, but you can't tell me more—"

"Until we get there," I finish for her.

She looks out the window and grows quiet. A half hour later, she's asleep.

❧

"ZOE, WE'RE HERE." I SHAKE HER SHOULDER GENTLY. A LINE OF spit trails from the corner of her lip to her shoulder. Before I can think not to, I reach out and wipe it away with my thumb. That's when her eyes open, and she stares right into mine. With my hand gently cupping her cheek and my thumb stained with her red lipstick, I try to speak but can't think of a single thing to say. Her lips part, and nothing comes out of her mouth either.

I clear my throat and draw back to my side of the car. "We're here. You, uh, fell asleep."

Before I do something I'll regret, I hop out of the truck and reach behind the seats for her bag. The sun is setting, and it casts a glorious pink and blue backdrop across the mountains. It's stunning, but all I care about is the eight-foot security wall that surrounds the property, the cameras that never stop running, and the armed guards who staff the security hut at the front gate.

"This is what you call a cottage?"

I round the truck to find Zoe staring at the house. I guess it's true that if she was expecting a rustic cabin, she might be disappointed. This place is an architectural marvel of glass and steel, designed by renowned architect Benjamin Foster to reflect and blend with the natural beauty around it.

"You don't like it?" I ask her.

She turns to me. "Of course I like it. Did you not just see the pit I was living in?" She points vaguely in a direction that isn't even close to the way we came from her old apartment. "It's just, I wasn't expecting the place to be quite so large or so..."

"Pretentious?" I fill in with a wince, trying to see it through her eyes.

She starts, "No! It's not pretentious, it's... It's...a work of art. A blending of livable space, architectural strength, and natural beauty."

My heart pounds. I love that she appreciates it. "Wait until you see inside." I take her hand, lead her up the steps, and through the front door that Patrick holds open for us. He bows when we enter. "Sir, there are several messages from—"

"I'll take care of it," I say. I've purposely been ignoring calls from the brotherhood. I've got no good news to share with them, and I'm not ready to hear the bad news yet.

"Shall I show Ms. Willow to her room?" Patrick asks.

"No," I say, too quickly and with far too much force. "I'll do it. We'll have dinner in the dining room in an hour."

"Yes, sir." Patrick takes off toward the kitchen.

"Wait, so this is your house? I'll be living under your roof?" she asks, sounding concerned. "I thought you said I would be provided with a place to live in after I was done with this job. One with a studio."

"This isn't technically my home. I don't live here year-round. And your place, well, let me show you." I lead her out past the pool to the small two-bedroom home behind it. It's a smaller version of the main house but still twice the size of her apartment. Technically, the thing started as a pool house, but no one would call it that anymore. I unlock the door for her and then hand her the key as we step into the open floor plan designed in white leather and natural wood.

"It's so light and airy," she says through a smile.

I love how excited her voice sounds, like I've just proven Santa is real. "It's yours."

I show her the chef's kitchen and then the second bedroom that's been converted to a recording studio with state-of-the-art equipment. She doesn't say a word, just sets her guitar case down and runs her red-tipped nails over the counters, the backs of chairs. I end the tour in her new bedroom.

She passes me as I set her luggage inside the closet, and I get a whiff of her scent. Creator, I have to squeeze my eyes shut against the swell of my inner dragon. Stupid. What did I think, I could stand in a room with her and a bed and be able to control my desire?

Claim her.

Sweat breaks out across my neck. I open my eyes and am relieved to hear her opening drawers in the ensuite bathroom. I take a step back and then another. Her scent fades with the click of the AC turning on. Another step and I'm safely outside the door. "If you need anything, Patrick can get it for you," I call to her, as I make my way toward the door. "Just give him a list. I'll need the keys to your old apartment for the movers. Anything you don't want brought here, we can put into storage."

I hear her testing a few of the drawers in the dresser.

"So, uh, I'm going to head back up to the house and let you settle in. Dinner will be in the dining room in an hour." I've done it. I'm about to walk out the door without having done anything I'll regret.

"Seb?" Zoe rushes from the bedroom, spots me near the front door, and hurls herself at me. Before I know what's happening, her arms are around my neck, and she's kissing my cheek. "Thank you. I still can't believe this is real! Oh my god, thank you!"

It's like I've been starving and the juiciest, most tantalizing steak has just leaped onto my plate. My arms wrap around her, one hand digging into her hair, my instant erection pressed against her belly. She feels it and looks at me, her eyelids fluttering.

Her breath is coming in pants, and so is mine. Our noses are so close, they'd touch if she flinched, and her lips... Oh god, those ruby-red lips. I long to taste them. I can smell her brand of lipstick. I can feel her breath on my mouth.

She's not pulling away, but inner turmoil turns her blue eyes to steel. If I kiss her now, if I give in to the urges of my inner beast, she'll assume this is part of the arrangement, some unspoken aspect required by a wink. I want her. Want her as my mate, if I'm being honest with myself. I'm not sure how that works with witches, but it's a one-way door for someone like me. Which means I have to be careful. And starting in a place like this would only complicate things for both of us.

I release her and clear my throat. "So, uh, I'll see you in the main house in an hour. Bring whatever you need to analyze the object. We'll start tonight."

"Okay," she says breathlessly, her eyes lingering on my face, even though she must have felt what's going on in my pants.

I slip out the door and draw in a deep, cleansing breath, relieved to put temptation behind me. And far too aware that, from now on, temptation will be my nearest neighbor.

Chapter Twelve

ZOE

I can't help fidgeting as Patrick clears the dining room table. I've just finished one of the best meals I've ever eaten in my life, but the tension between Seb and me is palpable. It's obvious why. When I hugged him, his body responded with an erection. It was a physical response to a stimulus he wasn't expecting. Nothing to be ashamed of. Oh goddess, Sebastian York has *noth-ing* to be ashamed of in the erection department.

But now, everything is awkward.

Once again, I have followed my instincts and probably fucked myself. Clearly, my hugging him like that without asking first was unprofessional, but also, he liked it. No denying he liked it, right? And I did too. I wasn't expecting it, but the moment I touched him, I wanted him. He *must* have felt my nipples harden under my shirt.

What I can't figure out is, if I did turn him on, why didn't he try to take advantage of the situation? I thought he was going to kiss me for a second. I wanted him to kiss me. But he didn't.

Have I found the one mythical male who has ethical boundaries and won't fool around with someone he's working with? Damn. The one person I wouldn't mind taking advantage of me won't take advantage of me. My bad luck.

As Patrick is walking back to the kitchen, I feel compelled to say something to break the tension. "Has anyone ever told Patrick he looks exactly like the famous jazz pianist Tangelo Fox?"

Seb grins. "It's a stage name. He goes by Patrick when he's not touring."

I laugh. "What?"

"Patrick is Tangelo Fox. He serves as my Firetender while he's writing new music. By living with me, he feeds off my creative energy, and in exchange, he serves me. It's a symbiotic and sacred relationship."

I lick my lips, trying to get my head around this. "Sorry, are you saying he works as your servant for free in exchange for just being near you?"

He shrugs. "More or less."

I blink slowly, shaking my head in disbelief. "That's insane. He's got to be worth millions. Why on earth would he be here fixing you dinner and washing your undies?"

Seb snorts. "Who said he washes my undies?"

"I just assumed."

"Maybe I don't wear any."

My face feels hot. I deeply regret the use of the word undies in this conversation.

His answering smile is dripping with mirth. "If you want to know why Patrick does what he does, feel free to ask him. He's a free person who does as he wishes. I'm sure he'd tell you all you want to know about the state of my undies."

While I'm recovering and trying my best to use X-ray vision to know for sure if he is wearing underwear, Seb rises from his seat and grabs a box off a nearby table. It's one movement. A human would push their chair back, stand, walk to the credenza, pick up the box. Seb slips out of the chair and retrieves the box with the grace of a dancer, or maybe a serpent. His movements are completely silent. He doesn't bump the table. The way he moves, it's clear he's not a man. He's a dragon. And I'm suddenly aware of him in a new way.

His relationship with Patrick is just one signpost that I am journeying into wonderland. I don't know the rules here. I don't understand his species. I need to remember that. I need to apologize for touching him without permission today.

"Sebastian, I—" My voice comes out as a croak, and he doesn't hear me. He gently squares the box on the table in front of me as if there's a live bomb inside it.

"Once you open this box, I won't be able to touch the contents. The ring inside is cursed and poisonous to my kind. Absolutely lethal. The vial inside contains water that seems to have a conflicting enchantment. Both are a mystery to us. We need you to use your magic to analyze these objects so that we can understand how they work."

"How they work? Can you explain more? What is your ultimate goal?"

He blows out a deep breath. "We want a way to defend ourselves against it. To be honest, we don't know what to ask for because we don't understand what is possible, only that this magic is killing us."

I try to process all of this. "The ring is poisonous to you. In what way? Like if it's put on your finger?"

He shakes his head. "It's true that if I touch it, it will burn me, but the real danger is that every member of the Saint's Order has one of these rings and can turn it into a weapon. If that weapon breaks our skin, it infects us with a poison that has to be extracted or we die."

I squint at him. Did I hear that right? "You say the ring transforms into a weapon. What sort of weapon?"

"Sometimes a sword, sometimes a dagger, sometimes a bow with arrows, sometimes a spear."

"Jesus Christ."

"Has nothing to do with it. Honestly, this magic is dark, Zoe. It makes my skin crawl."

I reach forward and pull the box toward me. He takes a big step back as I lift the lid, and I understand why the moment there is no longer a barrier between me and the ring. A deep sense of dread washes over me. The closest thing I can relate it to is when my grandfather died and I had to approach the open casket. My stomach drops, my skin goes cold, and I'm gripped by an intense unease. I reach out to hover my fingers over the ring, and I hear Seb inhale sharply.

"Is there any evidence that this will hurt me if I touch it?"

"I don't know. My brother's mate is human, but he won't let her touch it. The only people we know who have touched it are order members, after they've been initiated. We don't know if the initiation makes them immune to the effects or if the effects are what make them all murderous assholes."

I decide not to touch the ring, just to be safe. It's a relief, actually. The closer my fingertips came to it, the stronger the feeling of dread in the pit of my stomach. "I think I'll skip being the guinea pig on this one. I'd rather not be tainted by whatever dark energy is bleeding off this thing."

"Good idea."

I shift my fingers to the other side of the box, to the vial. Instantly, my skin feels cool, as if I've dipped my hand in ice water. This, I pick up and hold to the light. The water refracts with rainbow colors edged in gold. It reminds me of the light I've seen when I transcend to the Gold Room, the golden goddess's plane of existence.

"What is it? What do you see?"

"This—" I lift the vial a little "—is celestial in nature. I'm not sure of its magical properties yet, but the source of the magic is the goddess."

"The goddess?"

"Yes. The mother of all things."

"The creator. We call her, him...them, I guess...the

creator. You know for sure that the water flows from the creator, then?"

"No." I laugh, shaking my head. "I'll have to study it to know for sure. But if there were an office pool, that's the square I'd put my money on."

He snorts a laugh. "An office pool. I think I could arrange that. It might lighten the mood."

"We are going to need some mood lightening. The aura of this ring is dreadful."

"Truth. So, can you do your witchy thing? Take it apart and see how it works."

I exhale hard. "Yes."

"Excellent."

"But I'm not powerful enough to do it on my own. I'll have to use gold dust." I dig into my bag for the small urn I brought from my apartment.

"What exactly is gold dust?" He eyes the urn with curiosity. "The only time I've heard that term used is in relation to drugs."

I lift my chin. "That's right. It's a combination of salvia, mandrake, honey, and peyote."

His eyebrows shoot toward the ceiling. "Peyote? Are you telling me there's peyote in that mix? This isn't *like* a drug. It's an actual drug."

"I told you that the tool I'd have to use came with a price and could be addictive." I can feel my blood turn hot in my veins. I'm the one risking my health to help him. "You knew this before you brought me here. Why are we rehashing it?"

He takes a deep breath. "I thought it was addictive magic, not actual drugs."

I laugh until I snort. "Oh, I get it. You think that a witch's magic is all eye of newt and toe of frog? Wave a wand and presto?"

He frowns. "Yeah, I guess."

"It's not. It's grounded in science. Science and something more. Like you are something more."

"Oh."

I clear my throat. "Look, witches are born with the ability to access magic, but when we are children, it usually happens by accident. Most of the time, our first experience with it is right before we fall asleep. We enter a trancelike state where we can commune with the golden goddess in order to wield our magic. In our teens, we train to do this on purpose. We learn meditation techniques. We practice wielding the elements. By twenty-five, most of us can perform simple magic on demand. But complex spells and enchantments require decades of practice.

"What you're asking me to do—to view the magic that created this ring as if I'm X-raying its bones, then unlock this curse's secrets at a detailed enough level to know how you can neutralize it somehow—only one of our elders could do that without assistance. But the elders would never help you with this. Even if you could figure out who they are, the coven has sworn to stay out of this war between you and the Order.

"All of that to say, gold dust is a young witch's edge

in an emergency. This combination forces us into a strong altered state. These plants have a different effect on us than other humans. It vastly improves our abilities."

"But then you crash."

"Yes. I'm not sure how hard. You might have to do CPR. Do you know CPR?"

He nods slowly, his face paling. "And then you want more."

"Often. And you'll have to give me more. There is no way I'll get everything I need my first time ascending. This is too big of a job. Our goal will be to space the sessions so that we get what we need before my body gives out or I lose my mind."

He scowls but says nothing more.

I pull a mirror from my bag and open the urn to dump a small pile of gold dust onto it. It's a tiny amount compared to what I used to do, but for this first time, I just want to dip my toe back into this magic. I don't know what I'm dealing with when it comes to this ring. It's best I'm not under for too long. I rummage through my bag again and find my ceremonial dagger—we call it an athame—and use the edge of the blade to make lines in the dust.

I'd be lying if I said I wasn't excited for this. The truth is, I've wanted to do gold dust again ever since I went cold turkey. But I'm also dreading it. Wherever this job takes me, it will be a long road back to normalcy again. And I'm putting my future in the hands of this dragon I barely know. But oh goddess, I can't wait to do it one more time.

I lean over the mirror.

"Wait." Seb raises a hand. He has a strange look on his face as if he's…concerned for me. But why would he be any more concerned now than before? Everything that is happening tonight, he asked for. Hell, he paid for. "Give me permission to enter your mind if something goes wrong."

"I'm sorry, what? Enter my mind?" He's got to be shitting me.

"It's a dragon thing." He comes closer to me, crouching down beside my chair even though I can tell being so close to the ring makes him uncomfortable. "I know it sounds invasive, and it requires a fair amount of trust."

"To allow you into my mind? Yeah, I think so."

"But, if you…get lost or have trouble controlling this… this…" He gestures at the gold dust. "I can help you back. I can ease your symptoms. I'd only do it, you understand, if you need me. But I have to ask you now, because—"

"Because once I snort this, my mind might not be my own."

"Exactly."

I study his face for what is probably a minute but feels much longer. He didn't take advantage of me today, even though he could have, and if he's asking for my consent, that means he probably deserves it. The truth is, I might need help. I don't know how hard this is going to hit.

"You have my permission."

He smiles a shaky smile and nods. "All right, then."

With one more look at Seb and then the ring, I lean over the mirror again and breathe in the goddess.

Chapter Thirteen

ZOE

The effect of the gold dust is so much stronger than last time. It feels like pure starlight has been injected into my veins, a warm, sparkling effervescence twinkling in the mitochondria of my every cell. Gold washes over the room, giving every object in it a hum. The dense oak table sings in baritone. The Ficus in the corner whistles a light, happy tune with an underlying crackle that tells me she's ready to be watered. No walls or ceiling remain here. Nothing to contain me.

I'm temporarily lost to the wonders of the Gold Room, until my eyes fall on Seb, and I gasp. Like everything in this room, he's frozen, watching me with unblinking green eyes. But beside him is a massive dragon with scales the color of tree bark edged in gold. His dragon's bright gold eyes wink at me, and his tail flicks like a contented cat.

Seb is a dragon. He shifts into a dragon. It takes me a second to get my head around it, but I realize that the dragon, too, is Seb. The human-looking version of Seb is frozen on the earthly plane, but this inner dragon is here with me, on the celestial one.

The dragon chuffs and takes a step toward me but then stops, turning his face toward the box with the ring and growling. That's right, the ring. I'm supposed to be analyzing it. I direct my attention to the contents of the box and notice two things immediately.

First, the water in the vial is singing the most transcendent aria, radiating pure gold. Warmth infuses me, all the way to my heart, and I feel happy, truly happy down to my soul, just to have gazed upon it.

And second, the ring threatens to swallow all that happiness, to flush it into a black void of darkness and pain. Even on this plane, the ring makes no sound and puts off no light. It is completely silent and dark, a black hole of energy that drains away the giddy sense of belonging I achieved from looking at the vial of water. In all the years I used gold dust, I never once came across an object like this, like a hole in the fabric of this plane, like a vacuum, sucking all the energy out of the rest of the room. Nothing else shares these qualities, and I instantly know that what I'm looking at is pure evil.

As I study it, the hair on my arms stands on end. *Fuck.* What dark magic is this? I draw in a deep breath and exhale. *Concentrate, Zoe*, I tell myself. *You can do this.* Lifting my hands, I form two letter Ls with my thumbs and forefingers, then lift one elbow so that my fingers form a box, thumb to thumb. Finger to finger. A magical X-ray machine. I center the ring inside the perspective of this box, not touching it but trapping it within my focus and intention. My magic locks on to it, testing its boundaries. It feels cold and icky, but I get a clear idea of where the magic starts and ends.

"Show me the weave," I request of the goddess.

I'm shocked when a voice responds—a triune of voices—like three women speaking in unison. "Defiled. Unclean. Forsaken."

I turn my head, trying to find the source of the voices, but there's nothing here but light. I gasp. "You speak? Are you the goddess?"

A warm breeze caresses my cheek. "I am many but of one voice."

I have no idea what that means, but I don't have time to interrogate my benefactor. "I need to see the magic that fuels this ring."

The breeze that fluttered a moment ago against my cheek increases to a strong wind. "We shall end it. We shall dissolve it in pure light." The gold around me flares like everything is lined with lit sparklers.

"Wait!" I raise my hands. Although I've ascended to the Gold Room plenty of times, I've never heard distinct words before. Usually, I receive signs and messages, not words. As far as I know, this is unheard of. "I must understand it so that I can create a spell to defend against it. People are dying."

"It is death. It is destruction. It will corrupt you," the voice says, now from across the room, opposite the windows, as if whoever is speaking to me is circling the table.

"I know," I say. "I've sensed as much. But my friend's kind is being butchered by these things. I've promised to help him. Tell me how I can understand this dark magic enough to create a shield against it."

"Dragon," the voice says, now from the direction Seb stands. His brown dragon purrs and circles something I cannot see, like a cat rubbing itself against someone's leg. "This is your friend?"

"Yes. The rings are being used to kill his kind. I promised to help him."

"An old war. Darkness. One even the light may struggle to vanquish." A slight breeze comes from the direction of the vial.

"What is in the vial? Do you know?"

"A gift. An ancient one."

"Can it be used against the darkness?"

"Light only exists to shine."

Cryptic much? I wait for an explanation, but none comes. "But is there a way, a spell or enchantment, to use the water in this vial to protect against the ring?"

"Water nourishes."

Water nourishes? What the hell does that mean? I swallow, and the intensity of the gold in the room fades. The songs of the objects grow softer. I don't have much time.

"Show me the weave," I plead again. "I understand the danger, but I want to help."

"So be it." The voice seems to echo in the room as

symbols erupt inside the frame of my fingers. Foreign words, symbols, and sounds churn in the space around the ring. I latch on to the magic and pull my hands apart to enlarge the spell, my forearms straining with the effort.

I've underestimated this job. It's the most complicated work of magic I've ever seen. This ring contains layers of curses. No fewer than five separate spells by five separate witches are braided together. Each spell is attached to the others with what looks like needles or scaffolding. Booby traps. If I break one curse, the entire braid collapses, and I'm guessing this thing self-destructs. This ring is built to be a killing machine. A poison without an antidote.

It's meant to scare me away. But I grit my teeth and look closer. A charm is embedded in the steel itself, ribbons of darkness woven into steel. This must be what allows the ring to morph into the weapon of the user's choice. The way it's sewn into the physical design, it could easily break the ring apart and form it again into a sword or dagger.

Revolving above it is the shimmer of an incantation, a chant that I can no longer hear but whose cadence strikes me as something even older than Latin. I catch a random phrase of it before it sinks into the background, replaced by the acrid stench of the remains of a foul potion.

This ring was soaked in a fluid concocted of bitter herbs, soured fruit, and blood. No dragon's blood. I'm not sure how I know, but I sense it. The blood is the catalyst. The ring uses the dragon's own blood as fuel. Goddess, the reek of it slaps my senses.

I open my mouth to breathe through it, hoping to save my nostrils from the reeking evil, only to taste the next spell in the braid. It coats the back of my tongue as if I've inhaled a handful of sand.

By the time I cough to clear my throat, the most dreadful spell rises to the surface. Dark whispers wrapped in cackling laughter circle me. The golden room grows darker, the sounds taking shape as dark flapping runes that grow large enough to block out the light.

Someone has opened hell itself to finish this ring.

"Ah!" My arms grow weak, and I close my magical window slightly to give them a break. My heart pounds. My breath comes in pants. That last curse binds the other four together, and it is the deadliest.

I watch as the voices fade again into the ring, a black ribbon looping and diving. Now, I see it. Although the aura around the ring is consistently dark, I'd mistaken it for true black before. Each of the curses on this ring has its own distinct color. Yes, the voices are black, but as the metal charm bubbles to the surface again, I notice it's the color of tarnished silver. The incantation shimmers navy blue. The potion, with its bloody stench, is hunter green. And that gritty spell I'd tasted on my tongue, it's the deepest burgundy red.

I observe the strands rising and falling, again and again, each one blending into the next until the pattern repeats. All of them together are a nasty, angry tangle of magic that sounds like the scratch of claws across stone.

Braided magic, fashioned in the shape of a ring, no end and no beginning. Five distinct brands of magic. Five distinct spells. To break this entanglement, I'll need the antidote to each individual curse ready. I'll need to slip them into the braid without tripping the trap, and I'll need to execute the spells at exactly the same time to keep the ring from destroying itself and taking me and anyone around me with it.

The muscles of my neck strain as I desperately try to memorize every aspect. I never expected to find something so complicated, and I have no way to take notes because I need my hands to hold the window open to see the spell. However, I can't help but hypothesize about the origin of this magic. I don't think a witch made this. I don't think five witches could have made this. There's something far darker going on here. Something far more powerful lending its voice to the chorus.

"This was made by the destroyer, wasn't it?" I ask, praying the voices in the room haven't abandoned me.

"We do not speak of it," the voices hiss in unison.

"I'll take that as a yes." My head throbs. My arms ache. The Gold Room flashes in and out of existence. I can't hold it. My hands clap together over the box, and I list to the side, falling out of my chair as everything gold turns black. The last thing I see is Sebastian's worried face as he catches me in his arms.

Chapter Fourteen

SEB

Zoe's body seizes in my arms, going rigid and arching. She torques unnaturally in a way that would be painful if she were conscious. I carry her into my room and climb onto the bed, holding her to my chest. For humans, being physically close to a dragon has healing properties. Every instinct tells me that keeping Zoe close to me, touching me, will help her recover faster.

When Zoe snorted the gold dust, her pupils turned the color of liquid gold, as if someone had opened her head and filled her with molten metal. And then she was gone, there but not there. She murmured unintelligible things, stared at the box and moved her hands as if she were interacting with something that I couldn't see.

This is necessary. This could be the salvation of my

kind. But I hated seeing her like that, lost to some warped ecstasy.

A Taurus's greatest fear is the unknown, and I watched her dive into that gold abyss headfirst. It shouldn't have bothered me as much as it did. I barely know this woman. But seeing her like that and knowing it was hurting her, maybe not in the immediate sense but long-term, doesn't sit well with me. And now this, whatever this is.

She shivers in my arms.

"Zoe, are you okay? Wake up." I grip her chin and shake her a little. Something warm and wet seeps onto my lap. She's wet herself. I place my hand against her heart. It's still beating, thank the creator, and she's breathing, but she's out, limp in my arms.

I consider calling Morwyn, but the dragon doctor is busier than ever right now, moving his clinic to a new, secure location. Calling him out is a risk to both him and our kind. We need him ready in case there is another attack.

Zoe expected something like this would happen. I know the cause and the solution. As scary as this is, she just needs time to recover.

And I'll be here when she does.

IT TAKES ME THE BETTER PART OF AN HOUR TO GET ZOE cleaned up and into a pair of my pajamas. She's drowning in them, of course. I've always been a fan of the finer things. They're pure silk, and the neck keeps slipping off her shoulder, which might be sexy as hell if she were conscious. Thank the creator, despite having to undress her and bathe her, my inner dragon has remained subdued. He knows she's not well. Both of us are nothing but worried. My *appetency*, the mating fever that burns inside me during my alignment, is barely an ache as I lay her in my bed.

I grab her soiled clothes and take them to the laundry room. It's the middle of the night. Patrick is asleep. But even if he weren't, I'd want to do this myself. No one needs to know what happened to Zoe but me. I don't want to embarrass her.

I've just hit the start button when the phone in my pocket vibrates. Remus's icon appears on the screen, and I answer it in a hushed voice, not wanting to wake Zoe.

"Imani turned out to be a wealth of information."

"Oh? Did you get the list?"

"Got more than that. The organization she works for has been tracking an uptick in Order activity. The original list has doubled."

"Doubled?"

"According to her intel, the Saint's Order isn't just recruiting millionaires and billionaires anymore. She's seen rings on men of all walks of life recently, most of them linked to certain extremist political organizations."

I groan. "Great. So, they're duplicating like rats. Fuck me."

"Yeah. But that's not even the weirdest part."

"No?"

"No. There's been no announcement concerning Roman's death, Seb."

"What are you talking about? The fire was in the news. They said they'd recovered bodies."

"Not Roman's. We assumed Roman was among the dead, but as it turns out, forensics has now identified all the bodies, and they were all servants and security. No Roman."

"Connor watched him die. And wouldn't we have seen something in the news if he were alive? Roman was a media darling before the fire. Last I heard, a new CEO is leading his company. If he isn't dead, where is he?"

Remus gives a long, low groan. "Here's the really scary part. Imani is a genius when it comes to surveillance. She played some recordings for me. A few order members refer to a new leader as 'the destroyer.'"

The hair at the base of my neck stands at attention. "The destroyer?" I have to repeat it. There's no way I heard him right.

"That's what I heard, Seb. If Roman is alive and he's still leading the Order, he's taken the creep factor up a notch."

Dragons worship the creator. The creator is the origin of all life and light, and is said to be the maker of dragonkind. The destroyer is our devil. It is the source of all evil, of all death. I say *it* because we think of it as a negative energy or a power, not an actual being. We believe the destroyer took the form of a dark angel and gave the first ring to the first order member, an attempt by the greatest evil to counteract the creator, the greatest good. We've been at war ever since. If Roman is calling himself the destroyer, he's decided that he is the embodiment of everything that dragons hate the most. He's our bogeyman.

"So, what you're saying is, Roman survived the fire, has named himself the destroyer, and has amped up his attack on dragons. Great."

"Presumably," Remus says. "And from what Imani is hearing, the new recruits are restless. Reports of innocent humans being attacked by overzealous order members are on the rise. They know we're in hiding now, but they aren't giving up. Their hope is that if they wait long enough, they'll starve us out, and then they plan to slaughter us."

My head pounds. Dragons are almost universally wealthy. Our creative energy lends itself to attracting wealth. But even the wealthiest of dragons can't stay hidden forever. Full Throttle will move to replace me if I don't come back to work after my leave of absence. How we're living now is no long-term solution.

"Have you heard anything from Lucas?"

"No. I'm on my way back to you. Maybe he'll know something by the time I get there. How did it go with the girl?"

"She's still recovering. I'll know when she wakes up."

"Stay on her, Seb. We need a solution to neutralize those rings, now more than ever."

"Right. See you soon."

I hang up and slip back into my bedroom, turning off my phone so that it won't wake Zoe. The soft sound of her snores vibrates in the darkness, and I can't help but smile. I crawl in beside her and gently curl myself around her. I tell myself this is for her, that she needs my healing energy. But the feel of her tiny body next to mine drives away all thoughts of the destroyer and of the Saint's Order. The warmth of her, her breath, it's all that exists as I drift off into oblivion.

Chapter Fifteen

ZOE

I wake and turn over within the circle of a man's arms. Beautiful, muscular arms. A quick glance at the clock reveals it's almost three a.m. I rub an eye with one fist and prop myself up on my elbow, running my hand down the front of my chest. I'm wearing silk pajamas. Real silk. Definitely not mine.

"What the fuck?" I whisper. Within the nest of a plush comforter, the color of which is lost to the darkness, I stare down at the man who just seconds ago was wrapped around me like a shawl. I can't make out his face in the darkness, but there is no question in my mind that it's Seb. His smoky sandalwood and citrus scent is a dead giveaway.

I'm in Seb's bed.

In his pajamas.

And was, only moments ago, being spooned by Seb.

Goddess, did I have sex with him while I was on gold dust? Did he take advantage of me?

"Zoe?" he whispers softly. "Are you okay? Do you need something?"

"Why am I in your bed?" I ask, sounding somewhat defensive. He promised to care for me, not take advantage of me while I was completely out of my mind.

"You blacked out. You came out of your trance and collapsed. I thought about calling in a doctor, but I was afraid that would just complicate things."

Probably afraid they'd commit me like last time. At least that was a good call on his part. "I'm glad you didn't. But that still doesn't explain how exactly I ended up in your bed."

I hear him move. I sense he's pushed himself up, but I can hardly see. A sliver of moonlight sifts through the blinds on the windows, but it's not enough to make him out clearly.

"I needed to stay close to you to make sure you continued breathing. Besides, as I mentioned before, dragons have healing properties. I knew if I lay beside you, you'd recover more quickly."

"Oh." Is that a line or the truth? I don't feel like I've had sex, but... Shit, I'm just going to have to ask. "Seb, can you turn on the light?"

"You can't see in the dark. I forgot. Sorry." He leans over and turns on the bedside lamp, casting us both in a soft glow. I look down at myself and then back at him. He's wearing a set of pajamas that matches my own.

"Did we have sex?" I blurt, feeling my ears heat with

an intense blush. Now, I almost wish the light were still off. Then again, he can see in the dark anyway, so a lot of good that would do me.

"No!" he says quickly, adding a light laugh. "I only kept you here because you were unconscious, and I was afraid to leave you alone."

"But why am I in your pajamas?" I lift the oversized silk from my shoulder.

He winces and rubs his forehead. "You, uh..."

He hesitates, and I want to shake the words loose. *What? Got sick? Spilled something on my clothes?*

"You wet yourself. While I was holding you."

"Oh shit." Now my entire face must be red. I'm so embarrassed, I could cry.

"No one knows but me," he says softly. "Not even Patrick. I washed your clothes myself. Gave you a bath and changed your clothes. No one will ever know. Your stuff is in the washer, if you want it now."

His words are so kind, I almost feel guilty for suspecting him a moment ago. But really, what was I supposed to think? I barely know him. My brow lifts. "But, um, then, it was you who changed my clothes?"

The corner of his mouth twitches. "Yes." He clears his throat. "And bathed you."

I make a low, throaty sound.

"I couldn't very well leave you to marinate in your own piss, Zoe." His mouth twitches again.

"Just to be clear, one of the people in this room has seen the other person in this room naked, and that person is you." I scratch my jaw, my cheeks still feeling hot.

"Yeah," he says dismissively. "Does that bother you?"

I snort. "Why should it bother me that a near perfect stranger saw me naked?"

"I mean, I didn't see anything that concerned me," he says through a constrained smile. I glare at him. "No oddly shaped moles or suspicious rashes. Your tattoos are tasteful."

Fuck. My throat feels tight, and my voice comes out higher than usual as I say, "You saw my tattoos?"

He presses his lips together as if he's trying his hardest not to be smug. "Yup. The tree of life on your calf. The flock of birds on the back of your shoulder." He lowers his voice. "The dragon you have at the base of your spine. Interesting choice, by the way." The words drip off his tongue like hot honey.

Okay, if I blush any brighter, my face is going to melt off my skull. Pull it together, Zoe! You are a grown-ass woman! I mentally slap myself, take a deep breath, and will myself not to be embarrassed. "To be fair, I got that tattoo before I'd ever met a dragon in person."

He laughs. "Don't worry. It doesn't look like anyone I know."

I laugh too. "I hope not. It's based on a character in a book I read. Your dragon is beautiful, though." The thought of his dragon's rich brown scales, edged in gold, sends me leaping from the bed, everything I experienced in my gold dust trance rushing back to me. "I need pencil and paper, stat. I have to write down what I learned about the ring before I forget."

I race from the room toward the main part of the house. I think I saw an office off the hallway to the dining room.

"How do you know what my dragon looks like?" he asks, hot on my heels.

"He was there, in the Gold Room with me." I glance back at him. "Where can I find something to draw with?"

"Take a left. Office is at the end of the hall."

I take off at a fast clip.

"How do you know you were seeing *my* dragon and not a mental construct of a dragon?" he presses.

I laugh. "Oh, it was definitely you. His scales were a rich, glossy chestnut edged in gold, and he smelled like you. Plus, he was standing right next to you."

No sound comes out of his open mouth.

I raise my brow. "Wow, Sebastian York speechless. Never thought I'd see the day. So, I take it you're shy about who gets to see your dragon? Still doesn't make up for you seeing me naked, but it's something." I duck into the office and sit down in the high-backed leather chair. I reach for a drawer, but Seb beats me to it, pulling out the bottom one and handing me what I need.

As I start to sketch, he drifts back toward the doorway and leans against the wall. "It's not that I'm shy about it. I just didn't think it was possible. He usually remains inside me unless I let him out."

I stop, my pencil poised over the paper. "You can let him out? Like, in the real world?"

He nods. "I'll show you sometime. Not here, of course. Outside. He's...big."

"That's what they all say," I mutter, shading the side of the ring to try to represent the dark aura.

"Wait, you said he was standing next to me, but he wouldn't have fit in that room."

"The Gold Room is open. Things are there but not there. The walls of the room didn't really exist." My eyes flick up. "I wasn't really focused on his size, Seb, because I was trying to understand the threatening evil pulsing at me from the ring, but if it makes you feel better, he was plenty big. Impressively big." I turn back to my drawing.

Seb mumbles, "I know how big he is. I just wondered how it worked."

I start in on what I remember of the first layer, depicting the ribbons weaving into the metal.

"It's not something we usually show people," he grits out. I glance up, and he's picking at an imperfection in the paint on the doorframe.

"Either is my tramp stamp." I arch a brow.

His Adam's apple bobs. Seeing him vulnerable like this, it stirs something deep inside me. I was turned on this afternoon when I hugged him, but Goddess, him standing there with his hair mussed gives me the strongest urge to run my hands over his silk pajamas. I bet they'd be soft. Silk over hard muscle. I wonder if his skin would taste as good as he smells. Mmmm.

His nostrils flare, and he looks at me, his eyes widening. He clears his throat. "The ring. Tell me about it."

With a start, I refocus on the page and start drawing

again. "Right. It's the most complex and dark magic I've ever seen." I add what I remember about the second layer of magic. I use labels to break out the details: the symbols, the smells, the taste at the back of my throat, the tingle on my skin. Everything. "Honestly, I'm not doing it justice, but it's impossible to record in a two-dimensional drawing. And I can't remember all the details. Was it a lambda or a nu? Shit, I can't remember. I hate that I can't record what I see while I'm there."

"Why can't you record what you see? I thought you used it to write music before. You would have had to take notes while you were using. Hell, you did entire concerts while using."

I finish sketching and lean back. "Yes, but I need both hands to pull apart the enchantment on this ring in order to see the moving parts." I show him how I do it, even though now, without the gold dust, nothing happens. "It's as if I'm holding open a window. I'd have to close the window to take notes. Or record my voice. Maybe if I narrate what I'm seeing." I shake my head. "I didn't know what I was dealing with before. I'm going to have to go back in, and when I do, I'll be ready."

He scowls, looking concerned. "You came down hard, Zoe."

I shrug, rotating my drawing a quarter turn on the desk. "I have maybe a third of what I observed. There's no way I can analyze it or even start to experiment with antidotes to the magic unless I get this right."

When Seb doesn't say anything, I look up at him. "Are you okay?"

"Did my dragon...interact with you while you were studying the ring?" he asks, but his voice sounds funny. Almost strangled.

"Not exactly."

"Specifically, then."

"Huh?"

"You said my dragon didn't interact with you *exactly*. What does that mean, specifically?"

I frown. "He watched me and seemed to watch the aspect of the goddess I was communicating with. Honestly, it was nice having him there. I've never had anything conscious on that plane with me."

"Oh."

"Why? Is this still bothering you?"

He swallows hard, his hand tugging at one ear like the question makes him nervous. Is he sweating? "You should know, my dragon has taken a particular interest in you."

"Hey, are you okay? You look like you're going to be sick."

He laughs. "Don't worry, it's not catching."

I squint at him. "What do you mean that your dragon has taken an interest in me?"

He sighs, his silhouette cutting an enticing figure against the shadowy hallway. "It's just a thing with my species. Sometimes dragons can become...fixated."

I put the pencil down and stand from the chair, moving toward him. "Hey, you literally changed my piss-stained clothes. I think I can deal—" My head starts to spin before I reach him, and I sway on my feet.

He lunges forward and sweeps me into his arms before I can fall.

"I keep ending up in your arms," I say, blinking up at him. I mean it to be funny, but it falls between us, oddly intimate. The awkward moment is made even more awkward when my stomach growls.

"You're hungry." His brow bunches.

"Gold dust burns a ton of calories. And I could really use some water. Can you point me in the direction of the kitchen? I haven't had a chance to give Patrick that list yet."

"Point you in the direction..." He laughs. "Like I'd trust you to make it there without cracking your head open." He starts walking down the hall with me still cradled in his arms. "No. I'll give you the full-service treatment."

I can't resist laying my head on his chest and closing my eyes.

Chapter Sixteen

SEB

I'm not the type of person who has a lot of hang-ups around sex. It's a bodily function. A need. When we're hungry, we eat. When we're thirsty, we drink. When we're a dragon in our alignment, we fuck as often as possible. As long as all parties are consenting adults, there's no reason to be shy about it.

Only moments ago, I'd considered telling Zoe that I wanted her. I considered confessing that the reason my dragon was interested in her was that I desperately needed sex. That sweat she keeps noticing on my forehead is a sign of a serious fever with only one cure—her. For reasons unknown to me, she's the only medicine my dragon wants to take. Spooning her tight ass over the last several hours was like smelling my favorite appetizer baking in the oven. Now I've got clinical-grade blue balls and heart palpitations.

One thing stops me from sharing all that with her, though. She's not well, and it's my fucking fault she can't walk three feet without almost passing out. I'm not sure I can ever compensate her for what she's doing for us. What I saw on that paper of hers was the start of something seriously valuable to my kind. I knew when I roped her into this mess that she was taking a personal risk to help me. I just didn't realize how immediate and intense the side effects would be. I may be straightforward about sex, but I'm absolutely not going to seduce a woman who has a growling stomach and is fighting dizzy spells. I'm not a monster.

I sit her down at the breakfast nook and pour her a glass of orange juice. Then I dig under the counter for a frying pan. "What are you going to make?" she asks.

"The only thing I actually know how to make." I reach into the cupboard and pull out a box of pancake mix, holding up the box for her. "Sorry, I don't have blueberries, and I guarantee these won't be as good as Alice's."

"Do you have whipped cream?"

"Of course."

"They'll be perfect. They may not be Alice's, but I can eat them in the middle of the night in a pair of silk pajamas. That makes up for a lot."

"True. Chocolate chip or strawberry?"

She grins. "You're thinking small, Seb. Why not both?"

I chuckle, loving that she's feeling excited enough about this meal to joke with me. "Both it is." I grab a bag of sliced strawberries from the freezer and dump them into a pan over low heat, then add a little sugar and water. While that's cooking, I collect the ingredients for chocolate chip pancakes.

"How is it you only know how to make pancakes?"

"Mom cooked, and then Patrick cooked." Out of the corner of my eye, I see her cringe and backpedal quickly. "It's not that I think I'm too good to cook or anything. My brother Connor is a chef and makes the best food you'll ever eat. Cooking just never seemed important enough to learn."

"You have a brother named Connor? How many brothers and sisters do you have?"

"Oh, uh, Connor isn't my biological brother. I do have a sister, but she lives in upstate New York with my brother-in-law, Todd, and their two rugrats. Connor is a fellow member of the Zodiac Brotherhood, the band of warriors charged with defending dragonkind."

She rests her chin on her fists. "So that's why you were the one who came for me. You and your brotherhood are responsible for stopping the Saint's Order from killing dragons."

"That's right."

"How many of you are there?"

"Twelve, just like the Zodiac, but you'll likely meet Remus, Ellison, and Lucas in the near future. We're the four taking point on this one."

A pocket of silence opens behind me, and I dart a glance over my shoulder at her as I finish mixing the batter. "That wouldn't be the Remus who works at

Venomous Ink? I mean, Remus is a name you don't easily forget."

"Uh, yeah. He mentioned that he did the tattoo on your calf." I might as well be the batter dripping into the hot pan with that admission. Is she going to think we manipulated her into doing this?

"I knew he was trying to get into my head. I felt it," she says with a snort.

"He does it to ease people's pain. He didn't know you were a witch."

"Yeah, I bet. Tell me, have I run into any other brothers before I volunteered for this?"

"No," I answer quickly. "We didn't manipulate you, Zoe. I would've been willing to ask another witch if you'd referred me, but then you agreed to help us."

She nods. "I didn't think you manipulated me. I got that tattoo years ago. I'm just surprised. I thought you were the first dragon I ever met, but I was wrong."

"We are relatively rare compared to humans. We tend to live around art or art communities."

"Why?"

"Dragons are made of creative energy. We emit it. Being near us brings out innovation in humans, and I guess you could say it's our purpose. Creating is definitely wired into us, like a compulsion."

"So, you *have* to produce art?"

"Yes, but art is a lot broader than you might think. Designing buildings is an art. Agriculture can be an art. There's art in everything. I can't remember a time when I didn't love music, and I can play a great many instruments, but I'm a partner at Full Throttle because I also enjoy the art of the deal. The art of business."

"How many instruments?" she asks, repositioning herself and crossing her legs. The neck of my silk pajamas falls off her shoulder again, and this time, my dragon is particularly interested. I have to look back at the pancakes to keep my dragon inside my skin.

"About twenty, I guess."

"Twenty!"

I laugh. "It's not a ton when you consider there are over 1,000 different musical instruments in the world. And I'm a dragon, which means I can master any one of them if I put enough energy into it."

"Are you saying you can pick up any instrument on the planet and, if you tinker with it long enough, become proficient? Like, without lessons or years of practice?"

I shrug. "More than proficient. I could stand in for any musician at any event if given a few hours with their instrument and their music."

She shakes her head. "That's impossible. What, without even practicing?"

"Look, you probably learned to ride a bike in a day, right?"

She flips a hand through the air. "I had training wheels first, but yes, once they came off, I had it in a day."

"There you go. The arts are like that for dragons."

"Playing the piano is like riding a bike?" Her voice is incredulous, and she's shaking her head at me.

"That's a good way to think of it, actually. Twenty

isn't even that remarkable. Plenty of humans can play twenty instruments." I flip the first pancakes onto the plate and drop a second round into the pan.

"After years of lessons and practice, maybe." Her brows shoot up incredulously. "What is your favorite instrument to play?"

"I've always been partial to strings. There's nothing quite like an acoustic guitar." Gods, when I think back to the night I saw her playing at the Barrel Room, it gives me chills.

She grins. "Me too. I actually prefer it to electric when I perform."

"Definitely in my top ten. But if I have to pick one favorite, it might be the violin." I pour the warm strawberries into the first bowl I find and bring them to the table with a spoon and some maple syrup. I snag the whipped cream from the fridge and bring that over too. Then I turn back to the stove to finish up the pancakes.

"The violin? You play the violin?"

I nod. "As well as the viola, the cello, the bass, the harp, the banjo."

"The banjo?" She laughs.

"I'm partial to the violin. I had the privilege of playing a duet with Lindsey Stirling once. Positively magical. Thought she was a dragon until I met her in person."

As I turn to bring the pancakes to the table, I see a strange expression flit across her face, and if I didn't know better, I'd swear it was jealousy. But it's gone so quickly, I can't be sure. In any case, she mounds a pile of whipped cream at the center of her pancakes and digs in like she hasn't eaten in a week.

"My god, this syrup is incredible."

"It's the best. From a tiny maple orchard in Illinois, of all places. Someone gifted me a bottle a few years ago, and I've never gone back."

A few minutes later, at the end of her second pancake, she leans back in her chair. "I'm going to have to use gold dust again to get the rest of the details on the ring. I can't do it right away, though, or my wetting myself will be the least of our worries."

"You said the day of your audition with our label, you went into cardiac arrest?"

She nods. "I died... Twice." I wince. "I'm lucky to be here, actually. Each time I use it, the length of effectiveness shortens and the consequences grow worse. And it changes me. I'll get mean, manipulative, cruel. I—"

"You?"

"I burned my bridges with my family and most of my friends. I borrowed money, spent it all on gold dust, and never paid it back. I lied to people I loved. I drained my parents' savings to pay for rehab. That's why I'm here. That's why I need the house and the money you're paying me. Gold dust has taken everything from me. Well, almost everything. I'm still alive."

I reach across the table and take her hand, her fingers slightly sticky from where she was holding her fork. "Well, I know what's coming, and I promise I'll care for you. I'll make sure gold dust doesn't steal anything from you again."

"I'll have to wait to go back in. Wait until I'm stronger. Otherwise, I won't be able to get the most of my time in the Gold Room."

"How long?"

"A day? Maybe two?"

I nod. Dark circles have formed under her eyes. She needs rest. "I'll help you back to your house." I release her hand. A drop of syrup lingers on the corner of her mouth. Absently, I wipe it away with the pad of my thumb. I bring it to my mouth and suck the sweetness from my skin. Her eyes lock on my mouth, and I remove my thumb quickly, shifting in my chair.

"You're sweating again."

"It's a dragon thing. Don't worry about it."

She drains the rest of her orange juice. We stand and walk slowly toward the back door.

"Will you play for me sometime?"

"The violin?"

"Yes."

"Sure."

She smiles weakly.

I gather her things for her, including her outfit from the wash, and walk her past the pool to the door to her cottage. She fishes the keys out of the side of the black bag and lets herself inside, before taking her bag from me. Our eyes meet and hold as she slips the strap onto her own shoulder.

"Goodnight, Zoe," I finally say.

"Thanks for the pancakes. Again."

Chapter Seventeen

ZOE

When I wake up the next morning, my brain has its own heartbeat, and the pulse of it thumps directly between my eyes. Also, my bladder is ready to burst. In fact, I think my having to pee is what woke me up in the first place. I slide from under the covers, a movement that reminds me I'm still wearing Seb's silk pajamas, and race for the bathroom. I make it just in time, and the feeling of relief I get from emptying it is amazing.

Afterward, I walk into the kitchen and dig my phone out of the black bag, which is exactly where I left it last night, in front of the door. My stomach is growling again, and I still don't have anything to eat. I plan to wash Seb's pajamas—can you wash silk?—and bring them up to the main house with a list for Patrick. Maybe, if I ask nicely, he'll make me some breakfast.

But when I look down at my phone screen, I realize the problem with that plan. It's two o'clock in the afternoon. Patrick can make me eggs and toast, but I don't think we can call it breakfast any longer. We are officially into lunch territory. Shit, we are pushing high tea. Worse, my screen is covered with missed messages from Jeremy. Fuck, we were supposed to have a Zoom session this morning. I slept right through it.

Feeling light-headed, I stumble to the counter and pour myself a glass of water, then drain it in a few gulps. No wonder I feel like crap. On top of recovering from gold dust, I've slept for at least twelve hours.

I pour another glass of water and drink it down. Then I send Jeremy a message:

Sorry to miss our appointment! I had a job interview that turned into a job. Unfortunately, I will need to cancel our other scheduled sessions until I'm settled into this position.

I hit send. I'll call the office later to make sure my sessions get canceled. I haven't even had a chance to set down my phone when it rings. It's a video call, from Jeremy. I answer it but turn my camera off. I can see his face, but all he can see is a picture of me smiling next to a carved pumpkin from last Halloween.

"Zoe, are you there? Your video isn't working."

"This isn't a good time, Jeremy. I'm right in the middle of something. In fact, I just sent you a text."

"I saw it. I'm just really uncomfortable with you missing our sessions right now. You've been sober for a year. This would be a terrible time for a relapse."

I rub my head. If he only knew. "Thank you for your

concern. Your sessions have been truly helpful to me, but I lost my job at Regal and was blessed by the goddess to have another position pop up. I really can't afford to jeopardize it right now."

"Oh? Where are you working?"

I think fast. I don't want to lie to Jeremy, mostly because his witchy skills make him a human lie detector. But also, I can't exactly tell him everything. "I'm working for Full Throttle Records, assisting one of the producers with a special project." There. That's the truth.

"Wow." He tucks his chin in surprise. "I didn't even know you were pursuing a new career."

I hate this comment for several reasons. First, working as a call center rep definitely didn't make it my career. It was a job. The only one I could find at the time. Second, why would it surprise him that I'd pursue something in the music industry? Until the incident, I was a very successful singer and songwriter.

"Why are you surprised? Music has always been my passion."

Jeremy has helped me a lot over the last year, but when he purses his lips, he looks like an old woman trapped in a man's body. He's only a few years older than me, much too young to make that face. It's an unusually judgmental expression, considering I've done nothing wrong. "It's just that music is such a trigger for you, hun. Your parents have always been really adamant that they feel you would have never tried gold dust if not for the pressure the industry put on you to develop skills and talents you maybe didn't have."

What? My head pounds, and I can't hold back the words that bubble up my throat next. "I never used gold dust to increase my musical abilities, Jeremy. Every song I sang, I wrote and performed sober, before the gold dust. I used the gold dust to help our discoverability. I used it to gain popularity, not because I was lacking in talent. It was all about publicity for Raven's Wish."

He raises both hands. "Whatever you say, Zoe. I'm just reminding you that the music industry has been triggering for you in the past." His voice is annoyingly placating, as if I've flown off the handle, although I haven't raised my voice at all.

I smile so that he can hear it in my voice. "Not triggered, Jeremy. I'm just very busy right now and need to go. Thank you for your call and for your concern. I'll be in touch about future appointments once my schedule is set. Have a nice day!"

I move to hang up, but he raises a hand and makes an urgent sound. "I'm afraid that won't do. Your parents are paying me to ensure your ongoing health. I can't make you continue our sessions, but I must insist that you check in with me regularly, just for their peace of mind."

I laugh. "I can check in directly with my parents. In fact, I need to call Mom and give her an update."

"But, after everything, they want *me* to check in with you. You have to understand, you put them through hell, Zoe. They want me to assure them you're doing okay. You don't want to worry them, do you?"

I close my eyes and sigh through my nose, thankful that he can't see me. I hate this. Jeremy is going to be a pain in the ass. But he's right. If I cut him off completely, my parents will worry.

"Okay. But just a phone check-in, like today. Do you want to schedule something now?"

He offers a broad, self-satisfied smile. "No need for anything formal. I'll set a reminder for myself. Best of luck to you in your new position."

"Wait—" He's gone. *Shit.* I really wanted a scheduled call and not some random check-in. *Shit.*

My stomach growls. Shower. Clothes. Tylenol. Then find Patrick and food.

A knock comes at the door. Who could that be?

I peer through the peephole and then can't unlock the door fast enough. Patrick stands just outside with a silver tray with what looks like a pitcher of coffee, a carafe of juice, and a silver cloche that smells of bacon.

"Please tell me you brought that for me," I say.

He grins. "You are the only one living in the cottage as far as I know," he teases. I open the door wider, and he lets himself in. I practically throw myself into the chair the moment he sets the tray down on the table and already have the fork in my hand by the time he removes the cloche. It's eggs! And bacon! And buttered toast! I think I might cry, but first, I pluck a triangle of toast from the plate and stick a corner into my mouth.

Patrick is watching me with a note of joviality in his eyes.

"I'm really hungry," I say. "Thank you."

"I'm pleased you're enjoying it."

He folds his hands and leans against the counter. I

take another bite. Am I supposed to tell him he can go or something?

When he notices me watching him, he raises a hand. "No rush, but Sebastian said you'd have a list for me of things you'd like from the market. And also, the contents of your apartment will arrive today. I'll need to know what you'd like delivered here and what we should put in storage for you."

I take a bite of the bacon. Delicious.

Patrick comes to my side and pours me a cup of coffee, then takes the plastic wrap off the carafe of orange juice. I look up at him with a full mouth and eyes that must hold all the gratitude I'm feeling in my heart.

"I'll return in an hour." He bows and then slips out the door.

Chapter Eighteen

SEB

"This is a long list. They're so spread out," I flip the pages of the Saint's Order members Remus has brought me. Technically, he brought me a thumb drive, but I've always processed things better with paper in my hands.

"They are where we are," Remus says. "Imani thinks that part of the magic of the rings is that they are drawn to our energy, because they tend to end up wherever we end up."

"Because they're hunting us," I say.

He shakes his head. "She's into technology, Seb. Didn't even believe in magic until recently. She can see it in the data. Where we go, they go. They're either following us or following the art we inspire."

"You seem to have learned a lot from Imani."

He flashes me a perfect Gemini half grin, a spark of wickedness in his eye. "She's quite a woman."

"Are you falling for the human, Remus?" I jest.

He clears his throat. "I wouldn't call it that. But I wouldn't turn down a few more hours listening to her theories, I'll tell you that."

We both chuckle.

"Speaking of women, where is that witch of yours?" he adds.

I snort. "Not mine, and she's resting. She's onto something, though. This is what she saw last night." I show him Zoe's drawing of the ring.

"Creator defend us all. What do all these symbols mean?"

"She said they were spells. Layers of spells. It's complex. She needs to go back in to make sure she understands it all, and then she can recommend how best to defend ourselves against it."

Remus lifts his cap and runs a hand over his buzz-cut head. "Fuck. This is great news. So, when is that going to happen, 'cause we need a solution like yesterday."

I frown. "It's going to be a few days. Doing what she had to do to understand the ring had...side effects."

He squints at me. "What kind of side effects?"

"The kind that could kill her if she pushes herself too hard."

Remus whistles through his teeth.

"Yeah, so I need to stay close to her to heal her afterward. I have to be here to protect her."

Remus's nostrils flare. "Shit."

I look over my shoulder and then back at him, but I don't know what he's smelling. No one is here but us. "What? Is Ellison here?"

He snorts. "Brother, you are putting off mating scent every time you mention Zoe."

The sound of her name on his lips sends my dragon into a lurch. I stand and lunge toward Remus, my dragon pressing against the underside of my skin. Sweat breaks out across my forehead.

Remus chuckles behind his cupped palm. "Damn, you've got it bad, brother."

I lower myself back into my chair, feeling my cheeks heat. I bury my face in my hands, not even bothering to deny it. "Fuuuck. Why does it have to be her?"

Remus's hand lands on my shoulder. "We don't pick who we want to mate. The creator does."

I groan. "The creator picks for me. She gets to choose for herself. That's the problem. She could reject me. And then what? I pine for her while she puts herself at risk to help dragonkind?"

"How is that different from what's happening right now?" Remus shrugs his tattooed shoulders. "Unless you want me to call Mia to come take the edge off?"

I growl, feeling repulsed.

"Judging by the shade of green you just pulled, you are beyond accepting any substitutes." He balls his hand into a fist. "One thing I think we can both agree on, though, is if she is your mate, you can't rush things. If she rejects you right now, you're toast."

"No shit," I say sarcastically.

"So, you need to talk to her and start, you know, getting to know each other, but like in a way that makes her fall for you without scaring her off or jeopardizing what we're trying to do."

I level a flat glare in his direction. "Genius," I deadpan. "Wish I would have thought of that."

He chuckles and spreads his hands. "I'm just saying, sort it out, Seb. We need you at your best."

I nod. "I'll sort it out."

"Meanwhile, how do you want to approach this list?"

I stare at the names. There's really only one choice. "We go out in pairs. We go where we think they will be. And we try to remove three rings a night. It'll be a few nights before Zoe can try her magic again. You and I can take the first rotation, followed by Ellison and Lucas. On down the twelve."

"Rotation to do what?" Zoe asks. She's standing at the entrance to the living room, looking like an angel in a white sundress and red lipstick. "Sorry, I didn't mean to eavesdrop. Patrick said dinner was in twenty. Oh, hi, Remus."

"Perfectly okay," I say, then glance between her and Remus. "That's right, you two have already met."

She nods and offers him her hand. "Nice to see you again."

My dragon growls at a decibel I know only his dragon can hear. Remus stares at her hand like she's offering him the hot end of a cattle prod. He does not shake it, instead choosing that moment to pick up the stack of papers between us. He grips them tightly between both hands as if the idea of holding them with one hand or tucking them under an arm is preposterous. "Good to see you again too, Zoe." He turns back toward me and adds. "I will recap what we talked about with the other brothers while you...do what it is you have to do. We'll start tonight."

He gives Zoe plenty of space as he leaves the room. I catch her nonchalantly sniffing her armpit. "What's he talking about? What are you doing tonight?" she asks.

"Brotherhood stuff," I mumble. I can't take my eyes off her.

"What kind of brotherhood stuff? Is this about the rings? I could try again—"

"You said you needed two to three days to recover. You're going to take two to three days." My voice is abnormally low and gritty, and I sense my inner dragon has a lot to do with how authoritative that came out. I clear my throat and try to shove him back down.

She tips her head and offers me a smile charged with candlelight and daydreams. I feel that smile all the way to my toes. "Sometimes your eyes glow when you look at me," she says. "And then it's gone. Is that a dragon thing?"

"Yes." The word comes out choked.

She moves toward me, and it's like pure magic, like I'm in the woods and a doe has decided to lay its head in my hand. "What causes it? When they glow, they're like molten gold. It's like I'm seeing your dragon's eyes as they were on the golden plane."

My jaw feels tight, and I massage it a few times before admitting, "You are seeing his eyes. He tends to come to the surface when you're near me."

Her brows bob as if they can't decide where to land on her face, and then she crosses her arms and backs up a step. "Do I make you uncomfortable for some reason?"

I snort. "No."

"It's just, yesterday, when I hugged you—"

"You don't make me uncomfortable. You make me horny." The phrase charges right out of my mouth like a bull chasing a waved flag. Her cheeks warm with an easy blush. "Sorry. It's the Taurus in me. It's hard for me not to be direct."

She laughs. "It's okay. I like direct. It's always best to know the truth."

Oh shit. It's like she just gave my dragon a free pass. He surges to the surface, and the voice that comes out of me next is his. "Then the truth is, you're already mine, and if it were up to me, I'd take you hard against the wall." I slap a hand over my mouth.

Her jaw drops, and tiny smile lines form around her eyes.

I give my head a firm shake, dropping my hand. "Fuck! Sorry about that. He's really interested in you."

A laugh like the tinkle of wind chimes leaves her throat. "Holy shit! I'd say so. Um..." She steps in closer and places her hands on my chest. "Is it just your dragon who feels that way? Or is it you, Seb?"

God, she smells good, like clean linen and clementines. I place a hand on her waist and pull her closer, wrestling my dragon into submission. "It's both of us. I mean, it's me. He's a part of me. It's hard to explain to someone who isn't a shifter."

She laughs. "I think I get it. We are all bigger than this body anyway."

Her lashes flutter as she looks up at me, and for a moment, I forget about everything. I forget where we are, that we barely know each other, that she's here for a reason, and I lean down to kiss her.

"Dinner is served," Patrick calls from the next room.

I don't stop. I kiss her, and the results are lightning in my veins. Her lips are crushed velvet, heated and moist. I taste her lipstick and then her tongue as she opens for me and lets me in. Her nails scrape across the skin at the back of my head, dig into my hair. I'm pressed against her, moving her toward the wall, my arms holding her to me like she's the source of oxygen in the air.

"Yo!" Remus yells, his voice loud and clear and close.

Zoe draws back, panting, and runs a thumb under her bottom lip. That lipstick of hers deserves a gold medal because it hasn't smudged a bit. My eyes swivel to where Remus is standing in the door to the living room, and I growl loud enough to shake the walls.

"Chill out, bro. Dinner is on the table, and we have work to do tonight. Or have you already forgotten?"

I squeeze my eyes closed. I haven't forgotten. And he's done me a favor. He knows that if he hadn't come in here and acted as a speed bump, I may have ruined everything. I can't rush this. I nod. "Thanks, man."

He gives me an understanding smile and then heads back toward the dining room. I hold out my hand to Zoe. "Dinner?"

She tucks her fingers into mine and, through a demure grin, says, "I'd love to."

He gives me an understanding smile and then heads back toward the dining room. I hold out my hand to Zoe. "Dinner."

She tucks her fingers into mine and, through gritted teeth, says, "I'd love to.

Chapter Nineteen

ZOE

Seb wants me. The sexual energy coming off the dude is thick enough to make me feel light-headed. And holy hell am I into it. It's been a long time since I had sex. My last boyfriend, if you could call him that, was the drummer from Raven's Wish, and our time together was mostly physical. It was serious enough for him to attend Mabon festivities with my coven once, but we never used the L word. It was all about using each other, the convenience of meeting our physical needs when we were touring.

It ended when I entered rehab. I've never been someone to have casual sex, though, and by casual, I mean one-night hookups where you don't know the person's last name. I do think there has to be a spiritual connection. Maybe not love in the sense of hearts and flowers and permanence. But a connection. I had that connection with Alex. If I called him tomorrow and said I was in trouble, Alex would help me. Not because he loved me or wanted a relationship with me, but because we were and are really, truly friends with a history of being lovers.

I don't know Seb that well, but I think he'd make a good lover. The way he took care of me last night demonstrates a tenderness that appeals to me. The chemistry is through the roof. And the rumble I felt when he kissed me, it was like the best purr I've ever felt against my skin. That dragon part of him intrigues me. I sensed a connection in the Gold Room—a spiritual one. Maybe something that was there before we even met, although maybe that's too "woo-woo" even for me.

"When's your birthday, Zoe?" Remus asks. While I've been lost in my thoughts, we've all sat down at the dining room table, where Patrick has served what looks like lobster bisque.

"I'm a leap year baby," I say brightly. It's always good for a little light conversation.

"February 29th?" Seb asks breathlessly.

"Yep. I've been on this earth for twenty-four years, but technically, I've only had six birthdays." I give a light giggle and try the soup. Delicious.

"You're a Pisces." Seb says my zodiac sign with reverence, and I remember that he's a zodiac dragon. I'm sure my birth sign is important to him.

"Boring, right? The fish sign. Nothing exciting like a bull or a lion."

"Nothing boring about Pisces. You're said to be the

most spiritual of the signs. Known for your intuition and mysticism," Remus says.

I take another bite. "Spiritual... Yes, I am. People think we're human beings with a spirit, but I think we're spiritual beings having a human experience. It's like, when I ascend to the Gold Room, I'm not traveling somewhere new, I'm going back to where I've come from. What I was made from. I just have to navigate beyond the constraints of my human mind to get there."

Another few bites and I notice the table has grown silent. When I look up, Seb and Remus are staring at me, nodding.

"So that's how witches do magic? You astral project to the celestial realm? That's what you mean by the Gold Room?" Seb asks.

I shrug a shoulder. "Yeah, I guess. I mean, that's not the language we use as witches, but yeah. Why does that interest you so much?"

Seb smiles. "Dragons are celestial creatures. That's how you saw my dragon in the Gold Room. The bigger part of him is always there, unless I shift and allow him out here."

"It's just interesting to us because we thought witches were, like, different," Remus adds.

"You thought our magic was made of some mystical, unknowable force that had nothing to do with you, when really, witches and dragons just play different sides of the same coin."

They both nod.

I raise my wineglass. "Well, here's to learning we're more alike than different." We clink our glasses together.

Patrick rounds the table, collecting bowls and replacing them with plates of white fish and rice pilaf. He gives Seb a little wave on his way out.

"Does Patrick ever join you for dinner?" I ask, still marveling that this very successful musician just served me a plate of fish.

"Most of the time," Seb says. "He just has other plans tonight."

I look between them both. "Speaking of plans, what is this mystery mission you two are going on tonight? You've mentioned it twice now, and every time I ask about it, you change the subject."

Seb glances at Remus and takes a long sip of wine. "We are going ring collecting, in hopes of reducing the threat to our kind."

"Ring collecting?" I'm not sure what he's talking about at first, and then it hits me. I lean back in my chair, suddenly feeling ill. "You—you're going after more of those enchanted weapons? Are you for real? I've seen that thing up close. You don't want to be anywhere near one."

He frowns. "It's not a matter of want. It's a matter of necessity. We have to start culling their numbers. We're in hiding now, but we can't stay that way forever."

My stomach clenches, anxiety gripping me for reasons I don't understand. "So, what, you're going to hunt one of these Order members down and kill them before they can kill you?"

Seb darts a glance at Remus. "We're going to try to cut the ring off. We'd prefer not to kill anyone, just lower the number who can hurt us, until we have another option."

"Until I figure out a way to somehow neutralize the ring's power, you have to remove the rings physically or kill the men who wield them, is that what you're saying?"

He nods. I rest my head in my hands. "I should go back in tonight. You don't have time for me to do this on a schedule."

Seb reaches over and squeezes my hand. "You're not going back in tonight. Go to bed early. Heal. Get stronger. We'll try again in a day or two."

I get the sense that's an order and nonnegotiable. Probably wise.

We finish our dinner in relative silence, and then they both stand from the table. Remus mutters his goodbyes and disappears, but Seb lingers, collecting the dirty dishes. Patrick must have left for his event.

"Is your cabin comfortable? Did Patrick get you everything you needed?" he asks.

"Yeah. All stocked up." I follow him to the kitchen, where he places the plates in the dishwasher. "I don't want you to go tonight. That ring, it gave me the creeps."

He takes my shoulder and kisses my cheek. "This is what a zodiac dragon does, Zoe. We're warriors first, and we're going to fight to protect our people. But I'm flattered you care."

I don't know what to say. I just fold my arms and shake my head.

"Feel free to stay in the main house for as long as you like. There's a home theater in the basement." He walks past me and heads for his bedroom. And I'm left wondering why I have the strongest desire to throw myself in front of the door and refuse to let him leave.

Chapter Twenty

SEB

One perk of being a zodiac dragon is the ability to fold space. When we reach adulthood, our parents and the Oracle present us with a key that allows us to travel from place to place as easily as stepping from room to room. It also opens the portal to Cardinal Island, a realm of safety where we perform our most sacred rituals, train for war, and meet with our spiritual leader, the Oracle. Choosing a target, then, isn't about geographical constraints. We do it randomly, picking a name from the list Imani provided us and manifesting outside the upstate New York address of Ronald Folman.

"House is dark," Remus mumbles. Like me, he's armed to the teeth with concealed weapons, a gun in the hollow of his back, and daggers strapped all over his body.

All the lights are out in the massive home, and my

sensitive dragon hearing picks up no signs of life. I have one last trick up my sleeve, though, a talent that will ensure this house is empty. "Could be asleep. I'll check."

I reach out psychically, searching for a human mind inside the walls, one I can infiltrate if I need to. Dreamwalking isn't something I do on a whim, but it's useful when you're on a mission. A few minutes into someone's dreams, and you can learn a lot about them. Maybe more than they know about themselves.

But I don't find a single head in the house. Not even a wife or servant. The place is completely vacant. "They're not sleeping. There's no one in that house."

Remus does a quick Google search. "He owns a club in the city. Looks like our man is recently divorced too. I'm betting he keeps an apartment in Manhattan for late-night activities."

I glance at the address and the Street View picture of the club. "The Red Room? Who exactly is this guy?"

"According to his profile, he's a beauty industry entrepreneur. Looks like he owns a bunch of salons throughout the city. But this is his only club."

I look over Remus's shoulder at the photo he brings up of Ron Folman. The man has a scruffy beard and a comb-over. "Has he actually ever visited a salon?"

Remus adjusts his cap. "Let's go get us a ring."

I grab my key and leap. We arrive, shoulder to shoulder, on the sidewalk in front of The Red Room. Immediately, the scent of cigarettes and sex is almost overwhelming. The club is a windowless box with a line of men and women dressed in black leather that wraps around the block. "Well, this is a choice."

"Yeah," Remus says. "No judgment on the peeps into this lifestyle, but it's not what I was expecting from a member of the Saint's Order."

"Let's go." I lead the way toward the door, engaging my camouflage. Dragons can't make themselves entirely invisible, but we can blend into our surroundings in a way that's almost as effective. As I slip along the brick wall toward the door, my body reflects the wall, the wood paneling, the sidewalk. If a very astute human were looking right at us, they might experience disorientation, might notice the bricks shifting. But most of the humans out here are half drunk, and none of them is paying attention to the wall. We slide inside behind the bouncer, the thump of the music guiding us deeper into the crowd. People are gathered around windows in the dark hallway, watching couples performing in rooms on the other side.

Remus nudges me as we pass a scene where a naked woman, blindfolded and strapped to a X-cross, is being eaten out by a fully dressed man, while another dribbles hot wax on her breasts.

"You okay, man?" Remus asks.

He expects my dragon to be all about the peep show, given my alignment, but instead, it feels like that part of me is curled in the back of my head. If anything, I'm repulsed. "All I can think about is Zoe."

"Fuck. I'm sorry, bro." His eyes linger on the next room, where a woman is on all fours with a man behind her. I keep going, reaching out with my dragon senses, pushing into minds, looking for Ronald. I find him behind a door marked OFFICE in the back, and he's not alone.

I grab Remus by the elbow and drag him toward the door. He lifts an eyebrow, wiping the dopey smile off his mouth. He catches on quickly and snaps back into warrior mode. He tries the door handle. Locked.

I hold up three fingers. He nods. He's sensing what I am. Three heads inside. One of them is Ronald. I nudge into his mind and get a sense of him sitting behind a desk. But my hold only lasts a second. Pain shoots through my temple. I grab my throbbing head.

"It's the ring," Remus whispers.

The sound of a chair drawing back reaches our ears, a sound that would be drowned out by the music if we were human. Remus meets my eyes, and we flatten ourselves against the wall.

Footsteps.

The door opens.

Ronald Folman squints into the darkness, the ring on his hand glowing blue.

Silently, I slip inside the gap between him and the door, heart hammering. Two men in suits sit waiting for Ronald at the desk. *Fuck*, they have rings too!

Ronald turns around, staring right past us. I hold my breath and go absolutely still. He closes the door again.

"What was that all about?" one of the other men asks, pushing a pair of black glasses up his nose.

The other man, Latino and sporting a neck tattoo,

toys with his ring. "This thing is burning, true? Why's that happening, Ronnie?"

Ronnie's picture didn't do justice to his size. Yes, he is on the older side and has a belly, but he's as tall and broad as a linebacker. And that ring on his finger is glowing like it's radioactive. The energy makes the hair on my arms stand on end.

"Guys, you are about to get a hands-on lesson in dragons," Ronnie says, and then that ring on his finger transforms into a Thor-sized hammer. Remus and I spare each other a half-second glance, and then we move.

I draw the dagger at my thigh and come down on Neck Tattoos' wrist, the power of my blow severing muscle and bone but also knocking me out of my camouflage, or maybe that's the power of the rings in this room, because I see Remus flicker into being as well.

Neck Tattoo starts screaming, "He cut off my hand! He cut off my fucking hand!" He cradles his stub as Ronnie attacks. Remus blocks his blow with his blade as I try to pry my dagger from the desk.

Glasses is on his feet, his ring transforming into a bow and arrow. I laugh, but it's Ronnie who says, "Wrong choice, numbnuts. It's too close in here."

The bow turns into a sword. I abandon the blade in the desk and draw my gun from the small of my back. I aim and fire at the center of his forehead. Ronnie's hammer blocks the bullet, and it ricochets toward my head. I move at dragon speed, barely dodging the bullet as it whistles past my ear and embeds in the wall. I fire again and again, but the magic of those rings must be attuned to bullets because they block me each and every time. No way could a human pull that off.

"Jesus fucking Christ!" Glasses yells, distracted by Neck Tattoo, who has collapsed in the corner, I'd assume from loss of blood. It's everywhere. Across the desk, sprayed along the walls.

I toss the gun aside and go for the long blade down my back just in time to block Glasses's blow. He's clumsy and obviously new at swordplay, but that makes things even more unpredictable. He swings at my waist as if he means to chop me in half, and I leap straight up. Although his blade grazes my hip, it slices under my feet. I land on the desk, my boots squelching in the puddle of blood next to Neck Tattoo's severed hand. My sword comes around, and this time, I don't have the time or angle to aim for his wrist.

My blade severs his neck, and Ronnie yells as Glasses's body drops. It's two on one. Now, we have him.

But as I leap down from the desk, my sword aimed at his torso, Ronnie moves fast, faster than a human should be able to move. His hammer comes down on Remus's right arm with a sickening crunch. Remus howls in pain as the blow lands him on his back, his sword clattering from his hand.

Ronnie laughs. "You fucking lizards need to die!" His hammer aims for my gut, but I'm faster. I dodge the blow, moving behind him. I strike. Rage makes me lethal. I take off his right arm at the shoulder and growl as it splats on the linoleum. The hammer transforms back into a ring instantaneously. I have him by the throat and on the ground in no time.

"Who the fuck is running the Saint's Order?" I ask him. I have a million questions, but the way this asshole is bleeding, I don't have much time.

Ronnie's eyes meet mine, and the look he gives me is diabolical. "The destroyer," he rasps.

"Don't fucking give me that bullshit. Who took over for Stefan? Who is the grand master?"

The man's face turns white, and his eyes roll back in his head. "You will die in blue fire at the hand of the destroyer," he rasps, and then he passes out. I drop his sorry ass and move to Remus's side. My brother is whimpering, and he hasn't moved since the hammer crushed his arm. Blue veins branch around the point of impact. *Fuck!*

"It's my drawing hand, Seb," he says, his eyes wild.

"I'm getting you to Morwyn," I promise.

But he raises his good hand. "The rings, Seb! Don't forget the rings. Don't let this be in vain."

Right. I pull a thick black bag from the pocket of my pants and then use the tip of my blade to retrieve each of the rings and put them in the bag without touching any of them. It's harder than I expect, and I have to get creative to get it done, but I manage. As quickly as possible, I tie the three rings to my belt.

Boom. Boom. Boom. A loud knock comes on the door. "Ronnie? You okay in there? I thought I heard a scream, and not the good kind."

I hoist Remus into my arms, his face drawn from the pain. "Fuck, I'm cold, Seb."

"You're also heavy as hell."

Another pound on the door and then I hear a key in the lock. I reposition Remus so I can grab my key, and then I step.

The Red Room melts away, and I arrive at Morwyn's clinic with three Order rings on my hip and a broken dragon in my arms.

Chapter Twenty-One

ZOE

I hold the urn in my hand, tipping it this way and that, listening to the gold dust sift like sand back and forth in the metal canister. I want to ascend again. Every cell in my body is urging me to open the canister, draw a line, and take the goddess into my body.

Seb has been gone for hours. Although I've returned to my house—it's still so weird to say that—I can't sleep. Dressed in my coziest pink kitten pajamas, I've stationed myself in the comfy chair near the window, my legs curled under me. I watch for signs of life in the big house for hours, but no dice. Seb's still not back, which means he and Remus are going after more of those cursed rings. He's probably in a dangerous situation. Fuck, being anywhere near those rings is dangerous.

It shouldn't bother me so much, but I've caught feelings for Seb. That kiss we shared today was a long time coming. I wanted it to keep going. I know our relationship isn't conventional, but when I think of him, I can imagine a future so clearly. Imagine waking up next to him again and again until we're both old and gray. I'm dreaming, of course, romanticizing an attraction born of lust-soaked chemistry and proximity. But I won't deny my desire for him or my genuine worry for his well-being.

If you ascended, you could use your magic to open a portal to him. You could help him.

The whisper from the back of my brain is a darker version of my own voice. When I was going through rehab, I pictured that aspect of myself as a spider. A black widow with a swollen abdomen trying to lure me into her web with her lies.

All she does is lie, and I've learned to call her out. "Ascending to the Gold Room now will not help Seb," I say to the empty room. "Seb is a competent warrior. Opening a portal to him could cause more harm than good by distracting him from his plan. It would also set back our goal of finding a way to neutralize the rings by at least three days because I'd have to recover from this use. And, because I haven't waited long enough to use again, I'll come down hard, alone, with no one to care for me or call for help if my heart stops. It's a bad idea all around."

I sigh and toss the urn back into the bag. Thankfully, the spider remains silent. This match called in my favor.

I rise from the cozy chair and head toward the bedroom and the book I've been reading, but I stop short when the phone rings. *Shit.* Could that be Seb? Heart in my throat, I jog back into the kitchen and snatch my cell off the counter. "Hello?"

"Zoe, I hope I didn't wake you. I just heard the good news!" My mom's voice fills my ear, and I glance through the window toward the big house. All its windows are still dark. I chase away the disappointment of not hearing from Seb and try to get excited that my mom has reached out. She so rarely calls.

"Hi, Mom! What good news is that?"

"What good news?" Her voice catches. "I ran into Jeremy at the Beltane planning meeting, and he said you told him you'd started your dream job and had to pause your sessions with him."

I muster a laugh. "Well, yes. I'd planned to call you and tell you all about it, but I've just been so busy." I rub the bridge of my nose. Stupid Jeremy and his blabber-mouth. I haven't had time to get my story straight about all this. I obviously can't tell my mother the complete truth.

"So, is this the opportunity you mentioned with the dragon you met at that club?"

I am shocked she remembered. "Yes. Yes, it is. How did you guess?"

"He said you were hired by Full Throttle, and I remember you mentioned the dragon was from Full Throttle. I knew this would be a good opportunity for you. Very lucky."

"It has been. I'm learning a lot and have an entire studio at my disposal."

"What a boon! I hadn't even heard you lost your job."

Damn, is every single word I say to Jeremy parroted back to my parents? "I didn't exactly lose the job. Regal Health closed the location where I was working, so I decided to pursue this opportunity."

"Jeremy didn't tell us that."

"I only had a short conversation with Jeremy. Honestly, I wish he would have kept some of this confidential so that I could explain everything myself." My voice holds more than a little annoyance.

"Oh, please don't be cross with Jeremy, Zoe. You know he only has your best interests at heart. And given our history, he felt compelled to explain why you had missed your session so that we wouldn't worry."

"I guess that makes sense."

"So, tell me about the dragon," she says salaciously.

I glance at the house again. "Nothing to tell, really. Hey, Mom, it's getting late. I should go. Can I call you next week?"

"Wait! You are coming home for Beltane this weekend, right? Dinner is at seven, immediately followed by the bonfire. Everyone is gathering at our place this year."

"I'm not sure," I say.

"Not sure? You haven't missed a Beltane celebration since you were twelve and had that appendicitis. What's going on? Please don't tell me that dragon is keeping you chained to your desk like an animal."

"Of course not. Don't be ridiculous," I say. Fuck. I truly have no excuse. "Yeah, of course I'll be there."

"Six thirty for cocktails, dear. Do you want me to send a car?"

"No. I'll find a ride. I may meet up with some of the girls at the maypole earlier in the day anyway." Shit. I haven't even broached the subject of not living in my apartment anymore and really don't want to. There is no way to say "I live in my boss's pool house and can't disclose the location" that will not blow up in my face. Having Mom's driver show up at my old apartment to pick me up would be an absolute disaster.

"All right. Let us know if you end up needing that driver after all. Good night, darling."

I end the call, not missing the undercurrent of skepticism in her last statement. She knows I won't go to the maypole. There's not a single witch who will give me the time of day anymore, let alone drive me anywhere. I burned all my bridges, and she knows it.

My eyes fall on the bag and the urn again.

I can make it all go away, the spider coos. *I can make you the most popular witch in the coven.*

"I don't care about any of that," I spit out. And then I grab my keys and head back to the big house. I'm never going to sleep until I know he's home, and I shouldn't be anywhere near that urn right now.

I'VE JUST DRIFTED OFF WHEN THE SOUND OF THE FRONT DOOR opening wakes me. With a start, I remember I'm in Seb's bed. I decided my only hope of getting any rest tonight was waiting here for him. It seemed completely rational at the time, but now, as the thump of his boots draws near, part of me worries how he'll react. I mean, it is presumptuous of me to assume I'm welcome to sleep in his bed anytime I like without his permission. Shit. What was I thinking?

I sit up, my arms circling my knees as he enters the room, stopping short when he sees me.

"Zoe?"

"I—I couldn't sleep. I needed to make sure you got home okay." I lean over and turn on the light so I can see his face clearly. That's the only way to know whether I should be apologizing or getting comfortable. But the second I can see him clearly, I almost scream. Seb is covered in blood. His hair is crusty with it. "What the fuck!" I bound from the bed and rush over to him, but I'm not sure where I can touch him without hurting him. I hold my hands out and scan him from head to toe. "Is this your blood? Are you hurt?"

He just stares at me, like he's in shock. He doesn't speak, but I wonder if he *can* speak.

I've never thought of myself as maternal. Whenever one of my mother's friends would ask me if I wanted to have children, I'd say no. But something deep inside me snaps into place at the sight of him. Without saying a word, I take his hand and guide him into the bathroom.

I've used this room a few times, although I don't

remember the first. I was unconscious when Seb bathed me that first time. But it's a big room and well-appointed. I lead him over to the enormous shower and start the hot water. The tub would be easier with him like this. I suspect I'll have to get in and help him. But there's too much blood.

When I turn back to Seb, he's still watching me, his expression unreadable. I grab the bottom of his black T-shirt and try to pull it over his head, but it won't budge. Black straps around his shoulders hold it in place. It's not that they're hidden, I was just distracted before by all the blood, I didn't register they were there. I go to work removing a holster and dagger from under each arm, another from his back. The weapons are heavy, but he helps me with a few of them, that absent look in his eyes still lingering. Together, we strip them from his thighs, his calves. Fuck, he has knives everywhere.

And then I notice the bag tied to his belt. I reach for it, and his eyes go wild. He grabs my wrist.

"It's okay," I say softly, suspecting by the way it hangs that these are the rings he was after. Hell, I don't have to suspect. I know based on the feeling of dread I get when I glance in the bag's direction. "I won't look inside, but I'm going to take this off you."

He releases my wrist, and I untie the bag from his belt. Once it's off, I tie it closed again and then walk it to the other side of the bathroom and drop it in a corner. It's a relief to leave it behind when I return to him. Seb's eyes are dark and haunted, his hair flopping around his face as he looks down at me, but the sight of him shirtless sends my heart fluttering, nonetheless. He's incredibly attractive, even covered in blood. I try to ignore the heat blooming deep inside me as I kneel in front of him, sitting back on my heels to unlace his boots. It takes me a few tries, but I pry them off one at a time and cast them aside. I strip off his socks.

It's satisfying to see clean skin under his bloody clothes. He's really not hurt, just filthy and tired and... traumatized, I think. I rise up on my knees and reach for the button to his pants. My eyes meet his. "Is this okay?" I ask.

He nods. I unbutton and unzip, then grab the waistband and peel the blood-soaked material off him. He steps out of his pants, and I learn that Sebastian York does not wear underwear. I'm temporarily frozen by the overwhelming sight of his manhood. Seb is big. He's not even erect, and the length and girth of him are, well... I guess as a Taurus, hung like a bull is an apt descriptor. I try not to make a big deal of it, but despite my best efforts, a high-pitched squeak comes from the back of my throat.

I stand and busy myself adjusting the water to the perfect temperature. When I get it just right, I move out of the way, and he steps into the spray. For a minute, he just stands there, the water hitting his hair and shoulders, his hands braced on the wall. Red rivulets of blood course down his body. I could leave now. Unlike me, he's conscious and clearly capable of washing himself, but I find I can't move. I stand there in my pink kitten pajamas, staring at this god of a man and thinking, *he's mine and it's my job to care for him.*

It's a stupid thought. Sebastian York isn't mine. We're not even officially dating, let alone exclusive. We've known each other a matter of days. But I can't bring myself to leave. Instead, I tie my hair up with the elastic I keep around my wrist. Then I pull off my top and slide down my pajama shorts.

Seb's eyes latch on to me, scanning my naked body in a slow, languid way. He stops breathing and goes perfectly still, like he's afraid to scare me away.

I step into the spray and close the door behind me. His back is still to me, his hands braced against the wall, but his breath is coming quicker now. Grabbing the shower puff he has hanging on a hook, I squeeze in some body wash and start at his shoulders. He releases a deep moan of pleasure as I massage the soap over his back, his spine, his ass. I scrub the blood off each of his arms from behind.

When he doesn't turn around, I pour some of his shampoo into my palm and rise up on my tiptoes to massage it into his hair. He lowers himself and tips his head back, his eyes squeezing shut as I use my nails on his scalp. The most delicious sound comes from his chest, a vibration, a purr, a melody like the sexiest harp chord being struck.

I trail my palms along his back, enjoying the rumble of it through his rib cage. He uses the opportunity to rinse his hair, the last remnants of the blood circling the drain. But even when he pulls his head out of the water, his eyes are squeezed shut.

"You told me today that your dragon wants me," I say, reaching under his arm to run the puff over his chest. "Is that why you won't look at me?"

"Do you welcome me looking at you?" His voice is gravel and rust, so rough I can barely make out the words.

"Only if you want to."

"I want to," he growls. He pivots in my arms, and I see right away what he is hiding behind his closed eyes. His irises are swirling, molten gold. Dragon's eyes. And his skin is flushed and heated. Hotter than the water. Steam rises between us, and I hazard a glance down. The overwhelm I'd felt before at the size of him pales in comparison to seeing him erect. His proud length juts between us, and something deep within me clenches. It's like my body is whispering, "I know just what to do with that!" Even as my brain screams, "That's going to wreck you."

I tell my brain to shut the fuck up and run my soapy hands down his abdomen, all the way to the base of his cock. I circle him with my hand—well...as much as possible. My fingers don't reach my thumb.

He inhales with a hiss. He still hasn't touched me, and his eyes are closed again. "Zoe—" His voice is trashed. "If I touch you, if I kiss you, I don't think I can stop. If you don't want this, go now. If you stay, my dragon will claim you. It's taking everything in my power to hold him back right now."

I see the strain in his neck, in the muscles of his arms, in the way his abdomen flexes behind my knuckles. I grip him tighter, my lids dropping low as I look up at him through my lashes and slide my hand up his shaft, running my thumb over the head. "I'm not going anywhere, Seb. Claim me."

The words are barely out of my mouth, and I'm in the air. My legs instinctively wrap around his hips as his mouth crashes down on mine. Our tongues tangle as our mouths meld, my back thumping against the shower wall. It feels soft, and I realize his arm is behind me, protecting me from the hard tile, my head cupped in his palm. His other hand is on my breast. And his hips...god, his hips are circling against me, that massive erection sandwiched between us.

Our bodies are both wet as hell, and I grip his neck tighter to keep from sliding down him. He drops his hand to my thigh, catching me, holding me there. Carefully, I lower one leg to the shower floor.

I'm a tall woman, but Seb's taller. He has to bend his neck to touch his forehead to mine, but on my tiptoe, with one leg hooked over his hip, I manage to reach his lips and lose myself in another kiss. His knuckles trace down my sternum and over my stomach to my navel. My pulse thrums. And when his fingers find my center, I have to stop kissing him to catch my breath. He circles my clit with a feathery touch that sends lightning through my veins, and then he dips a finger inside me.

I tip my head back on a gasp, and I'm thankful for the cool tile, because my blood is on fire. Everything in me is burning for him, my skin, my individual hairs, my very cells call out for his touch. I grab his cock and pull myself up on his neck to position him at my opening. He lifts me until the head of him is tucked inside my folds.

I lick my lips, ready, so ready. Our gazes lock. "You're mine, Zoe Willow," he growls.

"Yours," I echo softly, urging him closer. He slides into me, stealing my breath.

Chapter Twenty-Two

SEB

T he creator must be rewarding me for what we did tonight. I have no other explanation for why I'm experiencing nirvana right here in my shower. I never expected Zoe to wait up for me or to lead me by the hand to the shower and wash me like I was a thing to be worshiped. And when she asked me to claim her, when she grabbed me and kissed me and drew me to her, it was as if the heavens had opened and the almighty himself was smiling down on me.

And now, in her, my dragon one with me inside my skin, I am a mated warrior. I have found my end and my beginning, and I want nothing more than to return the pleasure this brings me.

I thrust into her, starting slow, allowing her time to get used to my size. She's tight and wet. Her quiet mews of pleasure and tiny gasps building with my rhythm. I reach between us and tease that sensitive bud between her thighs, feel her hips respond to me with sharper and faster thrusts. I give her what she needs. Hard and deep, all the time rubbing where I instinctively know she needs it.

"Oh my god, Seb. Seb!"

She arches in my arms, and I catch her nipple in my mouth, fluttering my tongue across the tight bud. She clenches around me and cries out as an orgasm rips through her. My mating trill goes into overdrive. As her body clenches around me, I unleash myself, pounding into her until my own climax seizes me. I tip her neck to the side and bite, holding her with my teeth until I've emptied myself inside her. It's the way of my kind, and it will leave a mark. It's something I should have warned her about, but this entire night has been a roller coaster for me.

When I finally release her, her inner thighs are dripping with my seed and she reeks of mating scent. I help her back onto her feet, but she holds on to me.

"Wait. My knees feel like Jell-O." She rests her forehead against my chest. "Seb, that was incredible. I've never had sex like that. I've never..." She looks up at me. "Was it the same for you?"

I laugh and place a finger under her chin. "It was the most incredible experience of my life."

She smiles and steps into the spray, rinsing off the mess I've made of her. The water's gone cold, and our fingers are turning pruney. As soon as she's done, I shut it off and guide her back to the bed.

"Do you want me to go back to my place?" she asks.

"No fucking way. I want you right beside me."

"Okay," she says softly.

"Do you need anything to eat or drink?" I ask, corralling her toward the bed. There's no way I'm letting my mate go to bed hungry.

"No, I'm fine."

"Thank fuck. I'm exhausted." Without my saying another word, she crawls into bed and scoots to the opposite side. I crawl in beside her, loop an arm around her waist, and pull her to me with a growl of contentment.

With her head tucked under my chin, I start to drift off.

"Seb, what's that sound you make? That purr? It's really beautiful."

I chuckle. "I'm glad you think so. You're the only one who can hear it."

She looks over her shoulder at me, rolling onto her back to see me better in the dark, although I know I must be nothing but an indistinct shape to her. "What? Anyone could hear that."

"Stick your fingers in your ears."

She does and then looks even more confused.

"The call is coming from inside the building," I say with a chuckle. "Just settle down. It will quiet as soon as my dragon falls asleep. With how exhausted we are from tonight, it won't be long."

I lay my head back down, and she runs her fingers through the side of my hair. "You got the rings."

"Yeah."

"You don't seem happy about it."

I want to tell her everything, but I can't keep my eyes open. "Tomorrow," I say, pulling her into my chest. She settles down and falls into a deep, dreamless sleep.

WHEN I WAKE, THE SUN IS SHINING THROUGH THE BLINDS AND Zoe isn't in bed with me. I run my hand over her side of the sheets and find them cold. After a few deep breaths, I surmise that she's not nearby anymore either. She's been up for a while, then. Probably back at her place. I need to find her and make sure she's not second-guessing our mating last night.

Bed her again, my dragon rumbles. I think it's the happiest he's ever been, and I definitely feel better than I've felt in weeks. For once, I don't feel feverish. Hell, if I don't love the idea of luring Zoe back to my bed. I think of how she looked last night up against the shower wall, her neck flushed, her skin tacky from the steam.

I need to find her. Make sure she's okay.

I bound out of bed and complete my morning routine in record time, throwing on a pair of jeans and a merino sweater. Then I go looking for her. I don't have to go far. She's standing in my kitchen, fully dressed, with a cup of coffee in her hands. She doesn't look happy.

Only when she turns toward me do I notice who is standing next to her.

"Morwyn? When did you get here?"

"Just a few moments ago," the Virgo doctor says, his wild dark hair making him appear far more unhinged than he actually is.

"He says Remus is still recovering. You didn't tell me he was hurt last night." Zoe's brow furrows.

"It didn't come up," I mumble.

She looks down into her coffee and frowns.

Morwyn glances between us, his nostrils flaring. He smiles, no doubt picking up my mating scent. But before he can get distracted, I ask, "What's happening with Remus?"

"You got him to us just in time. We cleaned out all the infected flesh and pieced his arm back together. Now, we're just waiting for him to regrow the parts we had to eliminate. Unfortunately, some of his bones were crushed in the fight, so it's going to take a while."

"Crushed?" Zoe asks. "Will he be able to use his arm again?"

Morwyn nods. "Dragons heal much faster and more thoroughly than humans, Zoe. Even if I had to amputate his arm, it would completely grow back within the year. I didn't have to amputate, thank the creator, but there was considerable bone damage." His gaze falls directly on me. "We tried the water, Seb. It didn't work."

"Shit. Not at all?"

"Wait, what? The celestial water in the vial?" Zoe asks.

"Yes. We thought it might have healing properties because it repels the ring."

"It repelled the infection, all right. Would have

repelled it deeper into his bone," Morwyn says. "Thankfully, we tested it on excised flesh. But I can definitely say we can't use it in its raw form."

"No, of course not," Zoe says, as if the question is rudimentary. "What's in that vial is pure, unadulterated positive celestial energy. The ring reacts to it, yes, because the ring is pure, unadulterated negative energy."

We both stare blankly at her.

She holds up her coffee. "Boiling water will scald you, yes? And if I put an icicle in it, eventually the ice will melt and the boiling water will cool, but at the moment something frozen meets something extremely hot—"

"It can shatter," Morwyn says. "How could I be so stupid? We'd need a method to contain the curse and slowly infuse the area with a diluted solution."

Zoe tips her head. "Or maybe a drip or a pill. I'm not a doctor, but in witchcraft, we'd probably mix two drops of this stuff into someone's tea every day for a month, not put it directly on a wound. Not that I've ever worked with something so powerful, but I have worked with herbs like lemon balm. When taken in a tea, it helps with a number of ailments—anxiety, depression, indigestion. But if you make a bath bomb out of it, it does absolutely nothing for you. You could soak in it all day without any benefit."

"Brilliant," Morwyn says. "And now that you have worked with it, do you think it has broader applications than healing?"

"That's an unfair question, Morwyn. She's only seen it once—"

"Actually, I do have an idea. The first stages of an idea. But I'm not ready to explain it yet. Not until it's fully formed, you know?"

Morwyn nods, and I'm so proud of my mate, I can't even speak.

"On that note..." Morwyn turns to me. "I came to ask your permission to take Remus to Cardinal Island to accelerate his healing."

"Of course," I say immediately. "Whatever he needs."

Morwyn finishes the coffee in his mug and gives a little bow to Zoe. "A pleasure to meet you, Zoe. I'm so happy you've joined the zodiac dragon family."

She smiles and shakes his hand, but I don't miss the look of confusion that flits through her features at that last part. I interrupt by hugging Morwyn goodbye and telling him to tell Remus that I'll visit him on Cardinal Island. I walk him to the door, where he grabs the key around his neck and disappears.

When I turn around, Zoe is waiting for me. "What do you think he meant by that 'joining the family' comment? Like because I'm working with you?"

I hold out my hands to her. "We should talk."

But she just shakes her head. "When you told me that what I was doing could save lives, I didn't really understand until now. Remus might have lost his ability to draw, to tattoo, from his injuries. He might have lost his tattoo business. Either of you might have been killed or disabled last night. We have to move faster. I need to ascend again. This can't wait."

I scratch the back of my head. "Yes. What you're

doing could change our lives, Zoe. And yes, if you're well enough, it would be great if you went back in today, but—"

"I'm well enough. I can do this." She crosses her arms over her chest, and I can tell she's resolute.

I raise a hand. "But about last night. We should talk—"

She smiles. "I'm fine with what happened last night, Seb. We're both consenting adults. Sure, it was fast, but if you're okay with it, I'm okay with it."

My breath leaves my chest in a huff. Does she understand what it means that we're mated? "I'm okay with it. I would like to be okay with it again, very, very soon." I pull her against me and find her neck with my lips.

She giggles. "It'll have to wait. Once I ascend, I'll be useless for the next twenty-four hours, which means we need to do it now, today."

"Why?"

"Because there's something I have to do this weekend and something I have to ask you."

"Anything."

"Will you come to my coven's Beltane celebration?"

"Beltane?"

"May first. It's a fire festival to celebrate the halfway point between the spring equinox and summer. I have to go. I'd like you to come as my guest. Besides, it's at my parents' house and will give me access to some magical resources I can use to follow up on my theories about the ring."

I hate the thought of her going anywhere right now

with the Saint's Order on a killing spree, but if she has to go to this celebration, I will definitely be at her side. "I'd love to."

That makes her smile. "Then we should get started right away. I'll need time to recover. I'll get my bag."

Chapter Twenty-Three

ZOE

I'm back at the dining room table, my mirror and my athame in front of me. Despite myself, I'm excited about this. I've wanted to use gold dust again for days, and although I tell myself that this could be the last time, that it *should* be the last time, all I'm focused on is doing it one more time. I hate this neediness in me. This is how it started before, the wanting, the distraction of it, the way my thoughts would return like a boomerang and linger on the idea of doing it again. And then, one day, I couldn't stop myself from doing it. Couldn't stop until I was made to stop.

But when I look across the table at Seb, I have another reason to want to do this. I'm falling in love with him. It's fast, I know. Too fast for me to call it love yet. But the connection we shared last night was once-in-a-lifetime level. I have to do something to protect him. And

I have a plan. If I can finish deconstructing how the Order rings are made, maybe I can use the water in the vial to create a celestial ring that is its balance. One that can transform into a shield or become a weapon.

What could combat a dark ring better than one made of light?

And if you have to make multiple rings, that means more times ascending to the Gold Room, the spider says.

I ignore her and reach for the urn.

"Are you sure you're ready to do this again?" Seb asks. "We could wait another day."

He seems more anxious this time. I tell myself it's because of what happened last time, how he saw me wet myself. After last night, he probably can't stomach seeing me like that again. But it must be done. Without me, more of his brothers could be hurt like Remus was. It could be him next time.

"I'm ready," I say. Then I give him a wide smile. "Take care of me afterward, all right? And if I say something mean to you, don't believe me, okay? It's the gold dust talking. Every time I use, the hill of recovery becomes steeper."

"I've got you," he says softly.

I pull the box holding the ring and the vial closer to me, and then I pour a precious line of gold dust from the urn with shaky hands. I lean down and take the goddess into myself.

As always, the ascension is euphoric. My body goes weightless, and my soul feels like it's in perfect spiritual union with the beyond. Warm comfort surrounds me in a hug of acceptance and communion. And then the song of the Gold Room comes to me, each item humming in unison, singing me a song of welcome.

"Back again, daughter," the triune voice whispers. Three voices in unison representing the goddess. My blood tingles with the vibration of the words.

"I need to understand the ring so that I can create an enchantment powerful enough to destroy it."

"You have someone with you today," she says with a laugh.

I don't know what she's talking about until a large head nuzzles under my arm, forcing my chair back from the table. Seb's dragon is wrapped around me, watching me with its golden eyes, its chin resting in my lap like the world's biggest dog. I stroke it between its horns, and it purrs, exactly how Seb purred last night.

"Hi, sweetheart," I whisper to it, breathing in his familiar sandalwood and citrus scent. This is Seb. Just a different aspect of him. It's completely wild to me that his dragon can exist in the Gold Room with me. "I'm sorry, but I need to work on this. Can you wait beside me?" I gently push his head away. With a whine as if he's only a large dog and not a dragon as big as a small airplane, he flops on the floor beside me with his head between his paws.

I reach for the box and open it.

That black hole of energy stares up at me from the velvet, and I waste no time forming the window with my hands and opening it again. I try to memorize each part, mumbling my notes to myself. Quicker than I expect, my arms start to hurt. I allow the window to close, panting and shaking out my arms. The gold flickers. Already, I grow tired. When I hang my head for a moment to rest, I see Seb's dragon watching me from the floor.

"If I tell you something and show you what I see, can you remember it for me?" The great dragon rises, nodding. He seems excited to help. At my urging, he looks over my shoulder. "Okay, here we go. Pay attention." I open the window again and quickly narrate what I observe. The chanting, the smell, the symbols, the vibration, the ribbons, the darkness. I describe everything using the words of a witch, and the dragon studies the ring.

It takes hours. At least, it feels like hours. I grow so tired, I can hardly keep my eyes open. But when my body sways in the chair, the dragon rubs up against me, cheek to cheek. He licks up the side of my face and nuzzles me awake again. We finish as the last of the gold bleeds from the room.

I release the window and grab Seb's dragon around the neck. "Thank you. That's all I got," I tell the creature.

And then I fall.

Chapter Twenty-Four

SEB

I catch Zoe before she hits the floor, and I immediately sense something is different this time. This is so much worse than before. She's not breathing, and my inner dragon is losing his shit, sending cascading scales up and down my arms.

"Zoe! Come on, Zoe, don't do this to me." I pinch her nose, tip her head back, and fill her lungs with two breaths, then follow up with some chest compressions.

She gasps like she's swum from the bottom of the deep end and just reached the surface. Thank the creator. I draw her into my arms, relieved when she continues to breathe. In and out. In and out. My dragon is still on high alert, but she's with us.

Something warm and wet spreads out across my lap, and I realize she's soiled herself again. And her skin is ice-cold. She shivers in my arms, and then her eyes roll back in her head and her entire body seizes. I hold her on her side. Hold her hair back as she purges everything from her stomach, and it comes up black as tar. Fuck.

"Should I call 9-1-1?" Patrick asks. He's standing in the doorway, clearly horrified. I'm not sure he's ever looked so pale. "Or I could call Morwyn."

"No. She's going to be okay. Only, can you clean this up after we leave this room?"

"Yes, of course."

"And we'll take food and drink in the bedroom in an hour or so. Lots of calories."

He nods. "I'll take care of it."

I lift her off the floor and start for the bedroom, but Patrick stops me as I'm passing him. "You have calls from Crew and from Ellison."

"Tell Crew I have the flu and I'll call him back as soon as I'm well enough. Tell Ellison to come as soon as he can and to bring Lucas."

Patrick nods and heads for the closet where we keep the cleaning supplies. I carry my mate into my bedroom and then the bathroom. When we're beyond this, I'm taking her on a real date. Hawaii or Europe. Anywhere but this fucking bathroom.

I fill the tub with hot water because she's still shivering, even though her skin is slick from sweat. While it's filling, I undress her and then myself. We both sink into the tub.

I didn't do it this way last time. Before she was my mate, I cleaned her up quickly and efficiently while all my clothes were on. This time, I climb into the tub with her, sinking deep into the water with her head on my chest. Now that she's my mate, the skin-to-skin will heal her faster, and I can monitor her better with my arms around her.

I soap up the bath sponge I keep on the side of the tub and start running it over her arms, her chest, her stomach, the rest of her. Steam rises up around us. She's finally stopped shivering.

"You're going to be okay," I whisper in her ear. "I'll take care of you. Whatever it takes."

I wrap my arms around her and close my eyes, and that's when my dragon sends me a picture of the deconstructed ring. What the hell? I open my eyes again. My beast is restless, but for once, it's not after sex. He's as concerned for our mate as I am. When I close my eyes again, I see the ring again—not just as it exists in this world but the view from the Gold Room, through Zoe's magic.

"Creator, bless! She showed the ring to you." Carefully, I stand from the tub and take Zoe with me. I have her dressed in a pair of my pajamas and tucked into bed in a matter of minutes. Once I'm sure her breathing is even and she's sleeping peacefully, I rush to the office and retrieve her drawing along with a blank piece of paper and a pencil. I return to the bedroom and grab a large book from the bookshelf to use as a lap desk. I never work in here, but I won't leave her.

I place the blank paper over hers so that I can see her drawing under mine, and I start to add to it. This would go faster if my dragon could hold a pencil. He remembers what Zoe told him clearly, but he can only show me a little at a time. We are one being. One soul. But he's an aspect of myself that lives in a deep part of my consciousness. I can hear what he thinks, but in order for me to see what he remembers, I have to enter a state that's something like daydreaming, then come back into my conscious mind to transmit what I saw to paper. It's a slow and daunting process, but by the time Patrick comes in with a tray, I've made incredible progress.

"Ellison and Lucas will be here in the morning. They say they have news," Patrick says.

"Great," I say with dread. I'm not sure I want to know what their news is. I have enough to think about with my mate sleeping much too soundly in my bed.

I turn my attention back to my drawing, but Patrick clears his throat.

"Is there something else, Patrick?"

"Zoe left this in the dining room. It's been...busy." He hands me her phone. I can't open it, but there are twenty-four missed messages on the screen. All I can see is the top one. *Why aren't you responding to Jeremy's texts? What is going on? Call me right away.*

I frown and look up at Patrick. "I'll handle it," I say evenly.

He removes the dome from the tray, offers me a shallow bow, and leaves.

My inner dragon goes eerily calm as we look down at the phone. We are of one mind on this. I don't know who Jeremy is or why Zoe's parents want her to call him, but she is mine. And I'm a jealous and possessive bastard. I don't deny it for a second. Mom and Dad, I'd love to know. Jeremy needs to find another hobby, and it's time they understood as much.

I rise from the chair and walk to Zoe's side, positioning the phone in front of her face to unlock it. It takes me a few tries, but it works. Then I hustle out of the room and call her mother back.

"Zoe? Thank the goddess."

"No. Actually, this is Sebastian York, partner at Full Throttle Records."

"O-oh. Hello."

"Are you Zoe's mother?"

"Yes, I'm Anita Willow."

"Nice to meet you, Anita. I—"

"Is Zoe okay?"

"Why wouldn't she be okay?"

"She hasn't been answering her calls, and she didn't return *multiple* texts. Also, if she's okay, why would *you* be calling us?" I have to hand it to the woman; she actually sounds convinced of her own bullshit.

"I'm calling because it's three o'clock on a Friday, and Zoe is busy in the recording studio. Very busy. Your daughter is extremely talented, Mrs. Willow. I'm afraid we have to make use of the studio when scheduled, which means it will be impossible for her to call or text you during work hours and sometimes after, if she's recording late. She noticed your repeated calls and wanted me to return your call to make sure you and her father were okay."

"Oh." The woman sounds disappointed. I release a

slow breath. That "oh" says it all. Her parents expect her to fail. They expect her to fall back into the mistakes of her past. I hate that. Parents should love you unconditionally. They should believe in you when no one else does. And this witch is falling way short.

"So, are you both okay?" I ask her.

"Yes, yes, we're fine."

"No emergency, then? I see twenty-four messages from you and someone named Jeremy on her phone. Is this Jeremy having an emergency?"

"No. No. He's her doctor. Just checking in with her."

"Did she have an appointment or something?"

"Uh, no."

"Then, could you please share with Jeremy that Zoe Willow is a very busy recording artist, and unless there is an emergency, please do not expect an immediate return call or text."

"Okay." A pocket of silence opens between us, and I surmise that Anita Willow is trying her best not to voice her true worries to her daughter's new boss.

I throw her a bone. "She also said to tell you we'll see you this weekend for Beltane."

"We?"

"Oh, I'm coming with her. It will be a pleasure to meet you in person."

"Oh, yes. Of course. I'm so glad you can make it."

"I'll relay your excitement to Zoe as soon as she's done recording. Buh-bye." I end the call, my blood still coursing hot in my veins. I stride back to the bedroom and quietly place the phone down on the end table next to her. As I watch her, a soft niggle at the back of my brain wonders if I've done the right thing lying to her mother. After all, Zoe is currently passed out from the very gold dust her parents and doctor fear she's using. Worse, I didn't have Zoe's permission to access her phone or call her mother.

But I dismiss the intrusive thoughts almost immediately. No one gets to snap their fingers and call my mate like a dog. She isn't theirs any longer. She's *mine*. And I will care for her. Besides, now that I've completed the drawing of the ring, she might not even need to use again.

I lower myself back into the chair and watch her sleep, watch her breathe. I'll keep her safe. She's mine now.

Chapter Twenty-Five

ZOE

Darkness. A cave. Cold and dark. I walk forward, hands out to feel for a wall or a piece of furniture, anything to steady myself. My hands catch on a rope strung across the room, and I grip it. It feels weird. Unnatural. I try to release it, but it sticks to my palms. I start to panic, struggling to pull away. I'm stuck.

"Can someone turn the lights on?" I yell, my heart thundering in my ears.

Light rises in the room, and I see that my hands are not stuck to a rope at all but to a strand of a massive spider web, and right in front of me, so close I can almost feel the brush of her pinchers, is a black widow spider the size of a bear.

I open my mouth to scream, but my breath catches in my throat. I'm too terrified. I'm frozen from fear. And then I notice something odd. A gilded frame surrounds the spider. I don't understand what I'm seeing until I reach out a hand to touch the frame and the spider's leg moves.

The spider isn't in front of me. It's a mirror. I am the spider.

Welcome home, Zoe.

Now, I scream. Again and again. Squeezing my eyes shut as the terror bleeds out through my voice.

"Zoe? Zoe! I'm here."

Sebastian's arms wrap around me and squeeze. The bedside lamp turns on. But even with Seb's bedroom coming into focus, it takes several seconds to stop screaming. He takes my face in his hands, and I just lose it. My screams turn into sobs. He holds me as I weep into his chest.

When I finally simmer down and pull back from him, he wipes away my tears. "You need to eat something," he says, as if it is totally normal that I've soaked his shirt with my meltdown. He stands and moves to where a nearby tray awaits as if a waiter has only recently come by and left it there for us. I wonder what time it is.

I turn and tap my phone screen. It's two a.m. I've missed multiple messages from Jeremy and my mother while I was out. Shit, I am going to hear about this later. I thumb through them as I rub my throbbing head.

"I took care of it," Seb says, gently taking my phone and replacing it with a plate filled with fresh baked bread and a selection of meats and cheeses arranged with grapes and strawberries. I'm so hungry, I instantly scoop up a healthy serving of Brie with a slice of the bread and sink it into my mouth.

"It's still warm," I mumble passionately around the bite.

"I had Patrick bring in a fresh tray about an hour ago when I could tell you were waking up."

"How did you know I was waking up?" I shove another bite into my mouth.

He glances away from me as he sets my phone back down on his side of the bed and climbs back in beside me. "Your brain waves changed."

I pause with a piece of cheese halfway to my mouth. "You were monitoring my brain waves?"

With a snort, he shakes his head. "Not actively. I didn't enter your head or anything. But dragons can always tell. It's like..." He stops and thinks for a second. "Like you can hear someone breathing. I can sense your mind."

Weird. So fucking weird.

I take another bite of bread and cheese, coming fully awake.

He holds out a drawing to me, and my eyes widen as I realize he's completed the sketch of the ring. Everything I saw in the Gold Room is on this sheet of paper. "It worked! Your dragon remembered!"

He nods. I grab my phone again and snap a picture for future reference. I want to research these spells using the grimoires in my parents' library. But after I snap the photos, I see again the numerous calls and texts from Jeremy and my parents. "Wait... What did you mean before when you said you took care of it? What exactly did you take care of?"

He points at the phone. "I called your mother and told her you couldn't call her back because you were in the recording studio and that we'd see her this weekend for Beltane."

I drop the grape I'm holding back onto my plate. "You…you…you phoned my mother? How the fuck did you get her number?"

"From your phone. I used your face to unlock it and call her back when I saw her last message on your lock screen."

I am flabbergasted. There haven't been many times in my life when I would use that word. It's the type of descriptor you read in novels but don't often experience. But I understand flabbergasted because I am speechless with a combination of surprise, anger, and violation.

"Who is Jeremy to you? Your mother said he was a doctor, but what doctor texts his patients twenty times in a matter of hours?"

"This isn't okay, Seb," I say firmly. "I didn't give you permission to access my phone or to call my parents. What the hell?"

He looks confused. "But if I hadn't called her, she would have kept messaging. You don't have to worry. I explained that you had asked me to call and that you'd be working late. She isn't worried at all about you now."

"In the recording studio," I clarify, making sure I have all the details about the lie.

"Yes!" He grins brightly.

I shake my head, close my eyes, and release a slow breath. "I don't lie to my parents, Seb. I may not tell them everything, but I don't outright lie. What will happen if they ask to hear what I've been recording? I don't have anything to play for them, do I?"

"But you will," he says quickly. "We can work on something today."

I climb out of bed. I still feel woozy, but I can't stay in this bed tonight. "You don't get it, do you? It was presumptuous and a violation of my privacy and my boundaries for you to access my phone without my permission and contact my family on my behalf. And you lying to them has opened me up to having to compromise my morals to cover up what you did."

His hand goes to his chest as if I've shot him and he's patching the bloody hole. "I was only trying to help. I was afraid they'd do something rash if they didn't receive a response."

"That's not an apology," I say softly. As much as it softens my heart to hear him explain why he did what he did, this is a new relationship, and I need him to understand that he overstepped my boundaries.

He tilts his head, his eyes narrowing. "I am sorry that I lied to your parents on your behalf. I am not sorry that I called to tell them you were okay, just busy. Given the nature of our mission here, I felt like it was the necessary action for me to take to protect my mate."

What? "Your mate?" Even as I say it, the strangest sensation flows through me, a rightness at the word, but also an awareness that the label has deep meaning.

"Have you forgotten already? You accepted me as your mate yesterday night."

"We had sex. It wasn't like we got married." But I know as soon as the words are out of my mouth that they are a lie. Something more happened between us that night. I know it in my bones.

Seb looks like I've punched him in the stomach. His face is drawn in pain, and he has to steady himself on the wall. Slowly, he starts to breathe again. He reaches down to pick up my phone and slides it across the bed to me, where it remains beside the plate of bread and cheese. "I have made an error," he says, so low I can hardly hear him. "Please forgive me."

"I forgive you." I pick up the phone and the plate and head for the door.

"Where are you going?" he asks, and I see his eyes glow golden, know that the dragon who stood sentinel by my side in the Gold Room is watching me through his eyes.

"Home," I say. "I think I need to be alone."

I walk out the door, but not before I see the absolute devastation on Seb's face.

Good girl, the spider says. *It's for the best. If we keep him close, we'll only hurt him. A spider eats her mate.*

Fuck you, I think back to her. But as I make my way past the pool to my house, a part of me knows she's right.

Chapter Twenty-Six

SEB

Rejected by my mate. No way did I expect this. Part of me understood she might be shocked or angry about the phone thing, but I thought she'd understand, given the circumstances. I never thought she'd reject our mating.

She didn't say the words, my dragon protests. He means she didn't specifically reject the mating bond. But she may as well have. It was just sex, she said. Just sex. It was not just sex for me.

And now I'm torn into a million pieces. I might as well be bleeding out from a hole in my chest. I lie on my side in bed, staring out the window toward her darkened cottage as the sky gradually lightens. By the time the sun rises, I'm aching and hot with fever, my appetency returning with a vengeance.

Who the fuck cares? I may as well go up in flames. I won't be able to live without her.

A knock comes on the door, and Patrick pokes his head in. "Ellison and Lucas have arrived and are waiting for you in the dining room. I've served coffee and cinnamon rolls whenever you're ready."

"Okay."

"Sir? Are you all right? You look a little, um... Should I call Morwyn?"

"No. I'm fine. I'll be right out."

I can hear him breathing. He's not leaving. And then I hear him lift the still-full tray from last night and take it and the stand from the room. He's a smart man. I'm sure he sees that the food was hardly touched and that Zoe isn't in the room with me. Perfect. Now he'll tiptoe around me and treat me like I'm made of glass all day. Just what I don't need.

I slide from the bed and get dressed. It's a tedious task. My skin hurts. I have to force myself to brush my teeth. But by the time I join my brothers at the table, I think I've come together pretty well.

"You look like shit," Lucas says when he sees me.

I guess I haven't hidden it as well as I thought I did.

"Appetency," I say vaguely. No sense sharing about Zoe. Morwyn knows, but the brother is anything but a gossip. "It's hit me hard today."

"Call in another Taurus, brother," Ellison says. "It's uncomfortable, but you'll feel so much better afterward."

Even the thought of calling in Mia turns my stomach. Besides, I couldn't do that to Zoe. Rejected or not, I don't want to hurt her. Learning I was with someone else so soon after we were together would unsettle her, maybe cheapen what we shared. Zoe's not a dragon and doesn't fully understand the appetency that strikes my kind during our alignment. I won't do it.

I place the pictures of the ring at the center of the table and pour myself a cup of coffee. "With the help of Zoe, we've deconstructed the ring. It's complex magic."

"So, does she think she can create something to defend us against it?" Lucas asks.

I frown and reach for a cinnamon roll. If there's one surefire salve for a broken heart, it's butter and sugar. I'd better eat two. "Unfortunately, we may need to find someone else for that part. Every time Zoe uses her magic to study this thing, she becomes extremely ill. That's why I look like this. I was up most of the night making sure she came out of it. Going in again could kill her. I haven't spoken with her yet today, but we should be prepared. We may need to find another way."

Ellison scowls. "We should get to finding one, then, because Lucas found something in Maryland."

I make eye contact with the Leo, and he tosses a manila envelope in my direction. I swipe it off the table and tip the contents out beside me. A series of grainy photos spreads across the table. They are all taken from a distance, maybe using a drone or a telephoto lens.

"Where is this?" I ask, trying to place the opulent mansion.

"New sale on the coast. Property is registered to a corporate entity." Lucas massages his jaw. "I tracked the bakery bomber by rummaging through a few heads. He was seen exiting the private drive that leads to this place, which is why I decided to dig a little deeper, and I think you'll be as surprised as I was to see who is living at that mansion."

I flip to the next picture and focus in on the profile of a man standing on the balcony. "Who am I looking at, Lucas? It's pretty far away. This could be anyone."

"Look closer. Flip a few photos in."

I do as he suggests, and my heart lodges in my throat. I do know who this is, and the realization sends an icy chill down my spine, cold enough to temporarily douse my fever. "Who is this? It looks like—"

"Roman Cifarelli."

"Connor killed him. I saw his dead body pinned to the wall with his throat ripped out. We all watched his house burn down."

Coming to my side, Lucas shuffles through the pictures and points at a close-up of the man. He has three pale scars that pucker along his neck, and half his face appears melted by fire.

"By the creator, how is this possible. No human could survive that."

Ellison couples his hands together under his chin. "No human could survive...without magic," he clarifies. "And Roman had plenty of dark magic."

"And something else," Lucas says. "When I was investigating, a name came up again and again in the heads of people who had seen the bakery bomber. A waitress who'd served him lunch remembered him telling her that she should prepare herself for the return of the destroyer. She didn't know what he meant, but it gave her the chills. Really freaked her out."

I run through the pictures again. "Cifarelli Enterprises has moved on without Roman and Stefan. They've named a new CEO. Roman hasn't been seen in public since Connor put a sword through his chest."

"All true," Ellison says.

"Do you think Roman is calling himself the destroyer now? Opting for the big bad moniker and telling his followers that he rose from the dead would definitely galvanize his base."

Lucas and Ellison nod in unison. "We suspect the same thing," Ellison says. "Roman is playing dead, but he's still leading the charge, and he's targeting us like never before."

I flatten my hand next to Roman's damaged profile. "So, to temper the Order, we have to take out Roman. And now we know where he is."

"Yeah, we know where he is, but attacking him there will be problematic. The place is guarded around the clock by guys with rings. He must have secured a ton of Donovan's blood before he died because they are recruiting at a record pace—and not just the rich and powerful anymore. Any man who they can convince to join."

"We've found the same thing. We targeted a club owner who fit the profile, but his two friends, who definitely did not, also had rings. And they must have been recent recruits because they barely knew how to use their weapons."

"How many rings did you get?" Lucas asks, his eyes darkening.

"Three."

"Did you look at the inscriptions?" Ellison's mouth takes on a sardonic tilt.

"No. Why?"

"Because Lucas and I collected five last night, and we noticed something interesting."

Lucas leans over and digs in his bag, withdrawing a wooden box. He opens it, and we all groan as the energy from the rings hits us. But as he turns the box to face me, I see the differences. At first glance, they're all exactly the same: silver, with a Saint George's cross on the face. But that is where the similarities end. The metal of one is brighter white and more substantial.

"Is it just me, or does one appear to be platinum and the others silver?"

"It's not just you," Ellison says. "You can see the lesser rings are already tarnishing. And—"

"No inscription," I say. I stand from the table. "We should check the ones Remus and I collected."

I rush from the room to my bedroom and to the black bag of rings Zoe dropped in the corner of the bathroom that I moved to a wooden box for safety. Memories of that night come back to me like I've been fed into a shredder. The way she undressed me. Washed the blood off my skin. My eyes burn, but I can't allow myself to feel this now. I grab the box and rush back to the dining room.

I drop it on the table between us and open it, then use a fork to tip the bag so that the rings roll out, along with a bloody chunk of finger. The stench is awful.

"Fuck, Seb! You didn't have Patrick clean them?"

"Hadn't thought of it."

I push the bloody rings around in their filth with the tines of the fork until we can see their faces.

"Same story," Lucus says. "Different metal. No inscription."

I wrangle the rings back into the bag and drop them into the box. Once our respective boxes are closed, I promptly dispose of the fork I used to manipulate the rings in the nearest trash can. A collective sigh of relief rises up between us.

"Creator, I hate those things," Ellison says, scratching his arms like he still has the creepy-crawlies.

"What we know for sure is that there are now two classes of rings, which explains the video of the bakery bomber. The Saint's Order is recruiting members faster, which calls for creating rings faster." I pull over the drawing of the ring. "This thing has five layers of enchantments, one of which is a potion made from drag-on's blood. Roman is using his store of Donovan's blood to enchant as many rings as possible as quickly as possi-ble, but why?"

Ellison's gray eyes lock on me. "Isn't it obvious? To kill us. He's trying to outnumber us and hunt us down before we can recover from Donovan's death and the loss of the accord. Let me be the first to admit you were right when you sent the dragons into hiding, and also right when you ordered us to go on the offensive. The code red was necessary, no matter what anyone says."

"I've never been less excited about being right," I say, taking another sip of coffee.

Ellison leans back in his chair. "So, the question is, what's our strategy for fighting back?"

I take a moment to think. There's a reason I've been able to grow Full Throttle Records to be one of the top music producers of this era. I'm decisive and I have great gut instincts. But this is no easy decision. Thousands of lives are in my hands. "We stay in hiding, for now. And we keep hunting rings. All twelve of us."

"Fuck," Lucas says.

"I know, but the faster we neutralize them, the safer everyone will be."

Ellison shakes his head. "Shit. The dragon civilians are not going to like hearing that there's no end date to this code red."

"With any luck, that will change. Because I am personally going to hunt down Roman Cifarelli, and I'm going to cut the Saint's Order off at the knees."

Chapter Twenty-Seven

ZOE

Mate. Am I Sebastian's mate? I stare at the ceiling, alone in my room, feeling cold and lonely. I miss Seb. I miss his warmth. I miss his steadiness.

It was just sex. Don't mistake lust for love, the spider says. Her voice is so strong now, and the little sleep I've gotten since I left Seb's side has been polluted with her dark presence.

"Shut up!" I yell. "It was never just sex!"

You've known him for eleven days. It couldn't be anything more than that. He's a dream. He's a story you've made up in your mind.

"Maybe it is fast. And maybe it won't be forever. But even if these feelings I'm having aren't permanent, they're real. He was never just a hookup. He's brave and he's good and he treats me like a queen. Even if it's not forever, it could be the start of forever, and I'm willing to give it a shot."

There is one way to tell. You could ascend to the Gold Room and use your power to look into the future. You would know in minutes whether or not your relationship works out. You could peek in on your future children. You could know if this seed of love for him might actually last.

"No. I'm not doing that. I only ascended to help Seb. I don't use for personal gain anymore."

She laughs. *To help him? After he violated your privacy and your autonomy? He brings you here, of all places. A free home completely under his control. Sounds more like a trap. You're not his mate. You're his prisoner.*

"That's not true."

Oh? Just try to go to Beltane without him. See what happens.

I throw the covers off me and stomp to the shower. I need to wash the filth off me. The filth of that ring. Of my addiction and her chilling, spidery voice. Of the way I jumped into something with Seb I don't completely understand. Of how I hurt him last night, rejected him, when deep in my heart, I do feel an attachment to him, one that shouldn't be possible in such a short time.

I step into the spray and let the hot water pour over me, wishing it could take my skin off and I could grow back a different person. I remember hitting rock bottom with gold dust, but I don't remember ever feeling this low. It's like I've been dropped into a deep, dark well. I can see a tiny circle of light above me that must be my one-time happiness, but reaching it seems impossible. The walls are slick. I may never climb out again.

But I force myself to go through the motions of life anyway. I learned this the first time. The shower, brushing my teeth, eating, dressing, doing my hair, spraying on perfume. If I look normal and act normal, and I cross off the days standing between me and gold dust, eventually, normal will be normal, and the dust will become a distant memory once again.

My living room is filled with boxes from my apartment. Patrick offered to put anything I wanted into storage, but I haven't had a moment to unpack. But I find one marked closet and dig out my Beltane dress and saddle-brown ballet flats. It's a flowy, hunter green maxi dress featuring peonies and pomegranates in a pattern of spring greens. I wear it for Beltane every year. I fasten the necklace my mother gave me for the season around my neck, the gold disk that dangles between my collarbones depicting a rudimentary engraving of a maypole. I take a quick look in the mirror before digging out my leather backpack-style purse and throwing my wallet, phone, and some essentials into it.

At the last second, I toss in a notebook and a pen. I promised to help Seb, and no matter what is happening between us, I plan to make good on that promise. And that means I'm not going to miss the chance to research some things in my parents' magical library.

In the late afternoon, I head up to the big house and hear voices coming from the dining room.

"With any luck, it won't last long. Because I am

personally going to hunt down Roman Cifarelli, and I'm going to cut the Saint's Order off at the knees," I hear Seb say. Why does that name sound familiar?

"What about the witch?" another voice says. "Can she help protect you?"

"No. I won't ask any more of her. It's killing her. We need to find another way."

"Sounds like you've come to care for the woman. Are you making the right decision for dragons...or for her?"

"It's my call, Lucas. Yes, I care for her. I'd go so far as to say I love her."

The other voices hiss.

"Happy? That's what you wanted, for me to admit it, yes?"

"Does she feel the same way?" the voice asks softly, almost a whisper.

"No," Seb says. "She has rejected the bond. So, you see, I have no problem being the one to go after Roman, come what may."

"Damn it. I'm sorry, Seb. That's awful."

"No wonder you look like shit."

I stiffen, not even daring to breathe. It's true I got angry and left. Things were moving too fast for me. But I didn't reject him. What exactly is he signing up for?

I clear my throat and stride the rest of the way to the dining room, not surprised when the voices I heard before go silent. Seb looks like hell. He's got dark circles under his eyes, and his hair stands up in wild tufts. And when he looks at me, his eyes go dead. No spark. No gold.

"Hi," I say to the room.

Seb stands, his full attention focused on me. "You look beautiful. Stunning, really."

"Thanks, but..."

"Let me introduce you to my two brothers, Ellison and Lucas."

"Nice to meet you," I say politely, then I turn back to Seb. "I was wondering if I could get a ride to my parents for Beltane?"

He stands. "I'll take you. Let me get changed."

See. He'll never let you out of his sight, the spider says.

"Actually, I think it would be better if you could just have your driver take me, if that's all right. I know how busy you are."

His face falls, the beaten-dog expression taking over. It's like each of my words has been a knife in his gut.

"My apologies. I thought maybe...because you'd asked me—"

Oh, that's right. I did ask him. Instantly, I feel like a huge jerk, and I'm about to renege and ask him to come with me. But he's already pulled out his phone. "William will meet you at the front door in five minutes."

"Thank you." I walk away, my heart heavy.

If he'd wanted to go with you, he would have tried harder to come, the spider says.

Shut up. You were wrong. I'm not a prisoner, and he is letting me go, I think back to her. My heart squeezes painfully. I wanted Seb with me tonight, and once again, I've made a choice based on a lie my addiction told me. Now, I'm stuck with the consequences. Yanking Seb's chain and asking him to go now would just confuse things.

I see William pull up outside and open the door, but Ellison's whispered voice comes through the wall. "Are you really going to let her leave? Alone?"

"She'll be safe with her kind tonight. Besides, she's a witch, not a dragon."

"But how will you stand it?"

I walk out the door to Seb's low growl.

An hour later, I arrive at my parents' house just as the sun begins to set. When William drops me off, he gives me his number and promises to stay in the area until I'm ready to go. I walk up to the door alone, the smoky scent of bonfire flavoring the air.

For a second, I just stand there, listening to the voices inside. It's been a long time since I was welcome to enter this house without knocking. A long time since I called this place home. But as I raise my fist to rap on the heavy farmhouse door, emotion catches in my throat. I wish I were a person they could be proud of. I wish I weren't keeping secrets from them even now.

The door opens, and I'm surprised when I see Jeremy standing on the other side. He gives me a warm smile. Jeremy is only four years older than me. When I was a freshman in high school, he was a senior, and as witches, we grew up in the same circles. Only, he decided to pursue psychiatry, while I pursued my music career. And now, he's my doctor. It's weird, though, to see him in social situations like this.

"There's our girl," he says with a shake of his sandy

brown hair. "We were wondering when you would arrive. But where's the dragon?"

"Excuse me?" I ask. How would Jeremy know about Seb?

"Your mom told me you were working for a dragon and that he'd be coming tonight."

A flare of hostility goes off inside me, shadowed by a ring of protectiveness. It's a deadly time for dragons right now. Not that I don't trust Jeremy or my mom, but why is that relevant?

"Who told you my boss was a dragon?" I say lightly. "And he couldn't make it. Something came up." I shrug.

"He's not a dragon?" Jeremy asks. "Your mom seemed to think—"

"Oh, Jeremy. You know Anita. She always has to have something to talk about." I roll my eyes. "All you need to know about my boss and my new job is that it's going great. I've never felt more creative or productive. And I am looking forward to thanking the goddess tonight for the fruits of all the hard work we put in to get me to this point." I give him my warmest stage smile and walk past him toward the back of the house, where I know my family will be.

Jeremy strides along with me. "So, what have you been working on?"

"I don't want to talk about work," I say. I've planned this. I knew he would ask, and I don't want to lie, so I prepared the truths I could share. I look him in the eye and say, "Suffice it to say that I planted a seed this week that I hope will grow into the most beautiful tree, and

I'm just not ready to expose that seed to the sun. It needs time in darkness. I'll share when I'm ready."

He frowns. "There shouldn't be secrets between us, Zoe."

I snort. "Why? Because you're my therapist? I don't think that's how it works."

"No. because I'm your friend." He nudges my elbow, allowing his upper arm to linger touching mine. "We've known each other since we were children. You know you can tell me anything, right?"

I glance in his direction, and he looks sincere. But the way he's looking at me makes me uncomfortable. I'm sure I could tell him or my parents anything and they'd still care for me. We've been through a lot together, and I owe them for facilitating my recovery. Only, he's looking at me like I'm a woman and he's a man, not a doctor and patient. I'm relieved when we reach the back porch and my mother and father rush over to me for hugs and greetings. I answer their questions about Seb in the same way I answered Jeremy's, and they let it drop quickly.

Soon, I have a glass of May wine in one hand and a honey cake in the other and am being crowned by our coven's elder, Hazel Heartwood, her wrinkled face smiling up at me as she places the ring of marigolds on my head. I forget all about the weird interaction with Jeremy and lose myself in the celebration. I eat and drink and laugh, and when a pleasant buzz vibrates in my veins, I kick off my shoes and walk barefoot in the grass toward the bonfire. The heat soaks through my dress and into my skin, shining gold against my face. The connection I feel to the flames, to the wood, to the fresh green grass, to the air around me is euphoric, almost as good as the Gold Room. I dance around the flames, just breathing, just being.

"Have you made your wish yet?" Hazel asks, pausing my steps. She holds out a box of pencils and parchment.

"No, I haven't. Thank you." I take one of each with no idea what I plan to write.

"Your aura has changed," Hazel says with a smile.

"Oh?"

"It used to be green when you were a child, and then, of course, when you were sick, it was dark gray for a while." My face falls from the shame I feel. "I knew that wouldn't last, though," she says, squeezing my arm. "You're not the first young witch to overuse gold dust, you know. And you won't be the last. But you are strong enough to manage the effects. I saw that in you from the start."

I raise my eyes to hers. "Thank you for that."

"Besides, you're getting stronger. Your aura now is hazel."

"Hazel? What does that mean?"

"Hazel is a blending of green, brown, and gold. Green is growth. You're changing, sweetheart, maturing as you should. The brown is grounding. You know your worth and are emotionally stable. And the gold—" she grins widely "—that's a gift of the goddess. Celestial joy, my dear. You've been in her presence."

I don't deny it. "You've always been able to see straight into me."

She takes my hands between her own. "You've been blessed with a gift, Zoe. You can accomplish whatever you want to if you just trust your instincts." Her eyes drift back toward Jeremy. She lowers her voice. "Others in the coven may not agree with me on this, but I've never bought into the modern view of things. Our world is magic, not psychiatry. But I believe everything you need to succeed is already available to you. All you have to do is trust yourself to access it." She releases my hands and the small pencil and paper within them.

"I really needed to hear that."

She rises up on her toes and kisses my cheek. "Blessed be."

As she drifts off to spread her wisdom to someone else in the coven, I smile down at the parchment in my hand and think about what I should wish for. Thoughts swirl through my head, but only one face appears again and again. Seb. Seb is the reason I don't have to wish for money. Seb is the reason I don't have to wish for a job or for a home. Seb is fighting a battle that could end his life and the lives of his people. I like Seb. I could love Seb under the right circumstances. I came here alone tonight to prove to the spider in my brain that he wasn't controlling me. I am still my own person. He did not follow me. He did not insist on coming with me. Even if we don't end up together, I want to help him. I want him to know that I did my best.

I pick up the pencil and write, *I wish I were enough for Seb.*

I pause. I'd meant "magically" when I started writing. Enough to help Seb *magically*. I was referring to power. But as I was writing, I thought, it's bigger than that. I want to be enough for him. Worthy of him. Enough that he trusts me, always. Enough that what we've started lasts forever.

I fold the piece of paper and toss it into the bonfire, the corners glowing gold as it curls in on itself and blows toward the stars. I picture the goddess, sweeping all our wishes into the palm of her hand and smiling down on us.

I draw in a deep breath tinged with a rich, smoky scent and decide it's time to visit my parents' library.

Chapter Twenty-Eight

ZOE

Hazel told me to trust my instincts, and I'm so glad I did. I sit at the desk in my parents' library with no fewer than six grimoires open in front of me, and I know I've done the right thing. As I snap pictures of the pages, I am sure my idea will work. I can create a gold ring just like the Saint's Order one, a ring that will hold the goddess's celestial magic. The power of the creator to face off against the power of the destroyer.

And the best part is, most of it I can do without ascending. I don't need to be in the Gold Room to form the gold into a ring or to soak it in a potion. I can sing an incantation and draw the symbols to add the layers of enchantments. Five layers. A celestial counterspell for each of the dark ones in the original ring. The only thing I'll have to ascend for is to infuse the charms, enchantments, and spells I perform into the metal. But as long as

Seb isn't in a hurry, I think I can wait until I heal a little bit more before I do it. I can make him the defensive ring he needs without falling into a full-blown dependency situation. I'm sure of it.

Quickly, I finish taking my pictures and slide my phone back into my purse. I was lucky to quietly sneak in here without anyone seeing me, but the party will be winding down soon, and I need to get back out there before someone notices I'm gone. I close the top book and walk it to the shelf, carefully returning it to the spot where I found it. I do the second book and the third. I've just closed the fourth when the door opens, and Jeremy strides into the room.

"Hello," I say lightly. My stomach sinks at the sight of him. I hate that he caught me in here. I'm not doing anything wrong, but I don't want to answer his questions. I arch an eyebrow. "Ever heard of knocking?"

He smiles, but it doesn't quite meet his eyes. "I didn't think there would be anyone in here."

I giggle. "That's why you knock." I return the book I'm holding to the shelf. Behind me, he walks deeper into the room. "I'll be done in a second if you want to use this room."

He clears his throat. "No. I came looking for you when I noticed you were missing."

"You don't need to keep track of me, Jeremy. I'm a grown woman and perfectly healthy now. No babysitter needed." I mean for it to come out teasingly, but I can't keep the sharp edge from my words.

"That's strange, because it looks like you were planning to do magic before I've cleared you."

What the fuck? I whirl to face him. "First of all, my researching magic is not the same as my doing magic. Second, why haven't you cleared me? I've been sober and thriving for over a year."

He scowls. "Thriving? You're barely getting by on your own."

I jerk back. "What the hell does that mean? I'm gainfully employed. I've made a home for myself. I'm healthy."

He runs a hand over the spell in the last book, still open on the desk. "I wouldn't know that, would I? Now that you're missing our appointments."

"You don't have to worry about me. In fact, I'm here because of something Hazel said to me, and I feel better than ever." I reach for the book to pull it out from under his hand, when I notice a large silver ring on his ring finger that reminds me far too much of the Saint's Order rings. Fear catches in my throat like I've swallowed a fist, until I notice that the face of the ring is different. There's a pentagram instead of a Saint George cross and no inscription. "Where did you get that ring? It's new since the last time I saw you, right?"

He slides his hand off the book and behind the desk. "Not new. It used to be my father's."

"Oh."

"As for Hazel, I'd be careful taking her advice. She's from another time, really. So old, her opinion is hardly relevant anymore."

I snort. "Hardly relevant? She's the most powerful witch in the coven."

"That depends on how you define powerful." His words lash through the center of the room and send a chill along my spine. I close the book and slide it back on the shelf.

"I should take off. I'm going to say goodbye to my parents." I turn to leave, but his hand lands on my shoulder.

"Zoe, wait." When I turn to look at him, my cheek comes close to his ring, and I feel the gravity of the metal. It's that same silent, cold draw, like a black hole of energy, that I felt from the Saint's Order ring in the Gold Room. I yank my shoulder away from his touch before I can school my features.

"Where did your father get that ring, Jeremy?" The hair on my arms stands on end.

"Goddess, what is with your obsession with my ring all of a sudden?"

"Nothing," I say, as I step into the hall. "Just think it's interesting. Wondering if they have a female version."

"No. It's a family heirloom."

I nod and head for the stairs.

"I want to see you again," he blurts. I can't tell if he's asking me to set up an appointment or a date.

"No."

"Why not?"

I decide it's better to presume he's talking about an appointment. "I think, given our personal history, that I should see someone else professionally going forward. I'll talk to my parents."

A grin spreads across his face. "Then there's nothing stopping us from dating," he says hopefully.

I frown. "Yes, there is."

"What?"

God, this man is dense. "Me. I don't want to date you either. I'm sorry."

Rage colors his face, and I descend the stairs at a fast clip. He follows me. "You should be careful who you're fraternizing with, Zoe. Dragons are dangerous."

I stop in the great room at the base of the stairs and look over my shoulder. "What is with your obsession with dragons all of a sudden? Are you a dragon, Jeremy?"

He opens his mouth to say something, but I don't wait to hear it. I take off toward the backyard and am relieved when I find my dad straightaway. I manage to get him and my mom alone in a bedroom and tell them the truth. I reveal that Jeremy asked me on a date tonight and that I don't feel that seeing him professionally is appropriate now.

"I told you he was interested in her, Anita," my day says through a frown.

My mother shakes her head. "But are you also interested in him, though, darling?" Mom asks brightly. When Dad gives her a sour look, she says, "I only mean, might you have led him on in some way?"

I take her by the shoulders. "Not even a little bit, Mom. And you should know that I've been healthy for over a year, and by all accounts, he should have cleared me by now. I believe he kept me on because of his attraction to me."

"On my dime," my father says angrily.

"Are you sure? It sounds so devious!" Mom says.

"Look at her, honey. She's the picture of normalcy. He's been using her as a meal ticket."

When I pulled them in here, I didn't mean to trash Jeremy or his reputation, but I don't stop them from drawing their own conclusions. Everything I've told them is true, and I'm sick of being hounded by that watchdog.

I text William to pick me up and give both my parents a firm hug.

"I'll take care of everything," Dad says. "Don't worry about Jeremy."

"I love you guys. Happy Beltane."

They walk me to the door, where they see that William is waiting, holding the door open for me. I promise to call before slipping into the back seat. Only when the door is closed do I see a Jeremy-shaped silhouette in the front room window. His dark face follows us as William pulls away.

Chapter Twenty-Nine

SEB

I'm not sure how many episodes of *Schitt's Creek* I've binged, but I'm starting to hear David's voice in my head. *I am suffering romantically right now.* "You and me both, David," I say to the screen. It's late. So late, one could call it early. But I won't be able to sleep until she's home. Fuck, I might not be able to sleep anyway. My mating sickness is in overdrive. A few minutes ago, I filled a bag with ice for my head. It isn't cutting it.

Mine, my dragon growls. *Find her.*

"No," I mumble to myself. "Not mine. She rejected us, you fucking pain in the ass. We didn't explain to her what she was getting into in a way she could understand because you hijacked my brain and went all caveman in the shower."

Zoe in shower, he growls needily.

I move the already melting bag of ice from my head to my dick.

The sound of the front door opening has me tossing the bag aside and springing from the bed. Technically, Zoe could walk around the side of the house to get to the cottage, but cutting through the big house is the fastest way—and the best lit, considering the time of night. I walk to the end of the hall and peek around the side, feeling her psychic energy as she nears.

"Did you wait up for me?" She stops and turns to face me.

All I can do is nod. I'm capable of shifting into a two-ton dragon, and I'm twice her size in this form. But when I look at her, I feel like a child on my knees in front of a god. She probably doesn't even realize how powerless I am when it comes to her. Under any other circumstances, I could take out my frustrations on another woman, anyone who would have me. But as a bonded male, it will be a long time before my dragon will stomach another. I mated her. And if she were a dragon, she'd be mated to me. I could look at her and crook my finger, and she'd happily allow me to take her in any way I wished. But she's not a dragon, and she doesn't know the significance of what passed between us. And when I tried to explain it to her, she pushed me away. She rejected what we had together. I have no power in this scenario.

Like a dream, she turns and walks right up to me. "I'm fine, Seb. It went really well. I cleared up the lie without revealing the truth. Everything is fine."

"I'm sorry to put you in that position."

"You were just trying to help." Her eyes meet mine, and I see something in them I hadn't dared hope to see. Openness, softness, attraction.

Don't mess this up, my dragon growls.

"To be clear, if you'd been awake, I wouldn't have taken the liberties I did without your permission. I hope you know that I do respect your boundaries." I wipe sweat from my forehead. Fuck, I'm burning up. "My dragon is possessive. Even now, it's taking everything in me to keep my hands off you. And he's protective too. It almost killed me to allow you to go without me tonight, not because I wanted to control you, but because I wanted to act as your guard dog. But I can control myself...most of the time."

"Jesus, you look like you're feverish." She comes closer and puts her hand on my forehead, and I moan at the feel of her touch. "You're burning up."

"It's the appetency. Mating sickness." Shit. I have to address this with her so that she understands. "I took you as my mate. I thought you wanted it too. I thought you understood what it meant." A muscle in my jaw clenches, and I rub it to ease the pain.

"Mate. What does that mean to you?" Her hand is still on my face and I try to look directly at her, but it's like looking into the sun. I have to look away.

"It means that my dragon wants you and only you. It means that if he can't have you, he'll burn hotter and hotter until I'm out of my alignment or we both go up in flames. It means that I've handed you the leash to my soul, and while I understand now that you didn't want it, I can't take it back."

She blows out a huffed breath. "I have a leash to your soul?"

"More like a chain. You can break a leash. I'm dragon chained."

She arches an eyebrow. "And you're saying that sex with me is the only thing that will cure this fever that's burning you alive?"

I nod.

"Frankly, Seb, it sounds like a line to get me into bed."

I squeeze my eyes shut for a second. It does sound like a line. Creator, I feel a hundred years old. "Yeah, it probably does to someone on the outside." I take a step back from her until she's not touching me anymore. "In any case, it's not your problem. I'll handle it."

Her gaze scrapes down my body and locks on the raging hard-on that happened the second she touched me.

"How?"

"You touched me. Believe me, that's all it takes."

She laughs. "No, I mean how will you take care of it?" The lilt of her voice is sensual heat, her words dripping with hot honey. Her gaze sinks to my erection again. She doesn't turn away. "Show me."

My dragon surges against my skin, and it's as if someone plugged me in to a massive battery. Lightning ricochets through me. I grab the waistband of my silk pajamas and ease them down. Her breath hitches at the sight of my cock, and her cheeks warm to an impressive shade of pink. Yeah, she's interested, and fuck if I'm going to give her the opportunity to lose interest.

I close my hand around my shaft and stroke myself for her, running my thumb over the head and working the moisture there over my length. The way she watches me is an incredible turn-on. I pump myself harder, wishing I were in her. Wishing I could touch her and give her the same pleasure.

"Does it feel good?" she asks, and I notice her nipples through the fabric of her dress.

"Yes. For now. But it won't last. It's not the same," I grit out.

"Not the same as being with me?"

I slow my hand and shake my head.

She moves closer to me, so close she brushes my cock with her body, and I hiss in a breath. "Let me see if this helps."

She sinks to her knees and takes my cock into her mouth.

My dragon is doing backflips inside me. I dig my fingers into her hair, my thumbs brushing over the crown of marigolds on her head, and I am undone.

"This crown," I rasp. "You are a fucking queen. A fucking goddess." I thrust to the back of her throat, trying not to hurt her but completely incapable of restraining myself. She sucks harder. Takes me in deeper. Faster. And then her blue eyes look up and lock on mine.

I lose all control. My balls tighten. Two more thrusts and I empty myself down her throat. She swallows, but it's too much for her. It spills out of the corner of her mouth, down her chest, onto the floor.

She stands and wipes the excess from her lips with her thumb, then gives me a heated smile. "How's that? Better than your hand?"

I'm beyond words. I growl and pull her against me. My lips crash down on hers, and I invade her mouth, tasting myself on her tongue. It revs me up even more. I sweep her into my arms. She squeals when I throw her over my shoulder and start walking toward the bedroom.

"Damn, I guess you know what you want," she says.

I stop walking. I'm hard again, and it is actually painful for me to consider letting her go, but I ask, "Do you want me to put you down? Let you go?"

In answer, she slaps my ass, hard. "Don't you dare."

I make it to the bedroom in three steps and toss her onto the bed. I don't bother with the buttons of my pajama top, just pull it off over my head and cast it aside. Then I reach for her shoes, popping each of her ballet flats off at hyperspeed.

"How are you hard again?" she asks, giggling. She helps me remove her dress and then stands to slide her black lace thong down her legs.

I knock her hands away when she moves to take off her bra. "Have you seen you? It's amazing I'm not hard every time we're in the same room." I slide one of the black straps off her shoulder and then do the same with the other one. I wrap my arms around her and unclasp her bra, sliding it down her arms.

She reaches up to remove her crown.

"No. Leave it. I like it. Queen, remember?"

She grins and leaves it where it is. I pick her up by the waist and set her back on the bed, watching her as she repositions herself. "You're so beautiful, Zoe. Like a sunrise."

"A sunrise?"

"All that blond hair, the blue of your eyes, those pink lips. Every time I see you, it's like the sun coming out."

She sighs. "You dragons sure know how to sweet-talk a girl."

I crawl between her knees. "How do you take care of yourself, Zoe? What do you do when you think of me?"

Her smile fades and her eyes grow hot, and then her hand sinks between her legs.

Chapter Thirty

ZOE

My wish tonight was to be enough for Seb, and based on the way he's looking at me, that wish has already come true. I didn't plan for this to happen, but when I walked into the house and saw him waiting for me—saw him suffering—I felt it deep in my soul. It felt like we were two trees whose roots had grown tangled together and that, somehow, I was choking him off.

I guess I didn't realize before just how much I've come to need Seb. I was reminded tonight how much of a burden I've been to my parents and to my coven, but also that they still love me and believe in me. But Seb doesn't just believe in me; he's betting his life on me. He needs what only I can provide. And I need to be needed like that. I need to feel like someone in the world thinks of me, not just as a recovering addict but as a true partner and potential savior.

Yes, our relationship has moved fast, but only because we've fit together so easily. I need someone who believes in me, who believes I can overcome anything the world throws at me. And he needs to be loved so badly it hurts him. He needs physical affection, for sure, but I see more in what he wants from me. Seb needs a home, not in the sense of a building but in the sense of a heart. Right now, as he kneels on the bed between my thighs, I believe with all my heart that I can be a temple of peace for him. I can be a home and hearth.

He watches me reverently as I shamelessly start to play with myself. I'm soaking wet already. The feel of him only moments ago in my mouth has left me so achy with need that this isn't going to take long. I circle my clit until that beautiful purr of his rumbles against my skin again.

"I love the sound of your purr."

"Let's find out if you love the feel of it." He lowers his head between my legs and replaces my fingers with his tongue. And I do feel the purr. His tongue is a little rough, like a cat's, but also vibrating with the sound. It takes seconds for an orgasm to rip through me like wildfire.

And then he's over me and pushing into me, even as I come down from my first orgasm. The feel of him full and hard inside me is enough to have me climbing again. I wrap my arms and legs around him and draw him close, breathing in his smoky sandalwood scent.

This is more than sex. It's as if he's sinking into me,

as if our souls are entwining. And that purr is enough to have my eyes rolling back in my head, even though he's holding still.

"You're the only one who can hear my mating trill. The only one who will ever hear it. It's a song just for you."

I run my nose along his. "You say that. But you don't know me. Not really. You haven't seen me at my worst. You don't know how cruel I can be or how selfish. You don't know how little I deserve someone like you." My voice cracks, and tears run from the corners of my eyes as emotion floods into me.

He bends his neck and kisses them away. "You really don't get this mate concept, do you?" he says as he starts to move again. "I've chosen you. You're mine. All the cruel parts and the ugly parts and the parts you wish didn't exist. Your checkered past. Your unknown future. It's all part of you, Zoe, and I want it all."

His fingers thread into mine over my head. Like this, I'm spread wide, and we're as close as two people can get. "I want that too," I whisper.

His thrusts come harder, more urgent. "Then say you're mine. Accept me fully as your mate."

"I'm yours."

"Say you're my mate."

"I'm your mate."

His smile grows above me like he's won an incredible prize. He kisses up my neck to my ear, his thrusts coming short and fast now. "Then let me feel you come."

An orgasm rockets through me out of nowhere, and

this one takes my breath away. It's blinding white light and weightless pleasure. I throw my head back and cry out from the intensity. And then he's so deep it almost hurts, and he's coming too. My inner thighs are slick and hot with him.

We stay like that for some time, breathing together, breathing each other in. Every part of him touching every part of me. When he finally rolls off me, I say, "Now that we're mates, what does that mean exactly?"

It means we're connected, he says into my head. It takes me a minute to realize he never opened his mouth. I heard his thoughts. As much as that should freak me out, it doesn't. It's just additional evidence of this bond between us born of chemistry, mutual respect, and magic.

"Holy fuck."

"Yeah, it was." He glances down our bodies. "Do you want a shower before bed? I've made a mess of you."

"Yes, but I need to tell you something first. Tonight, I did some research in my parents' library. I think I have an answer to how to defend your people against that ring."

"You have a way to neutralize the Order rings?"

I shake my head. "Not exactly." I sit up in bed and take his hands. "I think I can create a sister ring, one that directly opposes every element of the Order's rings. It would be infused with celestial energy by the creator and capable of alerting you when its opposition is near and transforming into a weapon or a shield. It would effectively be a countercurse, an opposing ring that is everything theirs is, but is born of light instead of darkness."

His eyes sparkle with the possibilities. He studies me for a minute and then hauls me up and out of bed and into his arms. "That's it. We're cleaning you up and changing the sheets so you can get some rest. If all this is true, you're going to need it."

I lower my chin and look at him through my lashes. "Do you want me to spend the night here, with you?"

He cups my jaw and runs a thumb along my bottom lip. "I want you to spend a lifetime with me."

Chapter Thirty-One

SEB

When I wake and find Zoe contentedly sleeping within the curl of my body, I almost can't contain my joy. She's mine. She accepted the mating bond. I lower my nose and breathe in the scent of her sleep-warmed skin. My mating scent mingles with hers. I don't want to wake her. She needs her sleep. But I can't stop myself from spreading my fingers on her stomach.

She rolls onto her back and stretches, blinking sleepy eyes at me. I roll with her, over her, in her. She's naked, thank fuck, as am I. A brilliant late-night decision on my part.

"Oh, Seb," she says softly.

"Do you want me to stop?"

She kisses along my neck to my ear. "Hell no."

I don't stop. Not until she's arching in my arms for the third time and I'm spilling into her. My dragon breathes a contented sigh and curls at the back of my head.

After a few more minutes of postcoital bliss, she bounds from the bed and cleans herself up in the bathroom, then starts pulling on her dress.

"Dressing is highly overrated."

"I need to go back to my place to change and do my morning routine. We should get started right away. Do you have anything gold I can use to make you a ring?"

I frown. "You should move some of your things here. I'll clear a drawer for you and space in the closet."

"Did you hear what I asked about the gold?"

I nod. "We have time, Zoe."

"No, we don't. I heard you tell Ellison and Lucas that you planned to go after Roman Cifarelli soon, as soon as they could get you into where he's hiding. You need this ring before you do that."

I thought I could wait to broach this subject for at least a day. Our mating should be a deliriously happy occasion. The last thing I want to think about is Roman. But she's right. It's my responsibility to kill Roman. His death might be the only thing that could disorient the Saint's Order enough to disrupt this war, make room for an accord or at least balance the scales.

"I can do it without the ring."

"Why would you want to? I can do this. I can help you."

I can feel her anger rising. It's important to Zoe that I believe in her abilities, and I do, but I also love her more than I love my life.

"I know. I know you can. But I don't want you to rush ascending. After what happened last time, I'd rather you never use gold dust again."

Zoe grabs her head.

"What's wrong?" I put my hand on her shoulder.

"Splitting headache. The spider is back."

"The spider?"

She looks at me like she didn't realize she was saying it out loud.

"Can we talk about this over coffee?"

Twenty minutes later, she's dressed and sitting at my kitchen table with a massive cappuccino in her hands and a plate of eggs and bacon that Patrick was kind enough to cook for us steaming in front of her. She still looks tired. I pray to the creator that she's not coming down with something.

"You asked about the spider," she says, looking down into her coffee.

"Am I wrong to assume this isn't an actual spider? We're not talking about a pet or something?"

She laughs. "No. The spider is what I call my addiction. She's a voice in my head that convinces me the only thing that will make me feel better is using gold dust. After the last time I ascended, she told me you were using me, controlling me. That's why I had to go to Beltane alone. I had to know that I was in control. That I wasn't your prisoner here."

I tap the side of my cup. "It wasn't easy for me to let you go, not when I know there are Order members everywhere. I tried to remind myself that you weren't a dragon and therefore not a target, but I admit, I almost climbed the walls waiting for your return."

"I'm sorry. I didn't mean to worry you."

"If going alone gave you what you needed to accept the mating bond, I'm glad you took the chance."

"It did, and it also gave me the chance to face Jeremy."

My skin prickles. "The doctor who messages you at all hours? He was there?"

"He was. And you were right. He admitted to being interested in me."

A growl rumbles from my chest.

"Seb, do you want to hear the truth or not?" She tips her head and frowns.

"Yes, sorry." I clear my throat and beg her to continue.

"I talked to my parents, and they agreed to fire him. I never have to see him again."

"I like this story more and more."

She frowns. "But that means there isn't a witch to call if things go wrong with me. No one but you knows that I've used again. If it's worse next time, I'm on my own."

I shake my head. "Then there won't be a next time. We'll find someone else to make this ring."

She lifts her chin. "That's the best part. I don't have to use gold dust to make the ring," she says. "I can perform all the spells on my own, aside from two things."

"What are those?"

"I need dragon blood for the potion, just like they used Donovan's blood."

"And?"

Her face grows serious. "This ring will be enchanted with five layers of interwoven spells. Think of it like computer code. I can write the code on anything, but to make it work, I need to connect it, power it on. I can lay the enchantments, but infusing them with magic will eventually require my ascension."

"Or someone else's, right? You could build the spell, and we could find another witch to power it on?"

She sips her coffee. I really wish she would eat. I have no idea what she had for dinner last night, but she needs her strength. "In theory. But why would you risk it? I can do it."

"Because every time you use, the spider gets stronger." I take her hand. "The ring isn't worth you hurting yourself."

"And killing Roman isn't important enough for you to sacrifice yourself."

I whistle through my teeth. "Not the same thing. It's my Creator-endowed responsibility as a zodiac warrior to protect my kind. They can't stay in hiding forever."

She twists her fork in her eggs, brooding silently. I turn back to my coffee. "I'm your mate, right? Isn't that like a creator-endowed life partner?"

"That's one way to put it."

"Then it's my responsibility to care for you, right? To protect you if I'm capable of it?"

"Not at your own expense," I shoot back.

"Then I'll make you a deal. We make this ring together, and you promise to wait until it's complete to attack Roman, and I will try to find someone else from my coven whom I trust to infuse it. There is one person I could ask."

My dragon dances in my psyche at the way she openly refers to me as her mate. I am proud of the way she negotiates with me, my smart and worthy woman. "There will come a time when I can't put off what needs to be done," I say seriously. "But if it is within my power, I accept your terms."

I'm relieved when she smiles at me before digging into her eggs.

Chapter Thirty-Two

ZOE

It starts with gold. Seb has a ring that we confirm is solid gold. We pry out the gemstone and melt down the face of the ring. Aesthetics aside, gems have their own vibration, and I can't have anything interfering with the magic. After some debate, we decide on a star, and I engrave it into the face of the ring, a symbol of the creator.

"Now what?" Seb asks.

"Now, I create a potion using your blood and a collection of herbs designed to magnify the celestial powers inherent in it. The Order's ring does the same thing but with poisonous herbs that kill the healing qualities and amplify the deadly ones."

"They turn our own blood against us." He scowls.

"I came up with this idea for a sister ring when I finally understood the magic of theirs. When I was in the

Gold Room, it struck me how I could hear everything else in the room but that ring. It's like a black hole of silence and darkness."

"I remember you talking about that."

"I finally understood it the last time I ascended. The destroyer can only destroy. My coven thinks of that axis of power as a god, an opposing force to the goddess. But gods can create and destroy. The destroyer can't create anything, especially not life. He can only take it away. Their ring is all about death and destruction. But our ring will bring light. I will draw out the celestial magic in your blood that heals and provides you with long life. I'm going to build this ring to be everything that theirs is not."

Seb leans over and kisses the side of my head. "My brilliant mate."

I pull out my apothecary, the large wooden storage crate that opens like a tackle box and carries all the herbs, crystals, and other ingredients used in basic spells. I open it and start measuring herbs into the Dutch oven I have on the burner.

"Do all witches have one of those?" He eyes my apothecary with its many vials and drawers with a look of curiosity.

"Our parents gift it to us when we're thirteen."

"I thought you didn't get your powers until later in life."

"We don't become powerful until we learn to ascend on our own, but we learn the mechanics of basic spells and potions before then. Using licorice root to soothe a sick stomach doesn't take any power, and neither does mixing this potion. If you can follow a recipe, you can do it."

"We both know my cooking skills are less than exemplary, so I'll take your word for it." He kisses me in such a familiar way, it feels like we've been together, moving around each other in this kitchen for decades instead of days.

"It's time. I need your blood." I hand him a ceremonial knife with a bone handle. He extends his forearm over the pot and slices across the soft underside. Blood splashes into the belly of my makeshift cauldron. I lift a compress to stanch the flow, but by the time I bring it to his arm, he's already healed.

"That's quick."

"We're hard to kill without the poison of those rings."

We exchange a quick kiss as I stir the pot, and then when the concoction starts to sparkle gold, I turn off the burner and drop in the ring. "It has to soak for three days."

The sound of the doorbell at the front of the house has me looking over my shoulder. I hear Patrick's footsteps and then the door opening. "That would be Connor and Fiona," Seb says.

"Where is that fuckhead brother of mine?" a man's voice booms.

Seb takes my hand and leads me toward the foyer, where a blond man the size of a mountain stands. My feet shuffle at the sight, although he's not particularly threatening. But it's hard not to experience fear when a man is big enough to pound you into the ground like a stake with his bare fist.

"Hi, I'm Fiona," a small, auburn-haired woman beside him says, holding out her hand. I didn't even see her there at first.

"Nice to meet you."

"And this is my brother Connor," Seb says, pointing to the Viking beside her. "He's the Aries warrior of the Zodiac Brotherhood."

I shake the man's hand, aware of how mine gets lost in his bear-sized paw. Beside me, Seb stiffens, and I notice his scent grow stronger, sandalwood and citrus filling the foyer. Connor releases me.

"Morwyn was right, then. You're mated. Congratulations."

My cheeks grow warm. "How could you possibly know that?"

Fiona chuckles, the back of her hand held to her nose. "His mating scent is all over you. Even I can smell it, and I'm human. And Seb's dragon was sending a strong warning to Connor that he didn't like him touching you. Honestly, it reeks."

"Smells good to me," I mumble.

Connor and Fiona both erupt in raucous laughter like I'm the butt of a joke I don't completely understand. But Fiona places a hand gently on my shoulder and says, "It's a dragon thing. Our mate's scent is attuned to us and us alone. Believe me, now that you're mated, Connor will smell like a wet dog to you."

I do catch an earthy and unpleasant musk in the air, now that I think about it, and I curl my nose.

Seb takes my hand. "Coffee? We have much to discuss."

"Please," Fiona says, and Seb calls to Patrick to bring it into the dining room.

"So, what is this all about?" Connor asks. "Your message sounded urgent."

"It is." Seb looks toward me as we sit across from the other couple at the table. Patrick whizzes into the room, sliding a mug of coffee in front of each of us and leaving cream and sugar. Seb dumps a little cream into his before lifting his chin. "Zoe, tell them what you told Morwyn and me about the water."

"The water in the vial?" I raise an eyebrow. I did not expect to be discussing this with others from the brotherhood this morning. I thread my fingers together nervously. "It's more of a theory, really, based on general magical principles."

Fiona nods. "Then tell us about your theory."

"There are certain herbs and elixirs that witches use topically and certain ones we take internally. When Morwyn was here, he mentioned that he's experimented with putting the water on a wound that was poisoned with Order magic, and it only made the wound worse. When I tested a drop of water on the ring, the ring moved away from the water. The water in the vial is diametrically opposed magic to the magic of the ring."

"I don't follow. If it's power is in opposition to the

ring's, why couldn't it cure Remus's wounds?" Connor asks.

"Because I think the water has to work from the inside out." How to explain this. "We have a vaccine for polio, right? But if you put that vaccine into a person who already has polio, it won't cure the polio. A vaccine can only prevent infection."

Fiona's brow bunches. "You think the water can be used as a vaccine against Order magic?"

I blow out a breath. "I'm a young witch and I haven't practiced magic much in the last year, but we wouldn't call this a vaccine. A vaccine is injecting someone with a small amount of something harmful so that their immune system knows how to react to it in a subsequent exposure. This water isn't anything harmful. In fact, it's infused with pure celestial energy. I'd call it an aegis potion. Usually, something like this...we witches would drink it as a tea, and, over time, it would protect the drinker against certain curses. It might even speed healing in someone who is injured by Order magic."

Fiona's eyes go wide, and she turns to Connor. "Oh my God, Connor, that's why—" She brings both her hands to her mouth.

"Why what?" Seb asks.

Connor shifts in his chair. "When we were fighting Roman, just before I killed him, Fiona was shot by one of his fucking cursed bolts. Went right through her shoulder. But it healed almost immediately."

Fiona tucks her hair behind her ear. "It was wild because I felt it pass through me, but when I had a chance to look at the wound, it was gone. I thought maybe it hadn't hit me after all."

"So, have you been drinking the water on your land?" I can't keep the hope from my voice.

"Not exactly," she says. "I used to meet my sister there, though, and she'd often bring a meal to share with me from the convent next door. Sometimes there was tea or lemonade. If she was preparing those drinks using the same water, it means I drank a lot of it over time."

Seb grabs my hand and squeezes. "Let's start distributing vials of this stuff to the other dragons."

Connor holds up a hand. "We haven't tested this on dragons. Fiona is human. Just because it works for her doesn't mean it will work for us. Plus, what do we tell them? How much should they drink? For how long?"

Seb looks at me, and I shrug. "He's right. I'm a singer, not a doctor or a wise witch. I can only tell you that I would personally start with a few drops in my tea or coffee every morning and see how it goes. Maybe test it after a few weeks."

"We can't test it, though. It would be unconscionable to infect someone with the ring on purpose."

Connor frowns. "I bet Remus will agree to be our guinea pig, though. Fiona and I will take some of the water to him on Cardinal Island and ask him to drink it. See if it accelerates his healing."

"It's a good idea," Seb says.

"Thank you, Zoe, for helping us. We wouldn't have known any of this without you," Connor says.

I have to look away. I'm so used to screwing up, it's

almost painful to be called out for doing something good. My eyes sting as pride swells within me. How I would love to be right about this. Right about something.

"If you think that's cool, you should hear what she's working on now."

I listen to Seb describe how I'm creating the ring, and my stomach drops, forms into a knot, and gets tighter and tighter and tighter.

You'll never get this right without the help of gold dust, the spider says. *You barely know what you're doing. Flying by the seat of your pants. Making promises you'll never be able to keep.*

Shut up.

You'll never complete it successfully on your own. You want to use it. Remember how good it felt? How confident you were? The goddess could tell you exactly how to complete the ring if you went back to the Gold Room.

No. I'm done. If I do it again, I might do permanent damage. I recognize the warning signs. Seb's right, I can't do it again without potentially losing myself.

If you don't do it again, you'll have to ask Hazel for help, and there's absolutely no way she'll agree to it. She's a wise woman. The witches still have a policy of neutrality.

You don't know that.

"Zoe? You okay?"

I shake my head, coming out of my conversation with my spider. I haven't heard a word anyone has said since Seb started talking about the ring. "Sorry. Lost in my thoughts."

"Connor asked how long the ring would take to complete."

"About a week, I think. I've never done this before, obviously. But looking at the spells involved, that's my best estimate."

Connor nods slowly. "Well, all right. I'm looking forward to seeing this ring, little badass." He takes a huge gulp of his coffee and then turns to Fiona. "You up for a visit to Cardinal Island?"

She nods. "I feel good."

"Cool. Seb, I'll let you know how Remus responds. And shoot me a note when the ring is done so I can see it in all its glory."

I cross my arms over my stomach, and Fiona slaps her mate on his shoulder. "I'm sure Zoe will do her absolute best. It's her first time doing anything like this. She doesn't need any more pressure, Connor."

"Ah, she looks like a fighter to me. Maybe she likes the pressure. When's your birthday, Zoe?"

"February 29th. She's a Pisces," Seb answers for me.

Connor's face falls. "Sorry. Fiona's right. I'll, uh... You got this." He smiles and gives me a thumbs-up like I'm five.

After a few well-wishes, we see them to the door.

"I guess we'll know soon enough if your theory about the water is accurate."

"Yeah," I say, trying to sound enthusiastic, but inside, I'm praying I don't fuck this up.

Chapter Thirty-Three

SEB

Zoe attacks the problem of the ring like her life depends on it, but there's only so much she can do. Each of the layers of enchantments takes days to cure into the gold. It's all I can do to get her to eat and rest. She needs both those things. In the middle of the night, I catch her thrashing, caught in some nightmare. She calls out my name sometimes, not in the way she does when we have sex, but like she's scared for me. I pull her against me and she calms, but it's clear the idea of me facing Roman weighs heavy on her mind. I need to help her relax.

On the fourth night, with two spells in place, I take her hand and lead her out the back door. "Where are you taking me?"

"Your studio. Have you even used it yet?"

She snorts. "Uh, no. I've been a little busy trying to save dragons."

"Well, put on your dancing shoes. We're taking the night off." I half drag her toward her cottage. The place has been dark for days. She's stayed with me since our mating, moving her clothes and things into my place. But the studio is in her cottage. I know her. I know this witchy work she's doing on my behalf drains her, and I know what medicine will make it better.

Zoe needs to sing.

She lets us into her place, and I step around the still-unboxed items from her old apartment. "I can have Patrick put these into storage for you," I say.

She stops in the middle of them and plays with the edge of the cardboard. "Patrick has offered multiple times. I wouldn't let him."

"Why?"

Her eyes meet mine. "Everything I was before I met you is in these boxes. I'm just not ready to let it go yet."

I reach into the nearest box and pull out a stained plastic ladle, holding it up between us. "What part of who you are is memorialized by this ladle?"

Zoe starts to laugh and rubs her temple. "Honestly, I don't even remember that one."

"Hmm." I stick the ladle back in the box. "You can keep all of it, Zoe. You can decide to never unpack these boxes, or you can put everything inside them away in the cabinets. You can take your time sinking into your new life. Hell, you can even go back to your old one if you want, although I would absolutely hate to see you in that apartment building again. You are still everything you were before you met me. The only thing that has changed is that I love you. I've bound myself to you. My dragon is yours to command."

She wipes under her eyes and moves to me, reaching inside the box and grabbing the ladle. Spinning around, she opens the cabinet under the sink and tosses it into the garbage. "I'm really not that attached to who I used to be, actually."

I catch her as she runs back into my arms and kisses me in a slow, lazy way. But I stop her when my dragon starts to wake from his slumber. "As much as I'd love to continue where this is going, we came here for a reason. I want to hear your music. Where's your guitar?"

She smiles and almost reluctantly heads into her bedroom, returning with the instrument in her hands. I lead her into the converted second bedroom, which is now a recording studio, and gesture toward the door to the booth. "I don't know what you want me to do in there. I haven't played for weeks. I don't have any new material."

"So, play me your set. The same one you played when I watched you at the Barrel Room."

She looks down at her guitar, hesitating.

"Just for fun. It doesn't need to be perfect. But I can go first, if you're nervous." I step into the booth and pick up the electric violin I used to practice with inside this room before it was hers. I flip on the lights and double-check that the battery is charged. I unplug it from the wall and grab my bow. Then I tuck it under my chin.

She watches me from the other side of the glass as I draw my bow across the strings, getting a feel for the instrument again. I adjust one of the strings. When everything is ready to go, I look at her and wake my dragon. He fills my skin. He's never been very good with words, but this part of me is a wicked-good communicator when it comes to music.

I start with a low staccato, thinking about the moment when I first saw her, before we even met. Mimicking how I'd looked at her picture and my heart beat faster. Then I speed up, finding a lively and dynamic melody, a legato that embodies my enchantment with her the first time I saw her perform. I move around the room, expressing through dance what I can't with my instrument, building to something that emulates flight, the beating of my wings. She's never seen me in my dragon form, but I try to show her through the music. It's a big sound but graceful, the sound of wings catching wind, moonlight on scales, the passage of towns and cities under soaring claws.

My violin sings to her as I smile through the glass, and when I end on a high note, I can see she's crying. I set down the violin and rush to her, wiping her tears. "What's wrong?"

She laughs. "If you think I'm following that, Seb, you are out of your mind. Fuck, you're really, really good."

I shake my head. "You don't get it, do you?"

"Get what?"

"Why do you think Patrick works for me?"

"You said it inspires him."

I snort. "You are a dragon's mate, Zoe. Use it."

She narrows her eyes on me and slowly walks into the booth. After a few adjustments to her guitar, she experiments, picking out a few notes.

I press the intercom button and say, "Don't think too hard about it. Feel it. Let it out."

She nods. And then she starts to play. The sound is somewhere between folk and rock, her fingers picking at the strings in a way only a handful of musicians can. And when she starts to sing, I feel her magic again. She has power inherent in her skin. Whoever told her she lost it is a damn liar. She doesn't need gold dust. All she needs is to open her mouth.

"Silver morning melody—
Whispers wake me from my dream.
The way your dragon sings to me
speaks to my very soul.

And when you're over me
Like a sunrise over raging seas
Your beast calms this beauty
My broken pieces become whole.

Take me away
On wings of gold
Sing to me of
A world unknown
I've been lost so long
My skin's grown cold

But lend me your fire
Watch our dreams unfold."

I LISTEN TO HER WORDS AND AM SWEPT AWAY BY IMAGES OF being over her this morning, of my mating trill echoing in the room, buzzing against her skin. There's only warmth in her eyes. The music she's making is brilliant, and I'm tempted to record this, but I don't hit the button. This is for me. Just for me. This one, I'm keeping for myself.

Our eyes are locked through the glass as she strums the last few stanzas of her song, beaming at me with a smile I can tell comes straight from her heart.

That was beautiful, I think into her head.

"Thank you." She rests her guitar in the rack and comes to me, throwing her arms around me in the small space. I hug her back, wrapping my arms around her and lifting her feet off the floor.

"You can do this, Zoe. Plan your album. We are going to make you a star." I set her on her own two feet and smile down at her.

"It felt like... It felt like being in the Gold Room. It felt like I was channeling the goddess."

"It feels like sorcery when you sing. I think, with practice, you could learn to leverage the power in your voice. I'm no witch, but I can sense magic, and you have it."

"I'm beginning to wonder..."

"Wonder what?"

"When I was at Beltane, Jeremy admitted he had feelings for me."

A growl rips from my chest before she can get another word out, and I can only imagine what my expression does based on her reaction. "Tell me what happened. Did he touch you?" It's the dragon's voice, gritty and harsh, not my own.

She stumbles back, her smile melting into a frown. "Never mind. It doesn't matter."

"It matters to me," my dragon grits out.

"Seb, your eyes."

I close them and shake my head, taking charge of my inner beast once more. "I'm sorry. I didn't mean for it to come out like that. What happened with Jeremy?"

"Maybe it's best we don't talk about this."

I take a deep breath and blow it out slowly. "I'd really like to know."

She remains silent for a second and then says, "I mentioned before that Jeremy confessed he was attracted to me. I rejected him and fired him as my doctor." Her tone is almost clinical. It's a good thing, because I think if I heard even a hint of receptiveness on her part, I'd lose it.

"I remember."

"I wonder, though, if he was being honest with me about my limitations. I wonder if he was keeping me weak so that I'd be dependent on him."

Oh, how my dragon wants to pounce on this and rip Jeremy to pieces verbally before dissecting him physically, but I force myself to stay in control. "Is there a way you can test your abilities? See if you're right?"

"Yes," she says tentatively. "But not tonight. I'm tired. I should wait until tomorrow and set myself up for success."

I move in closer, my smile returning as I recognize the hours we have ahead of us. "So...what do you want to do tonight?"

She gives me a wicked smile. "I want to meet your dragon."

Chapter Thirty-Four

ZOE

Sometimes I wonder if I was born a thrill seeker. As long as I've been alive, I've passed up the slow and steady for any opportunity for risk-taking. Even when I was forcing myself to work at Regal, I was maintaining a side of nightlife, singing in clubs without any security, walking home or taking public transport at all hours of the night.

What is wrong with me?

I have another chance to wonder this about myself as Seb and I stand in the woods behind the cottage and he prepares to shift into his dragon self. I trust Seb and his dragon. I mean, technically, I've met the beast in the Gold Room. But the way Seb talks, I'm taking my life in my hands.

"Don't be afraid," he says. "He won't hurt his mate, but he may want physical contact."

"It's okay. I can hold my own. It was fine in the Gold Room."

"But he was smaller there, right? My dragon doesn't fit indoors. It might be a different experience for you here."

I look up at the moon and around the clearing we're standing in. "Plenty of room here. Don't worry about me, Seb. I asked for this. It's time, don't you think, that I know the other half of you?"

He nods and starts unbuttoning his shirt.

"I like this already."

He snorts and toes off his shoes, then strips off his pants. When he's completely naked, he runs both hands through his hair. "You're sure about this?"

"Yes." I don't get a chance to say anything else. What happens next is like a magician's trick, like pulling a long handkerchief out of a fist. Wings erupt from his back, and scales shingle his arms and legs. Talons sprout from his fists before spearing the dirt in front of him. His paws grow until they're wider across than my waist.

I blink and take a step back.

It's over.

I am staring up at a dragon roughly the size of an Airbus. "Holy shit," I mumble. Seb's dragon looks like he did in the Gold Room but much, much bigger. His scales may be the same deep, mahogany brown, but where I perceived them as edged in gold before, right now their reflective quality picks up the silver light of the moon. His eyes, though, are pure gold. Set in a head big enough to contain teeth as tall as me. Two beachball-sized eyes with the most beautiful irises of a luxurious, deep yellow are focused wholly on me.

From the head, the body stretches behind, to a long, whip-like tail. Seb's dragon isn't built like a dinosaur but like a serpent with legs, long and lean and muscular. Powerful but graceful.

I scurry back, unable to hold my ground as the scaled nostrils of the beast lower to my level. I don't stop until my back hits a tree. Two warm blasts of air blow back my hair. He sniffs me like a dog.

Unable to go anywhere, I raise a trembling hand and pat the side of his face. "Good dragon," I say hopefully.

He snorts and falls onto his belly, his head between his paws. I can't help but laugh. Resting like this, Seb's dragon looks like an enormous dog. He hears me laugh and laughs too, the sound coming out of his chest like a series of rough barks and snickers, not unlike what I remember from Scooby-Doo reruns. I can't help being swept up in it. Still laughing, I walk around his paws and scratch his side and then his belly when he rolls to expose it to me.

"How much do you understand in this form, Seb?"

The great horned head bends around to nudge my shoulder and licks me up the side of the head.

"Eww!" I jerk away, half my face covered in a layer of saliva.

That Scooby-Doo laugh comes again.

"All right, Chuckles, no more belly scratches until I see you fly."

He leaps onto his feet, a blast of air almost knocking

me down as his wings expand. With a slight dip of his scaly knees, he shoots into the air and circles above me, then backflips and barrel rolls.

"Show off!" I mumble, loving every second of the show. He's nimble and graceful, his wings directing him through the air like he's swimming in it. And when he finally lands in the clearing in front of me, I think that it's no wonder the Order learned to fear dragons. It's all I can do not to quake in my shoes.

The dragon walks toward me, his wings folding into his back, his scales disappearing. One second, he's a deadly dragon; the next, he's just a man again. A naked man. A naked man with an erection that would be frightening if I hadn't already become familiar with it. He stalks toward me with hunger in his eyes.

"Did I satisfy your curiosity?" he asks through a wicked grin.

"Uh, yes," I say. My hands land on his bare chest as he sweeps into me.

"Good. Now I want to satisfy mine." He spins me around and pulls me against him hard, so that my breath rushes out of me in an *oof*. With his front against my back, he reaches down to the hem of my skirt and starts working the fabric up my leg, until his fingers reach my inner thigh.

His breath skates over my neck and ear. "Do you know how beautiful you are when you come?" he whispers to me. "Do you know what it does to me to feel your hands on my scales in my dragon form?"

I lean against him, my lids sinking. "I'm beginning to."

"I want to feel you from behind. I want to hear you cry out my name when you come."

The arm banding my waist rises to my breasts, even as the one on my thigh finds my center. He moans at the feel of me, no doubt because I'm soaked. Having him touch me here, outside, under the moonlight—it's so hot, I already ache for him. He pinches one of my nipples as his fingers move my panties aside and dip inside me. The way he cups me strokes all the right places, and I moan.

"Seb… Goddess, how can I want you again already? The wanting is endless."

He draws his fingers out and moves his hand around the back of me. "I can think of worse things."

A sharp tug and I hear my underwear tear off my body. He casts them onto the ground beside us. "Hey! Those were black lace. I would have taken them off if you'd asked."

"I'll buy you a new pair," he says into my neck. "I'll buy you twenty."

My skirt is lifted to my waist, and in one slick move, he fills me. All I can do is moan as I'm stretched to my limit, the angle making it feel so much more intense. It's a good thing he's holding me up. My legs go wobbly. Besides, he's taller than me, and when he thrusts, he lifts me to my toes.

The hand that's not holding me up does a valiant job unbuttoning my shirt and drawing my bra cups under my breasts. The cool air hits my skin, and I give myself over to the pleasure of it, of the wildness. We're in the woods, under the moon, moving together like two beasts lost to instinct.

He's thrusting into me so hard, we fall forward. I squeal, extending my hands to break my fall, but his arm takes the brunt of it. Thankfully, he holds me to him, supporting his weight and mine, until he can gently set me on my hands and knees. We both laugh, but the humor doesn't last long. His hands hook on my hips, and he unleashes himself, his hips slapping against my bottom. One hand tangles in my hair while the thumb of the other presses against my most private entrance.

I inhale sharply at the invasion, and it pushes me over the edge. The orgasm seizes me like a tight fist, and my inner muscles pulse around him. I buck against him, wanton and wild, my fingers digging into the grass and dirt. "Mmmm, I love that," he whispers in my ear, bent over me. One of his hands drifts between my legs, teasing my clit and drawing out the orgasm. His trill is a loud buzz in the night around me, like a swarm of cicadas.

"Come for me, Zoe. Again," he orders.

It feels like the stars above me explode. Another orgasm rides the first, this one hard and fast and as if it's pulled from my toes.

He howls and thrusts until hot jets fill me, overflow me, and slick my thighs. The grass grows sticky with it. And goddess, the scent of him. It's everywhere, like the best cologne.

"You're filthy again, my mate."

I look over my shoulder at him, and he rumbles appreciatively, deep in his throat, when our eyes meet. "You seem to make me that way."

He lifts us from the ground and brushes off my knees. "Come, let's get you cleaned up and me dressed. Patrick is understanding, but we're in no shape for dinner."

Chapter Thirty-Five

SEB

I am guilty of occasionally poking fun at my brothers and their mates. I always thought the relationship that Connor had with Fiona was a vulnerability. While it cured their appetency, I thought it made them slaves to their emotions, dogs heeling at their mate's side.

I was wrong. My bond with Zoe has had a steadying effect on both of us. I'm bound, but not like a dog, like a partner. I'd never want it any other way.

Over the next several days, Zoe continues her spell on the gold ring. Once it finished in the potion, she nailed it to a board made of ash wood with symbols burned into the surface. She explained the magic behind the spell, but I couldn't follow it. All I know is that the entire house smelled like lilacs and honey for two days. She followed that up with dangling the ring from a triangle of sticks and feathers that spun in the wind. Even I figured out she was capturing the element of air somehow and transforming it into an enchantment.

Today, she wraps the ring in a banana leaf decorated in runes and buries it near a tree on the back lot. "Last one," she tells me as she pats the surface of the dirt.

"How many days do you have to leave it buried?"

"One should do. I'll take it out tomorrow. Then it's just a matter of raising the enchantments and fusing them."

"The picture you drew had five ribbons. You've only done four spells."

"The fifth is in the metal itself. The gold holds its own magic."

"So, have you found anyone who can fuse the spells?"

She turns to me, a twinkle in her eye. "I think I'm going to try to do it myself. Not with gold dust but with my own power, the power you feel in my voice."

I take her by the shoulders. "That's great, Zoe. But have you tried it on anything else yet?"

She slants me a coy smile and flings her fingers out toward an oak leaf that rests near our feet. I hear the air rush from her lungs and then a soft whisper of a song, almost like she's coaxing the wind to her aid. The leaf lifts off the ground and revolves between us.

"That's incredible!"

She flips her hand, and the leaf settles back to the grass. "Don't look too impressed. I'm not sure it will be enough to finish the spell, but if I'm not strong enough, I'll ask Hazel. She's a member of my coven who has always had a soft spot for me. I think she'll say yes, but

I've waited to ask her because doing so will necessitate my coming clean about everything that we've done so far and why. It will mean admitting you're a dragon and that I used gold dust to analyze the ring. I think she will help me, but the journey to get her there won't be pretty."

"You're strong enough," I say confidently. "When a human mates a dragon, it improves their health, their strength, and any magical abilities inherent in their blood. Draw on our connection. I believe in you."

She wraps her arms around my waist. "You are the world's sexiest cheerleader."

My phone rings, and I reluctantly unwrap myself from her to answer Patrick's ringtone. We have a brief exchange before I turn Zoe back toward the house. "We have a guest."

"Remus!" When I embrace my brother, he thumps my back with a fully intact arm. I stop to inspect it, noting that the blue veins are gone and all his bones are back in working order.

"Yeah, I'm back, motherfucker, thanks to that mate of yours." His gaze flicks to Zoe, and she smiles proudly.

"Excellent news."

"The healer on Cardinal Island said it would have taken me a year to regrow what I lost of my arm if not for the tea we made from Fiona's well water. What the fuck is in that stuff?"

"It's infused with celestial energy. I'm so glad it

worked," Zoe says, then strides right up to him and gives him a hug hello. The growl that rumbles from my throat echoes in the foyer.

Remus gently pushes her away. "Maybe it's best you don't touch another male for a year or two," he mumbles.

"Sorry." I shove my dragon down and tell him to shut the fuck up.

"Understandable." Remus takes another small step away from Zoe, who looks like she's fighting back laughter. "Thanks again, Zoe."

"Dragons." She shakes her head. "You're welcome."

We assemble around the table, where Remus tells us the story of his recovery. The conversation stays light until he reaches the end. "I've been cleared to full service, Seb."

"Full service," I parrot, not wanting to think about what that means. The truth is, I've been enjoying the bubble Zoe and I have been in all week as the rest of the brotherhood gave us space to finish the ring.

"The other brothers have filled in for our rotation long enough. They've obtained dozens of rings. It's time for you and me to get back on the horse. I told Connor we'd take the next one on the list tonight."

"Connor isn't in his alignment. You should have cleared that with me," Seb says.

Remus frowns. "I'm clearing it with you now," he drawls. "In what universe does Sebastian York shirk his zodiac duties?"

The Taurus in me cringes at that statement, and my dragon grows instantly defensive. "I'm not shirking my duties. I just don't appreciate being left out of the discussion."

Zoe clears her throat. "Seb and I have been working on a ring that will have powers in direct opposition to those of the Order's rings, blessed where theirs are cursed. If it works as designed, it will be capable of being used as a shield as well as a weapon against those who would do you harm."

"Connor mentioned that when he came to visit me on Cardinal Island."

"Good, then you understand. The ring is almost complete. Why not wait until tomorrow when it's ready?"

Remus sets down his fork and leans back in his chair, his face doing that half-smile thing that mirrors the masks tattooed on his chest. Gemini son of a bitch is arguing with himself again.

"One ring?" he asks her.

She sighs. "Yes. There's only one so far. I can make more after we test this one, but—"

"So, it will need to be tested, which will take time. Creating one for both of us and the rest of the zodiac dragons will take time. Getting vials of the celestial waters to civilian dragons will take time." I'm impressed by how calm and matter-of-fact he keeps his voice, but then he knows that the moment he comes off as threatening to Zoe, he'll have to deal with me.

"Yes, that's all true," she says, looking defeated.

Remus's gaze shifts back to me. "We need to keep thinning the Order. They're adding members at the fastest pace in a century. Dragons are getting restless. You've heard the complaints from dragon civilians. They're tempted to go back to their daily lives. This is a prison for them. I don't think we can wait on this, Seb. They need to know the brotherhood is doing something."

I nod. "You're right. I can't keep up the code red if I'm not actively doing something to make it safe for them, and our other solutions will take a few more weeks to implement. We'll go tonight."

Zoe's eyes widen. "I hate this. What if one of you is injured again?"

"Thanks to you, I'm so full of celestial water, an injury won't kill me. Unless, of course, they take off my head," Remus laughs.

The humor doesn't reach Zoe.

"I've been adding a few drops from the vial to my morning coffee," I tell her.

"We don't know how much it takes," she says quickly. "I don't like you putting yourself in danger."

I don't want to displease her, but I have a job to do, and I am nothing if not loyal to my responsibilities.

Remus's good humor quickly turns sour. "Zoe, I get that it's scary for you. But you mated a dragon warrior. This is who Seb is and what he signed up for. He was chosen for this by the Oracle herself."

I raise a hand, silencing him. "I'm sorry, Zoe. I know you'll worry, but I'll take good care of myself. I'll be back before you know it."

A tear forms in the corner of her eye. She sets down

her fork. "Fine. Go. Do what you have to do." She stands and leaves the table, heading toward our bedroom.

"Zoe!"

"Let her be, Seb," Remus says softly. "There is nothing you can say that will make this easier for her. She loves you. It's only natural that she worries for you."

"Right." I look down at my plate but can't bring myself to take another bite. Instead, I take a long drink of my wine. Then I level a stare on Remus. "We leave in an hour."

ZOE

WHAT THE ACTUAL FUCK IS HAPPENING TO ME? I FEEL LIKE I'M fifteen years old as I throw myself on Seb's bed, in the room that I've started considering our room. I know I'm acting childishly, but my feelings are out of control. Seb will be putting himself at risk tonight, and if something happens to him, I won't survive. I'm sure of it.

I rub my eyes on the nest of my arms, trying to keep myself from crying. But even having my face buried in the comforter doesn't stop me from sensing Seb as he silently walks into the room. His scent reaches my nose almost immediately. We're so attuned to each other now. It's a level of intimacy I've never experienced with anyone else.

His hand lands on my back, and I flinch. "I know you

have to do it," I say into the blanket. "But it feels like my heart is ripping in two."

He lies down beside me, running his hand down the length of my back. "I get it. You love me. You want me to stay safe, the same as I wanted you to stay safe during Beltane. Besides, you're a Pisces, so you're going to feel our spiritual connection stronger than most. I'm sure this is scary for you."

I turn on my side so that I'm facing him and raise an eyebrow. "Tell me more about what I'm feeling."

His brows lift. "Am I wrong?"

"I've never told you I love you," I say with more snark in my voice than I intended, but I don't appreciate him beating me to the punch, especially on this.

He props up his head on a fist. "No, you haven't."

"Are you the type of man that just assumes something like that, without any verifiable evidence?"

"Oh, I have evidence."

I scramble up to a seated position and fold my arms over my chest. "What evidence are you referring to, Mr. York?"

He mirrors my position. "You wrote me a beautiful song and sang it to me. You compared me to a sunrise."

"Who says I love the sunrise?" I scoff. "Besides, you wrote a song for me too, and that doesn't mean anything."

He smiles and nods. "Oh yes, it does. I love you unconditionally. I love you to the end of time and back again. I was telling you I loved you with every note I played on that violin."

I gasp at his declaration, struck mute by his sincerity.

"I love you, Zoe. If I haven't made it clear before, I do. This isn't just biology."

I throw myself across the bed, tackling him to the mattress, and deliver a long, passionate kiss to his smiling mouth. When I finally pull back, I'm not sure if we've been kissing for thirty seconds or three minutes. I've completely lost myself. "I love you too," I tell him.

My heart swells. The way he's looking at me is like my every childhood dream of what love should be. This is my endgame. This is forever.

I roll off him and climb from the bed. "Now that that's settled, go do your job before I lose my nerve and chain you to the bed."

He stands and kisses me on the nose. "Don't give up on that dream, little witch. The night is young. You can chain me to the bed later."

FRACCJINAKED

Chapter Thirty-Six

SEB

"You look ready for a fight."

Remus can barely stand still. Dressed in fighting leathers and enough weapons to take on an army, he fidgets beside me outside the Santa Barbara mansion that contains our next target. Unlike our last job, there are signs of life inside and a few cars in the drive.

"If I'm ever in bed for that long again, I hope it's because I've found a mate and not because I'm recovering from a run-in with the Order."

I grin, thinking of Zoe. "Definitely a better reason to stay horizontal."

"What's it like?" Remus asks. He's smiling, but it doesn't quite reach his eyes. We both know that we're less than a week out from his alignment. He's older than me, which means the symptoms of his appetency will be grueling. Almost unbearable. I pray to the creator that he finds a mate soon.

For a while, I just stop and think about how to explain it, and then it comes to me. "You know when you were little and you'd fall asleep on the couch, and your parents would carry you to bed and tuck you in?"

"I think I do."

"And maybe you'd wake up a little. Not all the way awake, but enough to hear them talking or laughing. You didn't know what they were talking about, but you felt warm and safe. You knew that you were loved."

"Yeah."

"That's what it feels like. She's this soothing presence, this source of warmth and connection. When I'm with her, everything makes sense. All my fears, my stressors, fade into the background."

"Shit. Sounds nice." He rubs the back of his neck, scowling.

"You'll find her, Remus. The perfect woman for you is out there somewhere."

He snorts. "I don't know, man. It's harder for Geminis. We're an air sign. We need change. I'm constantly second-guessing myself. If I'm at war with my own thoughts half the time, how will one woman ever be enough to keep me interested?"

"That's not narcissistic or anything." I laugh.

He shakes his head. "It's not all about me. I know it's not. But how will a woman ever put up with my moodiness? I have an intense need for freedom, Seb. It's part of my star sign. I just don't see how that meshes with a permanent relationship."

I shrug. "The creator has a way of sending us just what we need when we need it."

He groans. "So, this guy, Stanley Trainor, is some sort of film financier, eh?"

"Yep. He's produced a few too."

"How would you like to proceed?"

I scan the modern monstrosity in front of us. The place is mostly windows and is lit up like a jack-o'-lantern, making it not difficult to see inside. A small group of men appears to be meeting in the front room, but I can't make out any of their faces from this angle. I can only see from their knees to their necks. "What does Stanley look like?"

"He's the one with the ring," Remus says snarkily.

I level an annoyed look in his direction. We're too far away and at the wrong angle to gauge who has a ring and who doesn't. "Getting close enough to see the ring or rings without triggering them is the problem at hand." A server dressed in a black dress shirt with a silver tray balanced on one hand passes from the front room into what appears to be the kitchen. "I say we put on the camouflage and slide into the kitchen. Listen in on what the staff is saying about Stanley. See what we're dealing with and what it would take to cut the ring off his finger."

"Best plan yet."

"It's our only plan," I mutter.

Remus blinks out of sight and starts for the back

door. He knocks, and we flatten ourselves against the side of the house. When someone opens the door to look around the side, we slip inside.

The kitchen is enormous. State-of-the-art. A chef arranges some type of appetizer on a tray, something that looks like meat but smells like mango. "Who was that?" the chef asks.

"No one's there," the server says.

"Fucking kids. Get these out to Mr. Trainor and his guests. The guests must always have food and drink readily available at these meetings. Never hide in the kitchen."

"Understood," the server says. Picking up the tray, he heads through the door toward the front room. Remus moves to follow, but I hold him back. Something in the way the chef looks at the second server tells me there's some gossip coming we won't want to miss.

The moment the door closes, he turns to the second server. "How is Mr. Trainor tonight?"

"Fastidious as usual," the server says. "He gave the new guy hell for serving him wine in a stemless wineglass. I just poured it into one of the old ones and sent it back out to him."

"Excellent. Make a round with the cigars in a few minutes, and make sure there's always a tray within his reach. He's in one of his moods."

The server looks over her shoulder at the door and then back at the chef, her blond ponytail swaying. "Can't say I blame him, all things considered. I overheard him tell one of the other guests that four of their friends were murdered recently. What exactly are these people into?"

The chef raises one eyebrow. "You don't want to know." He nudges the tray toward her. "Go. And don't spill anything on that cream suit of his, or we'll never hear the end of it."

The door opens and we move, silently drifting through the door after the server and following close behind her into the main room. We skim along the back wall and settle into a shady corner.

The blond server offers her tray to a man with a mustache in a cream-colored suit who takes one of the canapés with a hand sporting a ring. This must be Stanley. I silently thank the creator that this room is big enough that our presence doesn't cause that ring to glow blue. I consider that a win.

Still, we are close enough that my dragon vision detects an inscription on the face. This is one of the originals. I nudge Remus. He taps my hand twice, acknowledging he saw it too.

Beside him, a familiar-looking young man with sandy brown hair takes a canapé. No ring, but I can't get a read on his opposite hand, which he leaves in the pocket of his jacket. Why does he look so familiar? Maybe an actor?

The third man stands from his chair and waves the server off. "We're wasting time," he says. "Let's get down to brass tacks. Are you going to sponsor my son or not?" As he moves toward the windows, an Order ring catches the light. Is the familiar-looking man his son? If so, there is no family resemblance in the man's silver hair and bulbous nose. But no, the fourth man who sits with his back to me stiffens in his seat. I'm guessing that's the son.

"Leave us," Stanley orders, and the two servers hustle back toward the kitchen. Once they're gone, he says, "It's not a yes or no question, Alex. It's a question of timing."

"I've contributed handsomely to the Order. You owe me this," Alex says.

The familiar man takes a bite of the puff in his hand. "It's not a matter of denying him a place. We need more blood, or we can't make more rings."

"Exactly." Stanley crosses his legs. "I have Scott on the list. It's just a matter of time—"

"If you need dragon's blood, hunt a dragon." Alex throws up his hands. "This is why the Order was founded in the first place. It shouldn't be that hard."

My spine tingles with the desire to attack, but the information we're suddenly privy to is too important. I grab Remus's wrist. He seems to understand. "Unfortunately, things in that regard are harder than you might think. The dragons have gone into hiding. And the only time they seem to appear these days is when one of us ends up dead."

"So now *we're* being hunted?" Alex scoffs. "Fuck this. I've seen an influx of rings all over LA."

"Made with the blood of the last dragon we had in our possession," Maybe-actor says. "That blood is now gone, and all the rings made are accounted for."

Alex charges toward the man and points a finger at

his chest. "How much would it cost to find Scott one that was already created? Kick someone else to the curb."

"Dad," the boy blurts. "No. I can wait."

Alex whirls on the boy, who has now leaned forward in his chair, showing his dark mop of hair. "You will never make it through an Ivy League school without that ring, Scott. You're not good enough."

"So, I'll go to a state school."

His father crosses the room and grabs him by the face. I really hate this guy. "Shut the fuck up. You will do no such thing."

Stanley raises a hand. "Release the boy, Alex. We'll find another dragon. We might even get permission to drain some blood from one of our members' beasts. A few remain in captivity."

Alex releases the boy and takes a long drink of some amber liquid. "Fine."

Stanley sits back in his chair and rests his hand on the armrest, his ring flashing in the overhead lights. This is my chance. I draw my dagger. Silently, I communicate that I'll take Stanley, and Remus moves toward Alex.

I creep across the room as the men move on to a discussion about a young actress appearing in Stanley's latest project. I lift my dagger and strike.

Stanley's fingers drop to the floor along with his ring, and Alex's hand drops along with the glass he's holding. The boy screams first, followed by the two men who are clutching their hands and wailing in agony.

The maybe-actor looks right at me, seeming to see

me despite my camouflage, his ring glowing blue on his finger.

"Jeremy, stop him!" Stanley yells as I move toward the blue glow.

"Jeremy?" My thoughts slow as Jeremy's hands do an odd dance, and the light from his ring grows brighter, not into the form of a weapon, but something else, something far more dangerous. It closes around me and squeezes me like a fist.

I hear shattering glass. And then I'm falling into a soundless black sea.

Chapter Thirty-Seven

SEB

*F*uck. It's the first word that crosses my mind when I wake up. I am in a world of hurt. Not only is there a blue cuff on my ankle, which means I am a prisoner of the Saint's Order, there's an IV running from my arm, draining my blood into a bag. And the worst fucking part of it all is that Jeremy, the fucking doctor who hit on my mate, is outside the bars to my cell, sitting in a comfy chair, reading a book. I squint at the title. *The Art of War*.

You've got to be kidding me. This guy might as well be wearing an I'M A DOUCHEBAG T-shirt. I try pushing into his mind, but my ankle starts to burn, and the entire cell is infused with blue light.

"Don't try to use your powers," Jeremy says. "You'll only hurt yourself. Oh, and the bars are charmed too."

I note the faint blue tinge to the steel. Fuck me. So I'm not getting out of here without help. "Where am I?"

He ignores my question. "I can't believe you're already awake," he says, snapping the book closed. "I have to admit, they said your kind healed quickly, but I had no idea just how quickly. The spell I hit you with would have knocked a human out for a good twelve hours. You were barely out for four."

"You're a witch," I say.

He snorts. "Let's not pretend you don't know who I am. Zoe is working for you, and I am her doctor."

Was her doctor, I think. But I don't correct him. The last thing I want is for him to turn his sights on Zoe.

"Tell me, Sebastian, did you disclose to Zoe before she came to work for you that you'd be digging around in her brain? She knows what you are, but does she know you've most likely infiltrated her mind?"

Infiltrated her mind. No, I wouldn't do that without her consent. But if he's asking, then he doesn't know she's my mate. At least there's that. I hope to keep it that way. "Why? Are you worried what I'll find in there? What kind of interest do you have in Ms. Willow?"

He lifts his chin. "The kind that makes me ecstatic to be the one who eradicates you from her life."

My eyes narrow. "Sounds like your interest in her goes beyond a doctor/patient relationship."

His smile shifts. "Maybe."

"Does Ms. Willow know her doctor moonlights for the Saint's Order? I think she'd be interested that the man who promised to heal her is secretly a killer."

"We kill dragons, not people."

"So, she doesn't know?"

He smiles as if it's his smug little secret. "No. But then, that's a recent development. My father did it for decades, and I only stepped up when he retired." He looks at the ring on his finger. "Some nice perks to the position, though. Perks she'll come to appreciate in time."

Not if I have anything to do with it. Pure rage courses through my body. My eyes drift to the IV in my arm, and I claw at it, ready to rip it out.

"Stop!" Jeremy holds up his hand. "If you do that, I'm just going to knock you out again and have to put it back in."

I leave it for the moment, but I stand to walk to the bars, thankful the tube is long enough to allow me some movement. Jeremy is smart enough to remain out of reach. "Are we alone down here?" I ask softly. I peruse the other cells, at least what I can see of them, and they appear empty. Instinctively, I try to screen the area psychically, and my ankle burns again.

"I told you to stop with the psychic shit. You're going to give yourself an aneurysm."

I grab my aching head, a low growl percolating in my chest.

Jeremy rubs the bridge of his nose. "If you're wondering about your partner, unfortunately, he escaped through the window with one of our rings. Someone is going to want to talk to you about that. You and your band of merry men have been a real pain in the ass lately."

I can't help but smile at this. Remus is free. At least

we have that. I can be replaced. Hell, my alignment is almost over anyway. The Oracle can name another Taurus to the brotherhood. Life will go on.

But even as I think it, my thoughts drift to Zoe. My death will hurt her, and I regret that. But I take solace in the fact that she's human and won't suffer the deadly fever a dragon mate would. What matters most now is that I either escape or ensure my death. I can't allow them to keep me captive. Now that I'm mated, I could live hundreds of years.

I gesture toward the tube in my arm. "So, is this the plan? Are you going to bleed me out until I'm dead?"

He stands, clasping the book in front of his hips. "What would that serve? If we keep you alive, we'll have a regular blood supply until you go up in flames. You're young. We might get fifty years out of you."

"Let me talk to the destroyer."

"Oh, I'm sure he'll want to meet with you in time. Right now, though, he's busy planning for the initiation of an army of new recruits, fueled by your blood." He turns and walks toward the exit.

"I choose the hunt," I blurt. "I have a right to be hunted to the death rather than imprisoned."

He looks at me over his shoulder, brow furrowed. "Rights? You have no rights, dragon. Donovan is dead, and the Order is no longer beholden to a peace accord. There is no more choice. You will live or die at the discretion of the destroyer, and right now, he needs you alive."

He turns for the exit again.

Fury blazes through my veins. I dig my fingers under

the tape holding my IV in place and rip it out of my arm, throwing it on the floor.

"You fucking asshole," Jeremy says, striding back toward my cell. Before he can reach me, I claw the half-full bag of blood from the hook on the side of the chair, toss it on the floor, and stomp on it.

Jeremy yells as the bag pops and blood sprays across the floor. He won't be using this to make rings anytime soon.

"Don't say I didn't warn you." Jeremy's ring glows blue, and a wall of magic barrels into me. My cheek hits the bloody floor, and then I'm out again.

Chapter Thirty-Eight

ZOE

The sound of men talking wakes me, and I have a few precious moments when the light flows through the slats of the wood blinds and I think Seb is behind me. But when I sleepily turn over, it's just his pillow. More low murmurs. Seb must already be up. More than one male voice is out there. Are his brothers here?

I stumble to the bathroom and do my morning routine. I'd meant to stay awake until he returned from his rounds, but I must have drifted off in the wee hours of the morning. He probably took pains not to disrupt my sleep. After all, today is the day I must charge the ring and combine the spells. Today, we find out if everything we've been working toward will pay off.

I dress quickly in leggings and a long-sleeved T-shirt and pull my hair into a ponytail. Then I go in search of

Seb. But when I leave the bedroom, the first person I see is Fiona. She rushes to me, her eyes rimmed in red.

"Fiona, when did you get here? Where's Seb?"

She grabs my hands in both of her own. "Now, I don't want you to worry, because the entire brotherhood is here to help..."

I try to see around her into the living room, but she holds my hands tighter. "Where is Seb?"

"He was captured last night, Zoe. I'm so sorry."

Terror tumbles through my body like shattering glass. My breath catches in my throat, and I yank my hands away from her and run for the living room. Eleven sets of eyes turn to me, including Connor's and Remus's, but Seb isn't among them. I zero in on Remus. "You were with him. You were supposed to back him up. What the fuck happened?"

Remus stands and walks toward me, tears welling in his eyes. "I'm sorry."

"Don't tell me you're sorry. Tell me what happened—and I mean every detail." I hold up my finger between us and say the words through my teeth.

He nods and gestures toward the hall. "Somewhere more private. The team is busy planning how to get him back."

I nod and quickly follow him from the room. The last thing I care to do is distract them from saving Seb. We wind up in the library down the hall, the quiet eerily like a tomb. "Now, tell me everything."

"It would be faster if I showed you," Remus says.

"Showed me?"

He closes his eyes for a beat. "I can play my memories for you, in your head. I think, in this case, I will never be able to describe for you with words what happened in a way that will explain why I couldn't help him, Zoe. I really want you to see it."

I nod. "Okay." I don't like the idea of having him in my head, but he's right. I need to see what happened.

He breathes out a deep breath. "Do you consent to me entering your mind?"

"Yes."

"Just relax."

I do, and in seconds, it feels like I'm standing against the wall while three members of the Saint's Order talk about initiating a fourth. One of them is Jeremy, and by the end, when my former doctor uses that cursed ring of his to knock Seb out and seal him inside a glowing blue cage, I want to scream.

Remus pulls out of my mind as easily as he went in. Tears drip from my chin onto my shirt. "I...I...know who that was."

"Huh?"

I swipe the moisture from under my eyes. "The witch who attacked Seb and knocked him unconscious. That's Dr. Jeremy Branch. He used to be my doctor. He must be providing magical services to the Saint's Order."

"Shit," Remus says. "It sounded like he's the one who was using Donovan's blood to make the rings."

A chill brittles my bones and causes my joints to ache, like fear has plunged me into a frozen pond. This is so much worse than I thought. "He's going to use Seb as his new source of blood."

Remus growls. "I need to tell the others. I'm so sorry, Zoe." He rushes from the room toward the other brothers.

I stand, frozen, staring at Seb's books and the desk where I'd first drawn the ring. *Jeremy, you brutal nightmare of a human being*. All this time. I pull my phone from my pocket and dial his number. I get his voice mail. I dial again. Voice mail again. I'm tempted to leave a message threatening to sever his balls from his body if he doesn't return Seb to me, but then I remember how devious he is. All this time, manipulating me. I shouldn't offer him any information that he doesn't already have, and that includes how much I care for Seb. He doesn't need to know.

I end the call and stare at my phone, then I dial my mom.

"Zoe, it's so good to hear your voice."

"Yours too, Mom. I, uh, have you heard where Jeremy is today?"

"No." She pauses for a beat. "We fired him, honey. It didn't end well. He's not checking in with me. Why?"

I roll my eyes toward the ceiling and think fast. "A few loose ends from our last session I wanted to tie up. I guess it's not important."

She huffs into the phone. "You know, I gave that boy the benefit of the doubt. I told myself that he was his own person, separate from his father. But, in fact, the acorn did not roll far from the tree. He was just as devious."

"I wasn't aware Jeremy's father was on your shit list."

"Oh yes. We went to college together. Were friends once until he started practicing dark magic."

A memory of another conversation I had with my mother lights up in my head. "Wait, is this the guy you said was using dragon scales in his spells?"

"Yes, I forgot I told you that. That was Jeremy's father. I knew he was into some dark stuff, but I never thought Jeremy would follow him down that path. He seemed so much more like his mother. And she was the sweetest woman, Zoe, truly she was."

I remember when Jeremy's mother died three years ago. I wasn't close to him, but whatever forces were at work in his life, he had indeed chosen a dark path.

"Mom, I have to go," I say. "I'm sorry. It's a work emergency."

"Okay, darling. Call whenever you're free."

I end the call, rage boiling in my veins. That fucker. By the goddess, I will make him sorry he ever knew me. My vision flickers to gold, and I know what I must do.

I run for the back door and out to the tree, digging in the freshly turned earth until I reach the ring. I unwrap it from the banana leaves and rest it in my palm, where it buzzes against my skin. The magic of this ring is ready. It wants to be released. I close my fist around it and return to the house, slipping back up to the main floor where I can hear the Zodiac Brotherhood discussing next steps with raised voices.

I slow my steps as I pass the front room where they are meeting. They don't know where Seb is. Ellison speculates he's been taken to the compound in Maryland where they saw Roman, whoever that is, but Remus is convinced he's close because they wouldn't want to risk traveling far with him. Too many opportunities for him to break free.

I frown. There is one way to know exactly where he is. A person simply needs a high enough vantage point to see everything.

Quickly, I pad to our bedroom and silently close and lock the door behind me. I take a seat on the bed, holding out the gold ring in front of me. I can't see the spells I've laid like I could when I was in the Gold Room, but I can feel them. I can smell them. I can hear them. This magic is alive, just sleeping. All I have to do is wake it and tell it to party.

I concentrate on the ring and then chant the spell to ignite the magic. Power flows through my voice, and symbols glow in the air around the ring. I can see the ribbons. But then I pause to take a breath, and the gold symbols fall to my palm like stardust and disappear. *Shit.*

I sit up straighter and try again.

Chapter Thirty-Nine

ZOE

Hours later, a knock comes on the door. "Yes?" I ask in a voice hoarse from singing. The ring still isn't activated, and I'm exhausted. Each try feels more desperate than the last.

"It's Patrick, miss. You must eat something, please. Seb won't forgive me if he returns and you are wasted away."

"I'll be right there," I croak. At least I won't have to explain myself. It sounds like I've been crying. I place the gold ring in the wooden box where Seb keeps his watches and rings and unlock the door. I'm surprised when Patrick leads me into the kitchen, although I can still hear the men's voices somewhere in the house.

"I thought you'd prefer a quiet meal here," he says.

I nod, unable to voice my gratitude any other way. He slides a big bowl of chicken ramen in front of me, braised chunks of bok choy and hard-boiled egg smiling up at me from under a nest of green onion. My stomach, completely uninterested a moment ago, wakes up and starts to growl. I slurp up a mouthful of the noodles and am immediately comforted by the rich broth and tender chicken. Is there anything better than soup when you're tired and distraught?

"Thank you, Patrick," I say.

He clasps one of my shoulders and gives it a supportive squeeze. "Seb is made of tough stuff. Don't underestimate him."

He slips from the kitchen, leaving me with the steaming bowl of goodness. I eat every last drop. When I check my watch, I see it's almost ten in the evening, and I can barely keep my eyes open. Seb, my mate, is counting on me, and I've failed him. I haven't even been able to ignite the ring, let alone transport it to him.

I could ask Hazel for help, but it might take another day. A day for her to charge the ring and another day for her to ascend to bring it to him, if she's even capable of doing both those things with natural magic. We don't have that kind of time. But the only other option is gold dust, and I promised Seb I wouldn't use again. Worse, if I break that promise, I might not come back from ascending at all.

That's all right, the spider says. *You'll be safe here with me.*

There has to be another way. I stand from the table and pad down the hall toward the front room, where I find Remus speaking to a young dragon he calls Mason.

They seem to come to an agreement on something to do with a place in Rhode Island. He sees me and nods before heading for the door.

"Remus, what's happening?" I ask.

"We've split up. I have brothers flying over all of the known Saint's Order properties where we suspect he might be held. We'll be looking for increased activity outside the building. If he's there, they'll have extra security."

"And then what? If they suspect he's being held somewhere, are they going in after him?"

"Not immediately. We're reconvening in a few hours. Once we know the target, we'll plan a coordinated attack."

"How long will that take?"

"It depends on what we're dealing with. The exact location and number of security guards. This safe house has a sufficient arsenal, so I think we'll have a plan in place in just a few days."

"A few days?" I can't believe my ears. "They could drain him dry in a few days."

Remus adjusts his cap, his frown mirroring the mask on his pec that peeks out from under his black tank. "I'm sorry, Zoe. That's the best I can do."

His phone rings, and he pulls it from his pocket, mumbling something about coordinates in response to the caller's question. I drift back toward the bedroom, too upset even to cry. I'm furious at Jeremy and achingly lost without Seb. There is no version of this situation in any universe or time or world where I allow

Seb to be left at the mercy of the Saint's Order for three days.

I need to help him, and I need to do it now.

I rush to my cottage and retrieve my black bag, before returning to the bedroom and snatching the ring from the ring box. I'm thankful not to see a single person as I carry both into the office. The ring, I set at the center of the desk. The bag, I drop near the legs of the desk chair. I feel like a robot as I walk back to the door and lock it, then sit down at the desk. I'm not strong enough to ignite this ring on my own, but I'm definitely strong enough to do it with gold dust.

I open my black bag and take out the urn.

When I remove the lid, I'm dismayed at just how little is left. It's enough to ascend and do what I need to do, as much as I used last time, but there will be none left of my stash after that. Perhaps that's for the best. I won't be tempted to use again. But it also means I can't mess this up. I have one shot, and I have to make it count.

I dump the gold dust on the leather desk covering and use my athame to draw the lines. I concentrate on the ring, lean over, and breathe in the goddess.

My ascension is quick, the walls of the office bleeding gold and every book on the shelves singing to me of its usefulness. I notice immediately that Seb's dragon isn't with me this time. The way it breaks my heart only spurs me into action.

"Please, Goddess, I beseech you for help charging the spells in this ring."

"You wish to bring the metal alive, my daughter. Breathe life unto it."

I take a deep breath and release it across the ring. Each spell rises, one by one, the scent of lavender and honey filling the room. The four enchantments float around the metal one, twisting into an infinity symbol and weaving themselves together and then into the ring itself. When the process is complete, the ring glows like a small sun.

"Sacred. Sacrosanct. Blessed," the goddess whispers in three distinct voices.

"Please, goddess, I must get this to Seb. He's in danger."

"Then open a door and take it to him," she says in a voice hollow as wind chimes. "But be warned, daughter. There will be a price for this level of magic. One only you can pay."

"He is worth the price."

The ring flies at me, and I catch it in my right hand. To my left, a gold door appears, covered in arcane symbols. I open it to find myself in a dark cell with Seb unconscious in a pool of blood at the center of the room. I rush to him, noticing the blue chains that bind him.

"Seb!" I call, but we're not on the same plane. He doesn't even know I'm here. But his dragon does. He appears in the room, his colors dull, his leg cuffed with the same blue cuff that resides on Seb's ankle. The dragon growls at something behind me, and I look over my shoulder. Jeremy is there, and although his body isn't moving, his eyes are. He's tracking me. He knows I'm here.

"You." His mouth forms in slow motion.

I'm running out of time.

I grab Seb's hand and slide the ring onto his finger. The golden glow is blinding, and I hear his dragon laugh as the blue cuff dissolves from his leg and Seb's. The chains break and drop to the floor. "Wake up, Seb. Wake up!"

His dragon plows back into Seb's body, and his eyes flip open, his irises molten gold. Our eyes lock. "Zoe?"

"Yes. I brought you the ring."

He looks down at his hand and then toward Jeremy. I glance back at my former doctor, just in time to see a pulse of blue energy heading straight for me. I move for the door, diving back through the portal into Seb's office. But the blue energy comes through after me, a cloud of blue fire, like the aftereffects of an explosion. It sears my skin and knocks me out of the chair my body is in, just as my soul reenters it.

I land facedown on the Persian carpet. I've descended, hard. Everything hurts. I manage a glance back to see the portal is closed. The gold is gone. I also notice that the back of my leg is burned and smoking.

"Ms. Willow?" Patrick's voice calls through the door. The doorknob rattles. "Are you in there?"

I can't answer him. The pain from my injuries, delayed by the gold dust, finally catches up to me. I gasp in a breath and then welcome a wave of darkness.

Chapter Forty

SEB

"Noooo!" I stand in my cell and instinctively cross my arms in front of my face against the dome of blue light Jeremy throws in my direction. My ring finger burns hot as the ring Zoe placed on it glows to life like a small sun. White light clashes with blue, sending it coursing around me as if I'm in a bubble. Unfortunately, it also collides with Zoe—the golden, translucent version of her I thought was an angel when she slipped the ring onto my finger.

I breathe a sigh of relief when the portal closes with her safely on the other side. I'm alone with Jeremy.

The witch's eyes widen when he realizes the gift Zoe gave me. He raises his ring, his lips drawing back from his teeth. A bolt of blue lightning flies at me, and I step out of its path. My feet splash in my own blood as I grab the bars of my cell with the hand wearing the golden ring. The blue metal turns to ordinary steel with a zap.

My gaze connects with Jeremy's, and a grin spreads across my face. He runs.

With one slam of my shoulder, I bend the bars and send plaster raining down from the ceiling. Another slam, and the door topples and I'm out. I bound after him, noting the terror in his eyes as I easily catch up with him and knock him to the floor. He tries to raise that fucking ring again, but I partially shift my hand into talons and hack it off at the wrist.

The ring and the hand it's attached to flop onto the concrete, blood blooming against the gray. Jeremy howls in pain, and I shove my knee into the center of his chest. "That was for the blood you took from me," I hiss, more dragon than man.

I lift the ring and concentrate. *Dagger.* What do you know? The metal obeys. The hilt of a gold dagger slides into my palm. I flip it so that the blade is facing his chest.

"Please—" Jeremy sputters, slapping at me with his good hand. "I can help you. If you kill me, you'll never heal Zoe. You have no idea what she did to herself to bring that ring to you. She'll die without my help."

I narrow my eyes and think about that for a second. But I can't trust a thing this asshole says. He's not the only fucking witch either. "Your filthy magic will never touch my mate," I seethe. "This is for Zoe."

I sink the gold blade into his heart. He makes a gagging sound and then releases a long breath. I watch the light leave his eyes.

I don't bother closing them as I stand and move toward the stairs, my dagger morphing back into a ring. Nice. She did it. It works exactly as intended. I can't wait to tell my brilliant mate that she succeeded.

But at what cost?

I climb toward a door, my dragon's roar in my head. We're worried for Zoe, but right now, that worry is laser focused on getting home to her, and that means going through whatever is on the other side of the door above me.

No surprise that it's locked. I back up a few steps and throw my shoulder into it, knocking it down and bursting onto the main floor. I'm in a house, but not one I recognize. A servant at the end of the hall sees me and screams. She disappears.

And then the fools rush in.

Blue weapons sprout from their rings, filling their hands with swords and spears and crossbows. I don't have time for this shit. My mate needs me.

I shift into my dragon form, and it ain't pretty. We take down walls and collapse floors on our way through the men. I flatten one under my foot, noticing the gold ring still around the talon of my paw, and laugh a fiery laugh. Drawing a deep breath into my lungs, I blow fire as arrows bounce harmlessly off my scales.

One man manages to slide into the rubble behind me and sinks a cursed blade into my hip. I yelp. With a simple shift of my body, I flatten him against the rubble. He pops like a balloon. I smash my way out the front door, just as my dragon shifts back into my human form.

I glance down to see that the blade is still protruding from my hip and reach down to yank it out. The wound feels like ice, so cold it burns, and blue veins spread from it like flower petals, but the celestial water in my veins must be working because I'm still moving.

"Sebastian York," a voice dark and slippery as motor oil calls from the house. "Current head of the Zodiac Brotherhood, if I remember my astrology. Although I never put much stock in fairy tales about the sky. You wouldn't leave without speaking to me, would you?"

I whirl to find Roman Cifarelli striding toward me. My wings unfurl from my back, and my hands ball into fists. But I wince when I see the man who used to be the handsome, playboy son of Stephen Ciferelli. He's badly scarred by burns that run up one side of his body, his hair missing on the left side of his head. And the scar from Connor's claws is three raised white ridges that span his neck, each with the tattered edge that comes from a severe wound.

"How are you still alive?" I sputter. "We watched you die."

He snorts, a crossbow forming in his hands, and he levels the bolt on my chest. "There's something you should know about me, dragon. I do the killing. I don't do the dying."

The bolt flies, and I cross my arms in front of my chest in the same motion I did in the dungeon, praying it has the same effect. The ring does not fail me. Golden light arcs, shielding me. The bolt falls harmlessly between us.

Roman's eyes widen.

"That's right, scumbag. Your little gift from the destroyer isn't quite so gifty anymore."

I find I still can't fully shift, thanks to the wound in my hip, but that's okay. This guy is going down if I have to do it with my own two hands. My ring morphs into a glowing golden longsword. I advance.

Roman's crossbow changes into a sword to match my own, although his is that deadly shade of blue. His gaze sinks to my injured hip. "Whatever gift the creator gave you, it won't protect you from the poison of my blade." He grins and repositions his feet, ready to engage.

Behind him, flames plume from the rubble that was once a mansion, toward the starry skies above. I point my chin at Roman, wanting to distract him more than anything. "Aren't you concerned about your people burning to death?"

"Not as concerned as you should be about that spreading rot in your hip."

I don't make the mistake of looking at my wound, and it's a good thing because his sword slices toward my neck. I block it, and the clash of enchanted steel against steel sends sparks flying and our swords ricocheting in opposite directions.

Diametrically opposed.

"Do you even know how to fight with a broadsword?" Roman taunts. He has no idea that every Zodiac brother has studied swordplay. I have years of practice with this weapon, and a dragon's strength and instincts too.

He settles into *ochs*, the point of his sword threatening me from high guard.

I smirk. "Enough to take off your head." I counter with *plow guard*, blade low but poised, feet light on the grassy lawn.

The first exchange comes in a blur. Roman slices down with an *oberhau*, forcing me to parry with my hilt held low near my hip. Sparks leap as our weapons collide again, and I groan as the hilt drives into my wound. My dragon growls in pain, but I immediately counter with a *cross-strike*, my blade sweeping horizontally toward Roman's temple.

"Fast, but sloppy," Roman barks, blocking my blow again.

I snort. "If there's one thing a Taurus never is, it's sloppy," I shoot back.

Roman lunges again, this time feinting high before driving up toward my ribs. I meet it with a sliding parry, then bind our swords together, the blades sparking like two live wires between us.

"You're exhausted. Drained of blood and infected with the power of the destroyer. You know you can't last long like this, Sebastian. Yield. I'd hate to have to kill you when your blood is so highly in demand," Roman says through clenched teeth.

"You'll have to kill me, Roman, or I'm taking you out. And this time, I'll make sure you're dead." I twist my wrists, disengaging, and thrust toward Roman's heart. The point enters his flesh, but Roman rotates away before I can pierce his rib cage.

He roars, and veins of light branch under his shirt, originating from the wound, but he does not lower his defenses. We circle, my bare feet feeling steady, grounded. He will pay for what my mate suffered. What she will suffer.

He's breathing hard, sweat cutting channels through dust on his face.

"It seems that my blade carries a different poison, and it's spreading fast, Roman."

In fact, I can see the branching light all the way down his torso now. This isn't a battle of swords; it's a battle of magic, a battle of rings. He makes a choking sound, and his sword lowers as his eyelids flutter. I take the opening. I attack. This time, I don't aim for his neck or his heart, but his wrists. I take off both his hands in a single blow and watch as the sword disappears and his clenched fists roll across the grass.

This time, Roman screams. He collapses onto his back, his arms trembling. "Destroyer, help me!"

I raise my sword above my head, its light shining over Roman like its own sun, tingeing everything gold. I can feel the creator's energy buzzing through me as I say, "Haven't you learned from that face of yours, Roman, that the destroyer can only destroy? It cannot heal. It cannot create."

He meets my eyes with his own and seethes, "Fuck you, dr—"

My blade comes down across his neck, severing it. I put so much power behind the blow, my sword lodges in the dirt. I draw it from the ground, the blade steaming.

Roman's blood burns off in white-hot flames. The sword disappears, and there is only the ring.

I look around, then search the area psychically to ensure we're alone. If anyone else was here, they're gone now. I tear off a section of Roman's shirt and use it to gather his hand and ring from the dirt. No way am I leaving it behind to be recycled. I give Roman's headless body one last kick, check the map of the stars above me, and take off toward home.

Chapter Forty-One

SEB

I limp through the door to the safe house, naked and covered in blood, and slam the door behind me. "Zoe?"

Remus appears out of nowhere, eyes going wide. "Creator bless us all. You're free!" He rips his phone from his pocket, hits a button, and yells, "Send a message to all zodiac brothers to return to the safe house immediately. Seb is back."

His automated assistant confirms the message as I hand him the blood-soaked shirt-sac I'm carrying.

"What is this?" he asks.

"Roman's ring."

"Holy fuck! Is his hand still attached to it?" Remus holds the bag away from his body.

"Yeah. He's dead. This time permanently, unless the

Order finds a way to reattach a head to a bloodless body. Now, where is Zoe, Remus?"

"She's in your bedroom. Morwyn is with her. There's something you should know, Seb. Seb!"

I shove past him and through the door to my room to find Morwyn and a group of nurses working over Zoe. She's unconscious, and her legs are wrapped in bandages. A fierce growl rumbles in my chest.

Morwyn advances toward me, his hands raised. "She's stable, Seb, but if she feels stress down your mating bond, you could set her healing back significantly. She only recently stopped thrashing. I'm guessing that has something to do with this." He gestures at the blood on my chest.

"What happened?" The two words come out like dual weights dropping between us.

Morwyn's astute gaze scrapes over me. "How much of this blood is yours?"

"Not much."

His perusal stops at the wound in my hip. "The fact that you're still standing means you've been drinking the water, but we need to treat that. Go get cleaned up and meet me in the kitchen for tea."

I get up in his face until our noses are touching. "Morwyn, tell me what happened to her," I grit out.

He folds his arms. "I will, once we get you strong enough to care for her. Now, do as I've requested. You're wasting time."

As soon as he mentions that he needs me strong enough

to care for Zoe, it's like something flips in my brain. Everything in me only wants her healthy again. I nudge past him to get to the bathroom and take the world's fastest shower, then put on sweats and a T-shirt because anything else would hurt like hell against my wound. It's not spreading, but it's not healing either. By the time I reach the kitchen, Morwyn has a cup of the celestial tea poured for me.

"This dose should take care of that infection," he says. "Drink."

"I'll drink. You talk." I glare at him to make sure he knows I mean business.

Morwyn nods. "Zoe was burned pretty badly by Order magic tonight. The burns are first- and second-degree. And thankfully, she isn't a dragon, so the curse isn't an issue."

"Good."

"But she's going to need time to heal."

"All we've got is time. I'll care for her as long as she needs me to."

Morwyn scratches the stubble on the side of his jaw, obviously procrastinating.

"And?" I prompt.

He blows out a deep breath, his eyes falling on the gold ring on my finger. "The ring!" His gaze flicks to mine. "She finished it!"

I nod. "It saved my life—or at least saved me from a lifetime of captivity. Roman is dead. I brought back his ring."

"Damn. It seems we owe her a debt of gratitude.

Remus had us all out looking for you, but we couldn't track your location."

"They had me under a compound in Colorado. Not a place we had on our known list. Looked new. Now, tell me what's going on with my mate, Morwyn, or my dragon is going to get involved."

"Zoe used something called gold dust to ascend to a plane where she could perform the magic necessary to get that ring to you."

"I'm aware. It's how she's been helping us this entire time."

Morwyn frowns. "She's used a lot of it, Seb. And afterward, when we found her, she was dead."

"Dead?"

"Her heart had stopped. Patrick performed CPR, and then my team and I took over, and we were able to revive her. But she never regained consciousness. She's alive and stable. Her heart is beating steadily. Her lungs are working. But although her eyes occasionally open, she's never responded to any stimuli."

I set down the teacup, a chill causing me to hug myself and rub my outer arms. "So, she just needs rest and to heal, right?"

Morwyn frowns. "We're not sure. She still has brain waves, but out of respect for you and her, I didn't enter her mind."

"Good choice."

"But I did try to elicit a response from her. I failed. I'm afraid she's suffering from postascendant psychosis."

I frown down into the remains of my tea.

"Judging by your expression and lack of questions, I'm guessing you know what that is."

"Yeah. She told me."

His brow wrinkles. "Has this happened to her before?"

"Once."

"Dammit, Seb. This condition comes about from prolonged overuse of gold dust. If she'd had this happen before, she shouldn't have been using—"

"Fuck off."

"Excuse me?"

"We sat around that table in LA and I told you all that I didn't want to use her, but the entire fucking brotherhood said she was our only hope. Zoe didn't use because she was an addict. She used to save us, to save dragons. And this last time, she used to save me. We all owe her our lives, not our fucking judgment."

Morwyn's back to scratching his jaw again. If he keeps that up, he's not going to have to shave that side of his face. "I'm not judging, just reassessing my prognosis."

"What does that mean?"

"It means we need to give her time to heal and then pray for the best. Pray she comes out of it. If you can get her to wake up, she's got a good chance."

"What do you mean, if?"

"In some cases, witches never come back from this, Seb."

"She gave me permission to enter her thoughts. I'll go in and get her out."

Morwyn shakes his head. "You may want to leave that one as a last resort."

"Why?"

"Her psychological state is fragile right now. She's alive, which means she's likely working hard to heal herself mentally as well. We don't know what is going on inside her mind, but whatever she's built so far is crucially important. If you go in and knock down a wall trying to get to her, you could collapse whatever house of cards she's constructed inside her head. You could end up ruining what recovery she's been capable of."

"Are you saying there's nothing I can do to help her?"

"I'm saying, you need to be patient."

The empty teacup shatters in my tightening grip.

Morwyn shoves his napkin into my bleeding hand. "You can do this. I know you can."

Chapter Forty-Two

SEB

I stand at the base of the two massive doors that lead to the Oracle's sanctuary, with Zoe draped across my arms. After days spent allowing her to heal and then trying to rouse her, I'm frustrated. I've heeded Morwyn's warning and stayed out of her head, but every day that passes, I grow more panicked.

Only one dragon can see all the possible futures and know which direction is the best to take—the Oracle. She has to help me. We can't go on like this.

I reposition Zoe in my arms and pound on the door. The wood is smooth under my fist, made from a type of tree that no longer exists on earth. Massive and solid, the door seems to absorb my knock, and I wonder if anyone inside can hear it.

But only a few seconds later, one of the two doors opens of its own volition, forcing me to give it room.

Once open, an acolyte greets me with a bow on the other side. Dressed, as all acolytes dress, in red robes with a veil that covers their face, this acolyte has no distinctive characteristics to set them apart from any other. "Good evening, Sebastien," they say in a soft voice.

"I need to see the Oracle."

"The Oracle sends word that you've broken the rules by bringing the human here without permission. She relays her deepest disappointment at your inappropriate behavior."

"You tell the Oracle—" I stop myself from saying something I'll regret and take a deep breath. "Please relay my deep contrition to the Oracle and ask if she might make an exception this one time for the woman whose magic ended the destroyer's reign."

The acolyte bows again and then disappears. The door closes between us.

Zoe *is* responsible for ending the Saint's Order's reign of terror, at least for now. After Roman's and Jeremy's deaths, the Order seems to have gone underground. Roman's body was found in the ocean off his Rhode Island estate, his death reported in the news as an accidental drowning. Jeremy was found just off a hiking trail in the desert a few days later, an apparent victim of dehydration and poor planning. Since their deaths, many of the most powerful Saint's Order members from Imani's list have stopped wearing their rings in public.

The brotherhood repealed the code red, and civilian dragons returned to their daily lives. That was days ago, and so far, there hasn't been a single incident. Just to be safe, Connor and Fiona have dispensed thousands of vials of celestial water to the heads of each of the major dragon families. It appears that, at least for now, Zoe has restored peace to our kind.

But if the Order should ever rise again, I still have the ring and a bottomless thirst for vengeance.

The doors open, and again, the acolyte greets me with a bow. "The Oracle recognizes the sacrifice of the human woman and agrees to grant you an audience. Please follow me."

The acolyte leads me through a maze of dark corridors until I feel like a rat who has lost his way searching for the cheese. And then with a sharp right, I find myself standing under a dome that magnifies the stars. A gold couch with turned legs sits at the center of a room of clocks, each one displaying a different time. One on the wall is shaped like an orange dog, its eyes looking left and right with every tick. It's disorienting, as if I'm in some sort of alternate reality where time itself doesn't exist.

The acolyte gestures toward the sofa, and I gratefully set Zoe down.

"My Taurus warrior," the Oracle says as she enters the room.

I lower myself to my knees, head bowed. "Thank you for seeing me. I broke the rules bringing Zoe to Cardinal Island, but only because I believe it is absolutely necessary."

"Necessary for whom? For you, I think."

"Yes. But also, our kind. She made this ring." I hold

up my hand to show her. "We owe our current peace to her."

I hear a snort, but then her voice softens. "Perhaps. Rise, dragon."

I do, and my gaze falls on the Oracle for the first time in years. By human standards, she's unremarkable, an older woman with wild, dark curls and eyes the color of espresso beans. When she smiles at me, she reveals a crooked eyetooth and wrinkles around her hooked nose.

She's surprisingly diminutive for a thousand-year-old dragon who can see the future. But then, dragons understand that with age comes wisdom and that the part of the ocean you can see from the shore is just a sliver of that which you cannot see.

The Oracle is ancient and cunning. If anyone knows how to save Zoe, it's her.

"Oracle, please—"

She waves her hand through the air, her joints bulbous with arthritis. "Save it. You wish to know how to bring your mate back, yes?"

"Yes."

She turns her eyes up to the stars, their dark color reflecting the pinpricks of light from above. Time ticks on, the clocks around us reminding us constantly of every moment. I know better than to interrupt her.

Dragons believe the Oracle is capable of seeing every version of reality that branches off this one. All I need is one where Zoe wakes up. One future. I will walk any road to get there.

Finally, she lowers her chin and turns back to me.

"There is a way. You must go into her mind and convince her to come out."

Dammit, Morwyn! I should have done that days ago! "I have her consent." My eyes dart along Zoe's body, so quickly I feel like the dog clock on the wall.

She frowns, and her voice carries a pensive melancholy as she adds, "You should know that the stars say there is a fifty-fifty chance you will never come out of her mind. But if you don't go in, there is no chance she will survive."

My throat bobs on a reflexive swallow. "I don't understand. Do you mean there's something inside her mind that could trap me?"

"Yes. Despite appearances, she's incredibly strong. Only, her strength has shifted into the darkest part of herself."

"And if I get trapped?"

"Your mind will no longer be your own. You will be like she is, trapped inside, unable to function. Unable to eat. Unable to sleep. Unable to communicate."

"We'll both die."

"Yes."

"What should I do?"

"You already know what you will do." She gives a low, solemn laugh. "My dearest Taurus dragon, nothing stops a bull charging in to save his mate."

I slide a glance over my shoulder at her. "I meant, should I take her somewhere else or do it here?"

"Ah, the particulars. Take her to Taurus House. You have my permission to remain with her on Cardinal

Island. You have three days. After, I will send an acolyte to check your status, and we will take action if it appears you have failed."

"You'll put us out of our misery."

She nods slowly.

I lift Zoe into my arms.

"Good luck, warrior. You know, Zoe is a Pisces. A leapling. Very special, intuitive, extraordinary. A water sign. You are earth. Nothing contains water better than earth."

Tell that to the Grand Canyon, I think. "I'll keep that in mind."

Chapter Forty-Three

SEB

I rarely stay here. Every warrior in the brotherhood has a house on Cardinal Island where we can stay while we train. Modern conveniences, though, have made them far less appealing or necessary. Now we use them only when a new dragon is ascending or we have to meet with the Oracle for something. Still, the bed is comfortable, and it's safe. I lie down next to Zoe and run my hand along the side of her face.

Then I close my eyes and enter her mind.

It begins with darkness, then a thick fog. When the smoke clears, I'm in some kind of a cave, crisscrossed with silver thread. What the hell is this? I reach out and touch one of the strands, and my fingers stick to it. When I pull my hand away, the string vibrates with the pluck of disentangling myself.

With terrifying speed, I am lifted off the floor from

325

above. Before I even have a chance to scream, I am pinned to the center of what I now know is a web, by eight black legs that dexterously begin to roll me. Spools of silver silk wrap around my arms, my legs, my mouth. Tighter and tighter. The more I struggle, the faster she works, this spider who is easily three times my size, with pinchers as long as my forearm.

A conversation comes back to me. Zoe once said that her addiction was a spider in her head. Fuck, has she become the spider? I turn my head to the side and manage to free my mouth.

"Zoe, stop!"

The spider pauses, her pinchers hovering near my neck. *The fly knows our name.*

"We need to talk. Can we just talk?"

The fly wants to talk to the spider? The spider's voice seems to come from inside my head. *You've walked so carelessly into our trap, little fly, and we are so incredibly hungry.*

I take a second to get over the description of me as little. I'm not as large as Connor, but no human would ever call me small. Which reminds me that I'm a dragon, and I have the ability to change this dream.

She begins to spin me again, but this time, I concentrate. A dagger forms in my hand, and in one fast, upward stroke, I cut myself out of the bundle of silk. I drop to the floor and toss the silk off me. Only because this is a dream does it not stick to me. I lift the dagger between us.

My blade is gold and shines as white as the sun.

Although my dragon abilities allow me to create things within dreams, I have unwittingly drawn on the power of the ring Zoe gave me rather than my imagination.

She scurries back into the upper shadows of the cave. *Too bright*, she hisses. *You'll burn us, you filthy fly.*

"I'm not a fly!" I yell. "Zoe, it's me. It's Seb, your mate."

Zoe is no more, fly. Her pincers snap. *Only spider remains.*

"No. She's in there. You said *we* before when you were referring to yourself. Both of you are in there. Transform back so I can talk to Zoe. I need to talk to Zoe."

Where were you when she was burning? the spider hisses. *I took care of her. I helped her survive the pain.*

"The pain is over. It's time for Zoe to come out again. She's safe."

The spider scurries forward, its multiple eyes focusing on me. "You know nothing about us, fly. I keep her safe. I am here when no one else is." For the first time, the words are spoken aloud, and I notice the use of I, instead of us. This is good. I'm getting somewhere.

I lower my blade and transform it back into the ring. I hold up the gold between us, thumbing the back of it. "Do you see this ring? You made this for me, Zoe. It saved my life. It saved my people."

She moves closer, sniffing the ring. I take it as a good sign that she doesn't yank me into her web again.

I shake my head and pace to the other side of the cave. "I never wanted you to have to do what you did. I knew that the first time I heard you sing. Some part of me knew that you were my mate. It scared the shit out of me. I wanted to keep you as far away from the war as possible, even if it meant we could never be together. But things got so bad, we didn't have a choice. I had to ask you for the name of another witch, and I was terrified when you agreed to help us. Inside, I wanted to die. Because I knew my dragon was attached to you, and I knew you'd be in danger. But you did it, Zoe. You saved us. You saved all of us. And now, I need you to save me one more time. Because if you don't wake up, neither will I."

Drops of water rain down on the cave floor. The spider is crying. Its black legs curl in on its abdomen like it's dying. "I can't save you, Seb. I can't even save myself."

I watch her, terrified, as her abdomen seems to shrink and prune. She's dying. What happens if Zoe dies in this dream? I don't want to know. What I need is something to help her remember, to fill her with the magic I know is in her bones.

The gold ring on my finger winks in the light, a light that has no source in this dark cave. "The first time I heard you sing, I knew I loved you. When did you know you loved me, Zoe?" I whisper. She doesn't answer, but I remember. It took her longer because she's human. But I remember the moment she knew she loved me.

My ring transforms into a golden violin. I catch the bow in my opposite hand and draw it across the strings. The gold puts off its own light and reflects in the eyes of the spider. She's watching, but what I need her to do is listen. I play the same song I played for her that night in the recording studio, pouring my heart and soul into the notes and chords. My body moves with the music, not exactly dancing but emoting exactly what I want her to feel. I want to sweep her away. I want my music to say exactly what words never could. I play of love, of kisses by moonlight, of moving through the world at her side.

I'm sweating by the time I play the last note.

But when I look back at her, I'm struck by how little my music has mattered. In fact, she looks worse, shriveled in on herself. Her web turns brittle, and she falls, a plume of dust filling the cave when she hits the floor and her body comes apart.

"Noooo!" I drop the violin and cover my face with my arms as the ground begins to shake, and chunks of cave fall from above. I spread my wings to shelter my head.

A woman's cry has me turning back toward the spider. Zoe sits where the spider once was, her head under the shelter of her arms. She looks so thin, so frail. But she's herself again.

I rush to her and pull her into my arms, her fragile body curling into my chest, naked and shivering. "Seb?"

"Yes, it's me." The cave is crumbling, and I grunt as a boulder hits my wing. "I need you to wake up now, all right?"

"It'll hurt," she sobs. "I have no more gold dust. It's going to take so long to heal."

Another stone drops, and I bend over her, taking it on the back. It hurts like hell. "With me, you'll heal faster," I say. "All you have to do is wake up. I promise you, I'll take care of you."

Our eyes lock as more stones fall around us. One punctures a hole in my wing, and I wince. Zoe sees the hole and seems to finally understand the danger. Her eyes widen as she looks at me and then beyond me to a giant chunk of rock that promises to fall on both of us as the world inside her mind crumbles. She grabs my face and then vanishes from my arms.

I follow her out of her head.

Beside me, on the bed, she opens her eyes. I take her in my arms as we both start to weep.

Chapter Forty-Four

ZOE

Twelve weeks later...

Would I be bragging if I said my magic saved an entire species from a devastating war? Maybe, but it's also true. When Seb killed Roman, he forced the Saint's Order underground. Dragons have returned to civilian life, but there hasn't been a single act of violence since.

Seb and I moved out of the safe house and into his Holmby Hills estate. Although we're already mated, he took Beyoncé's advice and put a ring on it. We're planning a wedding in Italy next year.

"One more time, Zoe," Crew says over the speaker in the recording studio. "It's brilliant, but I think you can take it to the next level."

He's right. It's the end of the day, and I'm getting

tired. But then Seb walks in and stands behind Crew, our eyes locking through the glass. And this time when I sing, that golden edge returns, and it almost feels like I'm ascending. This time, when I reach the bridge, goose bumps march across my skin.

> *"...Take me away*
> *On wings of gold*
> *Sing to me of*
> *A world unknown*
> *I've been lost so long*
> *my skin's grown cold*
> *But lend me your fire*
> *watch our dreams unfold."*

Tears run down Crew's cheeks. We finish recording, and he just shakes his head. "That's it for the day, Zoe. Brilliant work."

I'm beaming as I set down my guitar and rush out the door, straight into Seb's arms. "This album is going to blow the roof off the charts," he says, swinging me off my feet.

"Let's not count our sales before they've hatched," I say through a huge smile, but in fact, I feel it coming like a blessing on the wind. This is my best work, and I have to believe people will feel that when they hear my voice.

He says his goodbyes to Crew and the rest of the team and ushers me out into the hall and toward the parking lot, where William is waiting to drive us home.

"It's late. Do you want to grab some dinner to celebrate?"

We slide into the back seat, and I run my hand along his thigh, the muscle flexing under his tailored slacks. "I thought you could make us something?"

"You know I'm only good for one thing."

"I'm eating what you're fixing."

The divider rises between us and William. I glance down to find Seb's finger on the button, and he raises an eyebrow.

"Are you cooking up something right now, Mr. York?"

"Only if you're hungry," he says playfully.

In answer, I throw a leg over him and straddle his lap. I moan as we fit together, his hard length rubbing against me in just the right place. I reach between us and undo his fly, springing his massive erection from its prison. It's been weeks of this, of not getting enough of each other, of wanting only more. Seb promises it will ease up eventually, but for now, it's all I can think about.

"Chocolate chip or strawberry?"

"You're thinking small again, Seb. Why not both?" I say into his mouth. He pushes my skirt up above my hips and moves the crotch of my panties aside. I'm just glad he doesn't rip them off me. "As long as there's plenty of whipped cream."

He enters me in one hard thrust. "Anything you want."

I lose myself to sensation as I ride my dragon all the way home, showing him with my body what I know in my heart.

I have everything I've ever wanted.

And the way he kisses me, I know he does too.

THANK YOU FOR READING THE ZODIAC DRAGON BROTHERHOOD Series. If you enjoyed DRAGON CHAINED or any of the books in the series, please consider leaving a review.

Want more from Genevieve Jack? Try A BARGAIN WITH THE SHADOW PRINCE.

Eloise is desperate for help to keep from losing her ancestral home to her cruel ex husband. When her witch best friend offers a spell to summon a supernatural advocate, she gratefully accepts — only to learn that the devilishly handsome Damien calls to something deep inside her.

USA Today bestselling and multi-award winning author Genevieve Jack writes wild, witty, and wicked-hot paranormal romance and romantic fantasy. She believes there's magic in every breath we take and probably something supernatural living in most dark basements. You can summon her with coffee, wine, and books, but she sticks around for dogs and chocolate. Her novels feature badass heroines, fiercely loyal heroes, and fantasy elements that will fill you with wonder. Learn more at GenevieveJack.com.

Do you know Jack? Keep in touch to stay in the know about new releases, sales, and giveaways.

The Zodiac Dragon Brotherhood

Legacy of Fire

Dragon Ascending

Dragon Chained

The Treasure of Paragon

The Dragon of New Orleans, Book 1

Windy City Dragon, Book 2,

Manhattan Dragon, Book 3

The Dragon of Sedona, Book 4

The Dragon of Cecil Court, Book 5

Highland Dragon, Book 6

Hidden Dragon, Book 7

The Dragons of Paragon, Book 8

The Last Dragon, Book 9

The Angel of Paragon, Book 10

The Three Sisters Trilogy

The Tanglewood Witches

Tanglewood Magic

Tanglewood Legacy

A Shadow's Bargain Series

A Bargain With The Shadow Prince

Battle for the Shadow Prince

Bartered by the Shadow Prince

Bride of the Shadow King

His Dark Charms Duet

Lucky Me

Lucky Us

Knight Games

The Ghost and The Graveyard, Book 1

Kick the Candle, Book 2

Queen of the Hill, Book 3

Mother May I, Book 4

Logan (companion novel)

The Wolves of Fireborn Pack Trilogy

Fated Bonds

Feral Instincts

Forever Mated